MURDER
HALF
BAKED

MURDER
HALF
BAKED

KATHLEEN DELANEY

Seattle, WA

CAMEL
PRESS

Published by Camel Press
PO Box 70515
Seattle, WA 98127

For more information go to www.camelpress.com

Cover design by Sabrina Sun

Murder Half-Baked
Copyright © 2011 by Kathleen Delaney

ISBN: 978-1-60381-828-5 (Trade Paper)

Printed in the United States of America

For my father, Lee Delaney, a truly good man and the best story teller I've ever known.

Acknowledgments

A big "thank you" to all the bakeries, from the California coast to the outer banks of the Carolinas, that I visited while writing this book. They let me poke around in their kitchens, never tired of answering my questions, and were unfailingly generous in sharing their knowledge and their Cherry Danish.

Chapter One

The vintage Cadillac sailed slowly through the cemetery gates like a battleship looking for its berth. The elderly driver peered over the long hood, carefully navigating the narrow roads, searching for the parking lot he always used. The walk from there to the grave was a little longer than he liked, but there was enough space to easily turn the car around. Today, cars were short. Compacts, they called them. Or SUVs, whatever that meant. Everyone stuffed them full of kids, dogs, and toys. In his day, the dog stayed home. So did the kids, if you could swing it. No one drove big, comfortable cars like this one anymore. Why, he had no idea. Didn't know what they were missing, that was for damn sure.

He was in luck. The lot was empty. Last time there had been that stupid woman. He'd never understood why she made such a fuss. Her silly little car was barely dented. Slowly he maneuvered so that he faced the exit and stopped. He sat for a moment, took a deep breath, and pushed open the door.

Gravel crunched. He hated gravel. Why couldn't they pave this lot? The roads were paved. Didn't the groundskeepers know gravel could trip people? Especially people who used canes. Not that he had to, of course. Use his cane. It was just that, well, sometimes lately … He hung onto the driver's door as he inched his way to the back one, swung it open, and took out the hated cane. There was a small hill to climb, and, as much as he didn't want to admit it, he'd need it to get himself and his flowers to the grave he'd come to visit. Flowers. Where were the flowers he'd brought? Damn it. They'd fallen over. Water had seeped onto the mat, soaking the back floorboard. He'd told that fool girl to prop them up with something. She hadn't listened, of course. No one did anymore. He took the roses, red as usual, out of the container, examined it to make sure there was some water left, and placed them both on the ground. He pulled out the floor mat and laid it flat beside the car. Maybe it would dry a little while he was gone.

He stuffed the roses back in the plastic vase and picked up his cane. Should he fill the container from the faucet at the head of the path? No, it'd just slop over and get his trousers wet.

This was the old part of the cemetery. Families who had lived in this town for over a hundred years were buried here. Granite monuments were scattered liberally over the slight hill, many with generations of names inscribed on them. Others, like the family plot he headed for, had marble statues on pedestals. Angels mostly, guarding the dear departed, waiting to take the next in line to heaven. He wondered if he would get into heaven. A small smile turned up the corners of his mouth. Sure he would. Francis would lobby for him. Almost there. Just up the path a little way and around the bend. He paused for a moment to get his breath. He loved this moment, going toward her, being with her again.

Everyone said that time would dull the ache, but it hadn't. Even after two years, the hole she had left in his life was so huge, the cavern so great, he couldn't see the other side. Francis. He had been everything to her. The children she'd wanted had never come, so she had devoted her life to him. He wondered fleetingly if she thought he'd devoted his life to her. Stupid. Of course she had. He'd never looked at another woman. So what if he hadn't been much on sweet talk. She knew.

Something was wrong. He struggled forward, staring ahead. Was he in the right place? There should be an angel standing there, almost directly over Francis's grave. But there was no angel, just the pedestal. Where was the angel? Oh God. There it was, lying on its side. What happened? Kids. He hurried forward, anxiety filling his chest. That was Francis's angel. He'd always hated the damn thing, but she loved it. Her parents were buried under it, and her sister, May.

A branch lay across the fallen angel. A big branch. He looked up. A white scar marred the side of the old oak tree that sheltered the graves. That storm on Thanksgiving night. Must have broken off then, landed on the angel, and knocked it right off its pedestal. It seemed intact. No. It was missing an arm. He looked around. No sign of it. He leaned heavily on his cane as he examined the angel. Probably could be fixed. If they could find the arm, of course.

A shadow fell across the grass, and a figure emerged from behind the neighboring monument. He stared at the person for a moment, surprised. He squinted a little, trying to focus. Eyes weren't as good as they used to be, but after a moment he was sure.

"What are you doing here?"

"Waiting for you."

"You're supposed to be ..."

He never finished. The missing angel arm hit him across the side of the head, crushing his skull, splashing brain tissue and blood on the grass, the path, and the body of the fallen statue. He only had time to think "why?" before he folded slowly onto Francis's grave.

Chapter Two

I stood in front of the full-length mirror in my bedroom, trying to decide if I should laugh or cry. "I look like an aging Scarlet O'Hara."

My friend, Pat Bennington, said nothing, but the twitching around the side of her mouth said laughter.

"Mom, I'm … Oh. Oh!" My daughter, Susannah, walked into the room and came to an abrupt halt. Her mouth twitched as well. "I hate to mention this, but Halloween's over." She took another look at my ruffled, hoop-skirted dress and smirked.

"Laugh and I'll—"

"What. Hit me with your hoopskirt?"

"Strangle you with my corset."

"You're not serious."

"About the corset or strangling you?"

"The corset. Even Grandma wouldn't … that *is* the wedding dress she sent you. It's not one you picked out. Is it?"

I gave her my most withering look, which she ignored. Instead she picked up the broad brimmed hat that lay on the bed, flared out the veil, set it on my head, and stepped back.

"You don't need to say it. I look like an aging Scarlet O'Hara."

"More like Hush … Hush, Sweet Charlotte."

How nice. I took another look in the mirror. All I needed was cobwebs, and I'd be a dead ringer for Miss Haversham. I removed the hat and started to throw it on the bed, but Susannah grabbed it and with a giant whoosh placed it on her head. With her long dark curls and deep blue eyes, she really did look like Scarlet—a young, seductive Scarlet. I didn't.

"What do you think?"

"Not even close," Pat replied.

"You're right. I think I want a simple wedding. No frills or ruffles." Susannah grinned at my reflection in the mirror and took off the hat.

"What wedding?" I whirled around to confront her, hoop swaying, ruffles coming close to sweeping clean my nightstand. "You're way too young to start thinking about weddings."

"You were my age when you married Dad."

"I was older," I stated, somewhat inaccurately. "Much older. Besides, look how that turned out."

"I plan on choosing more carefully."

Pat grinned for the first time since I'd shown her the dress. As well she might. It was her son, Neil, who was Susannah's current, and only, boyfriend. "One wedding at a time." Pat pushed me away from the mirror and started circling me, picking up the organza skirt, fingering the taffeta underskirt. Susannah started circling the other way, examining the bodice of the dress.

"This is actually pretty." Susannah ran her fingers down the beadwork across my front. "If the sleeves weren't so funky. Shorter maybe, or at least not so puffy. And if there was about twenty yards less material in the skirt …"

She and Pat stood back and stared at me, nodding and muttering. I felt like a store dummy.

"What do you think?" she finally asked Pat.

"I think we can do it." Pat nodded and circled me again. "The cream color is nice. So, if we take the ruffles off the skirt, bring down the bodice over the underskirt—it's pretty but sort of bunchy looking—change the sleeves … "

"And ditch the hat. Yep, that should do it." Susannah acknowledged me with a grin. "Good thing Pat spent all these years rescuing costumes for the Little Playhouse, or we'd really be in trouble."

"What are you going to do?" I couldn't help being suspicious. After all, it was my wedding dress. Even if I hated it, I should have some say about what happened to it. Shouldn't I? Besides, what would I tell my mother? She was convinced that the reason my marriage to Doctor Brian McKenzie hadn't worked was because we'd eloped and she hadn't been able to give me the huge wedding she'd been planning since my christening. So, when she learned I was going to marry Dan Dunham—whom she'd known since his birth and had picked out for me when we were both toddlers— she'd insisted on sending me a wedding dress. She said it was the least she could do since she and my father now lived in Scottsdale, Arizona, and wouldn't be around to help me with all the wedding plans. I was so relieved she wasn't coming early that I accepted her offer almost eagerly. Mother always means well, but she gets carried away. Like with this dress. I took another look at myself in the mirror and shuddered.

"Okay. Start snipping." I'd figure out something to tell her.

I stepped out of the dress and handed it to Pat, who immediately spread it across the bed. It covered the whole thing and part of the floor. She and Susannah pinned and plotted as I watched. After awhile I got tired of standing there in my bra, panties, and that stupid hoopskirt. Besides, I was getting cold.

"Do you need me?" I asked. "For, maybe, a decision about how the dress should look? Something like that?"

"I think I'll take it apart first and see what we can do." Pat was doing something with seams and barely noticed me. Susannah, on the other hand, was staring at me intently. "I think this wedding stuff is getting to you. You've lost weight."

I looked down at myself, then at my reflection and smiled. At least one good thing had come from all those sleepless nights. It wasn't just worrying about the wedding that had ruined my appetite and set me to tossing and turning at three in the morning. It was the whole idea of marriage. My first had been pretty grim. Twenty years of gradual disintegration, finishing up with an abrupt demand by my devoted husband for a divorce. I'd been scared to death to say "yes" to Dan, fearing that the same thing would happen. But Dan wasn't Brian and, after a lot of sleepless nights, I'd decided that life with him was infinitely preferable to life without him. Even if that meant marriage, which to him it clearly did. But I still had butterflies in my stomach when I thought about it. Or maybe they were bats flying around in there. Anyway, it had all been great for my waistline.

The screen door slammed and a "where is everyone" followed.

"Up here," Susannah called down the stairs, "laughing at Mom's wedding dress."

"Doing what?" Aunt Mary puffed a little as she came up the stairs, paused at the landing, and entered the room. "Good God, what's that?"

She walked over to the bed where the dress lay and poked at it, lifting up one ruffle before dropping it back on the bed. "This isn't—"

"My wedding dress."

"My sister has finally lost her mind."

Pat hoisted the dress up, and all the ruffles sort of fluffed out, cascading onto the floor.

"Ruffles? At your age?" She sounded torn between horror and hilarity.

"I'm not that old."

"You're too old for ruffles."

There was a loud ripping sound, and we all jumped.

"Pat Bennington, what on earth are you doing?" Aunt Mary demanded.

"See, no more ruffles." Pat held up what looked like a

whole bolt of filmy stuff and laughed. Susannah joined her. So did Aunt Mary. Somehow the joke escaped me.

"I'm getting dressed," I announced. "In real clothes. I hope no one minds."

"We don't." Susannah's grin made me grumpier. "And quit worrying. We'll tell Grandma all those ruffles made you look fat."

I stopped trying to untie my hoopskirt and stared at her. Why hadn't I thought of that?

Strains of Beethoven's Fifth sounded faintly.

"Isn't that your cell?" Susannah asked, looking around.

"Yes. Where is it?" I started combing through all the material covering the bed.

"Watch it," Pat said. "You're going to have beads all over the bed."

"Here." Aunt Mary held it out to me. "It was on your nightstand. If it was a snake, it would have bitten you."

Why did people say that? If it were a snake, I'd have been galloping down the hall, hoop skirt and all. The screen said my office was calling. I forgot all about snakes.

"Really? It just came in? Sure. I have a two o'clock appointment but I'll pick it up before then. Thanks."

They were all watching me.

"Good news?" Susannah had tried on the hat again and was watching me in the mirror as she fluffed out the veil around her. "Actually, this isn't too bad."

"Yes it is." I watched her in the mirror. She looked lovely. I could see her coming down the aisle, radiant, Neil beaming as she came closer—. No. That vision had to wait awhile. Years.

"I hope it's good news," I answered. "I've got an offer on Minnie's little condo in Sunset Village."

"Minnie who? Mouse?"

"No, smarty. Patterson. I can hardly believe it. We just listed it. I haven't even had it on caravan."

"Caravan?" said Aunt Mary.

"Sort of an open house for agents."

Aunt Mary pushed aside some skirt and sat on the edge of my bed. "I didn't know Minnie was still living by herself. I thought she'd gone into assisted living after Ben died. Why, she must be in her nineties."

"She is, and she should have gone somewhere before this. Her place is … not in the best shape. She's almost blind and doesn't remember things very well. But she wouldn't budge. Or she wouldn't until last week. She left the teakettle on and it burned up. Almost set the kitchen on fire. Scared her and panicked her kids, who aren't all that young themselves."

I tugged at the knot holding my hoopskirt up. It finally came undone and fell to the floor in a heap. I kicked it in the general direction of the corner and pulled on knit pants and a baggy, oversized sweater.

"If the condo is in such bad shape, why did you get an offer so quickly? You keep complaining about the market being so slow." Susannah was full of questions today. They would be easier to answer if she'd take off that blasted hat. It distracted me. "I've no idea. It had everything going against it." I was on the floor, putting on socks, anxious to get to the office, but paused for a moment, thinking back. "Her kids want her out of there as soon as possible. They already have an apartment reserved for her at Shady Acres, the new assisted living place up on Montgomery Hill. But before she can go there they need to sell, and of course they also want top dollar."

"Shady Acres isn't cheap." Aunt Mary bounced a little on the bed, more because her feet didn't quite touch the floor than because I hadn't priced Minnie's Sunset Village condo high enough, even thought that was clearly what she thought. That's what everyone thinks when an offer comes in right away. "They're going to need every penny to keep her there."

"It's the first of December, the slowest time of the year.

We're in a declining market, which means prices are falling with the speed of water over Niagara Falls, and Minnie's place … well, it smells. We finally settled on a price only a little too high. But I got a long listing." I examined my toe. The red polish on it showed gaily through the hole in my sock. I rummaged in my sock drawer and found a pair of gray ones with snowmen on them. I thought they were cute when I bought them. "If this offer is even close to good, they will be convinced forever that they listed it too low."

"Surely not. They'll be grateful you did such a good job."

"You were sitting there thinking I didn't list it high enough."

"I was not."

Sure. I smothered a sigh.

"I thought you had an appointment with Anne Kennedy today to talk about Grace House."

"I do. At two o'clock." Aunt Mary eyed me critically, letting me know I wasn't presenting the perfect picture of a dedicated real estate agent. "And I don't think she'll care if I'm not in pantyhose."

"Let's hope she likes snowmen." Aunt Mary stared pointedly at my socks.

"This is a small town. No one dresses up. Besides, it's cold." I tried to remember where I'd left my briefcase. Surely not on the bed. I'd never find it under all of that. No. Downstairs. In the kitchen. Beside the hutch. "Anyway, all we're going to do is talk. I'm not sure what she wants."

"She wants a larger house." Aunt Mary gave a little bounce and let the bed propel her onto her feet. "She has to turn women away because they don't have enough room. I told Anne you were in real estate, seemed to know what you were doing, that you'd help her find a bigger house and sell the one they're in. You will, won't you?"

That wasn't a question. It was a mission statement. My mission, and I knew from experience that I'd better accept it.

"I'll do the best I can. Do they have to sell the one they're in before they can buy?"

"The board is discussing that."

"I really have to know. The market is heading south, fast. It's almost Christmas and—"

"Who's Anne Kennedy?" Susannah interrupted.

"She's the director of Grace House."

"They need a bigger place?" Pat said from around a mouthful of pins. "How sad that there are so many women who need help!"

"What's Grace House? Is it one of those safe houses for women who get abused? Can I take the veil off this thing? " Susannah had been fingering the veil attached to the bridal hat again in a much too speculative manner but dropped it to give Aunt Mary her full attention.

"No. Although some of the women who come to us have been abused. Grace House is set up for women who are in transition. Many of them married *too young*." Aunt Mary pointedly eyed the veil in Susannah's hand. Susannah grinned. "Most are divorcing or separated from their husbands, and almost none have job skills. Some have never had a checking account. Their husbands always handled all the money. Lots have children. The only thing they have in common is the need for a breathing spell while they figure out their next step."

"And Grace House does that?" Susannah's grinned faded.

"We provide them a place to stay and counseling while they live in the house. We also help them to get a job and manage their money, and to find an attorney if they don't have one."

"Why do they need attorneys?" Susannah looked as if she were going to take notes. I hoped those notes would be for a class, not for future reference.

"Mostly to get their once loving spouses to pay child support or alimony. It's amazing how many men think their

11

obligations end with the divorce decree."

"And Mom's going to help them get a bigger house? Awesome."

"Not if she doesn't get going." Aunt Mary pushed back her sleeve and looked at her watch.

I got the message. I grabbed my jacket and headed for the stairs but stopped at the doorway. "You said the board is talking about how you're going to finance a new Grace House. Remember what I just said about Minnie's. It's December, a terrible time to get anything done. More than that, the economy is in a nosedive, and the real estate market is the nose cone, which means it's going to hit bottom first and hardest. Selling the house they're in now before we buy another one would present a real logistical problem. That doesn't mean we can't do it, but it would take longer and the process would be harder. I'll go talk to Anne, but I think you—the board members—have decisions to make before we do anything. And another thing. I'll do my best, but I have a wedding coming up. So—if you could all just keep that in mind?"

"Everyone on the board is coming to your wedding. They're aware of how jumpy you are just now."

What? Me? Jumpy? But before I could respond she went on:

"We have options. Francis Sadler, the founder of Grace House, left us a legacy, and Owen is supposed to come up with more money."

"Good luck," Pat muttered around her mouthful of pins. "The good doctor will attach so many strings to any money he donates you could use it as a May Pole."

Aunt Mary laughed. I didn't. This didn't sound like fun.

"Francis loved Grace House," Aunt Mary said firmly. "It was her idea and her baby. Owen always, finally, did what Francis wanted. And he will again. That money will help. But go talk to Anne. She's the director. I'm sure she has a plan."

I started to make a caustic remark about plans but took a look at her face and thought better of it. Anne Kennedy had better have a plan, and it had better be a good one. Christmas was only three weeks away, my wedding only four. My parents and Dan's parents would be arriving way too soon, and I had barely made a dent in my Christmas shopping. I had found a caterer who thought barbeque tri-tip, served with packaged salad and ranch dressing, was the height of elegance. I was looking for another caterer. Just to make things really interesting, I had two escrows due to close within the next two weeks. Both sellers had decided they didn't want to move until after the holidays, and the buyers wanted to be in for Christmas.

However, the wedding invitations were in, they were actually correct, and Aunt Mary was busy addressing them, blessed woman that she was. And I had been to Ianelli's Bakery and ordered my cake. A simple, dignified but beautiful cake, one that would set off a simple but beautiful wedding of two people in their forties who had each been married before.

"Mom."

I turned, curious at the tone in Susannah's voice, instantly wary of the expression on her face.

"Mom, I think you might want to stop in at Ianelli's when you get a chance."

"Why?"

"Oh, I think Rose Ianelli might be a little confused about which cake you wanted. I was in there, getting a Danish, and the cake she showed me didn't look like the one you described."

Pat took pins out of her mouth and stuck them on the front of her T-shirt. "How was it? The Danish. The last ones I got there weren't very good."

The hand gesture Susannah made meant only one thing. Mediocre. But I didn't care about Danish. I did care about the cake.

"What did Rose say?"

"She showed me a picture. I didn't say anything, but you probably want to go check."

"I'm sure it's nothing that can't be straightened out quickly. Rose is the sweetest thing on earth."

Aunt Mary was right. Rose was indeed a sweet lady. She was the one who had talked my mother into letting me have a Barbie cake for my eighth birthday, the kind where the cake is Barbie's skirt and she sticks up out of the hole. The top half of Barbie rising from that mound of frosting seemed to make my mother a little nervous, but I got my cake. "Right. Thanks for telling me. We did look at a lot of pictures. I'm sure there's no problem."

I'd stop by the bakery when I got a chance, but probably not today. Right now my mind was on Minnie and the offer on her Sunset Village condo. She needed to move, even if she didn't fully realize it, and getting an offer this soon had to be good news. I hoped. In any case, I needed time to go over it, talk to the agent who brought it in, then contact Minnie's family. Fingers tightly crossed, I headed for the stairs, my briefcase, and the car.

"Wish me luck," I said as I left.

No one answered. They were all clustered around the dress, muttering. Susannah was still wearing the hat, but the veil was gone. Good.

Chapter Three

Real estate agents don't need three wishes. Two will do just fine. First we wish that our sellers will listen to us and not insist on pricing their property so much higher than the market value that it is impossible to sell. The second is that an offer, when we get one, is "clean." That has nothing to do with soap, but lots to do with conditions that make it difficult, if not impossible, to close the sale. For instance, a buyer wants you to take the house off the market while he sells his, only his isn't on the market yet. He'll offer it for sale as soon as he finishes painting. Or a buyer has little cash, needs ninety-five percent financing, but hasn't bothered to talk to a lender. Of course they also want you to take the house off the market while they try to qualify for the loan. Although sometimes, like now, the market slows down to the point where, in desperation, we actually look at those kind of offers. I had my fingers crossed that Minnie's wouldn't fall into one of those categories.

I read the offer on her place three times before I really believed it. Almost full price, all cash, just the usual inspections, and they were willing to close in forty-five days, which meant after Christmas. I even knew the buyers. Pat and Bobbie Olmert were buying it for Bobbie's recently widowed mother who had moved in with them after her house sold. She had the cash, and if she didn't have enough, Pat and Bobbie could, and would, make up the difference. The buyers' agent and I agreed on the escrow officer we would like to use, she planned on using my favorite home inspector, and we even agreed on the termite company. I'd called Minnie's family, fully expecting them to want to counter full price, but they were thrilled with the offer. They agreed to pick up the paperwork late that afternoon, take it to Minnie to sign, and bring it back in the morning. And ... they actually thanked me! Two hours and we had an agreement. Which was why, still stunned, I was sitting in my car, in front of Ianelli's Bakery, with half an hour to go before my appointment with Anne Kennedy.

Ianelli's Bakery was on Center Street, in the heart of the old part of town. Exactly two blocks long, Center started at Elm and ran out at the park. It was the first street in Santa Louisa and had some of its oldest and most historic buildings. The ugly gray stucco building where Ianelli's Bakery was housed wasn't one of them. It's only attractive feature was a large picture window that had been filled for as long as I could remember with plaster replicas of baked goods. A huge wedding cake was always center stage, flanked by a couple of birthday and holiday cakes, rotating depending on the season. There were always trays of what might be cinnamon rolls in front, a cream pie of some sort beside them. A basket of assorted Italian cookies and candies claimed the spot nearest the door. I stared at the basket, thinking I hadn't seen any of the cookies or any of the other Italian pastries Sal Ianelli used to make since I'd moved back. Too bad. My mouth still watered at the thought of Sal's Lady Kisses.

I pushed open the door and was met by the tinkling of the old bell, the wonderful aroma of fresh bread, and an empty shop. I stopped and looked around. Even though I'd dropped by several times in the year and a half since I'd returned to Santa Louisa, it had always been a hurried visit. I had been gone over twenty years and I'd found many changes in my little hometown since my return, but I hadn't really thought much about the bakery. Now, in this empty room, I stopped and looked around.

The long glass counter still sat in the middle of the floor, the door to the kitchen area directly behind it. There used to be wicker baskets on the counter filled with freshly baked bread. Long loaves, fat round ones, dark brown wheat, and special breads filled with cheese or olives. My mother always bought white bread. Sal would say, "Sliced, Mrs. Page?" "Yes, thank you, Mr. Ianelli," she'd answer. The wicker baskets were gone and so was most of the bread. The only loaves, a pale brown color, were stuffed into plastic bags fastened with a little wire tie and piled haphazardly on the low counter next to the cash register.

The old wood floor still covered the front part of the store and it still didn't lie very even, wavering across the room to end in a slight dip in front of the big window. The walls were still covered with travel posters of Italy, the same ones that had been there when I was little. My favorite gondolier still pushed his black boat through the canals of Venice, but somehow he didn't seem as romantic as he had then. The edges of his poster, the edges of all of them, had started to curl slightly and the colors had dulled. An accumulation of years of dust and flour? Whatever it was, they no longer made me want to catch the next plane east. The round oak table and the two bentwood chairs that sat in front of the window had also been there when I was little, but the table hadn't been piled high with catalogs. Customers used to sit there, chatting with Rose and drinking small cups of thick, rich coffee liberally laced with cream. I sniffed the air. Not a hint of coffee. I walked over to the long glass case and looked in. Where were the fruit tarts? The ones filled with peaches, apricots, pears, and cherries, all piled on rich custard and topped with glaze? My mother didn't buy one often, but when she did … And where were the cannoli? The wonderful cannoli stuffed with ricotta cheese? I hadn't known it was cheese back then. If I had, I probably wouldn't have eaten them. Cheese! Ugh. Think what I would have missed! I searched the case. I sure was missing them now.

What was that other thing she used to buy? Bread

pudding. That was it. It came in a little tray and you could get a sauce to go over it. Mother always worried about my sister and me eating it, so it must have been laced liberally with liquor. Rum maybe? Whatever it was, it was heavenly. I wondered if Sal still made it. And the cookies. Where were the cookies? Oh, there were cookies on one of the shelves—chocolate chip, oatmeal, peanut butter—but no almond, no little puff pastry strips, no round honey balls, or crescent cookies. The cakes were there—carrot, lemon, chocolate—but they didn't look the way I remembered. The top shelf held trays of Danish. Had they been there when I was little? I didn't think so, but they looked familiar. Everything in the case looked familiar, yet somehow wrong. It took me a moment, and then it hit me. They all looked like the choices offered at the new supermarket. Only these were more expensive.

Rose Ianelli rushed out of the back room with cries of, "Ellen. I didn't hear you come in. Sal, come quick. The bride is here." She rounded the corner from behind the counter to smother me with a big hug. Rose was not a tall woman, and the years had left her plump and soft. Except for her arms. The hug she gave me squeezed the breath right out of me, and her cries of "the bride" made me flush with embarrassment. I thought of brides as young, radiant, romantic. I had been married and divorced, had an almost grown daughter, and was crowding middle age. My groom was a widower, his light brown hair lighter than it used to be. Silver strands among the gold? Yep. And there wasn't quite as much of it. But there was a little more around the waistline. It didn't matter. He was still tall and handsome and had the cutest mustache … None of that made this second marriage romantic.

"Susannah told you about the cake? I was going through the book, and when I saw it, I just knew it was the one for your wedding. Your wedding and Dan's." Rose's eyes glistened. "It's so perfect. Gina, don't you think it's perfect?"

A woman I'd never seen before stood at the end of the bakery counter wrapped in a large white apron. Her dark brown hair was pulled back into a tight ponytail, her face was devoid of makeup, and her long brown eyelashes wore no mascara. It didn't matter. She was beautiful. Beautiful and lush. "Perfect," she answered Rose.

"Ah, Rose." My curiosity about this new employee was momentary. She wasn't why I was there. "About the cake—"

"You want to see a picture. Of course you do."

She grabbed me by the hand and immediately dropped it. Her hands were lightly coated with flour. "Did I get flour on you?" She whipped her hands down the front of her own apron before she examined me. "Good. No flour." She picked up my hand again and pulled me over to the oak table piled high with ringed notebooks. It wobbled on the uneven floor as she pushed them around, looking for the one she wanted. I thought the whole pile was going over, but somehow it stayed on the table. Rose pulled out the biggest one, labeled "wedding cakes," slapped it down on one edge of the table, and flipped it open. "Here."

I stared down at the most garish cake I had ever seen. Instead of the four tiered all white cake I had chosen—the one with pretty little loops and curlicues on it, with tiny fresh roses and baby's breath cascading down one side—this one had green holly with red berries looped all over it. Gold pillars— *large* pillars—separated each layer so that the bright red frosting poinsettias could not only sit on top but fill the openings.

"I've already started them. Wait. I'll get them."

She trotted off toward the back room, leaving me to stare at the picture of the cake. I was still forming my protest when she came back, carrying a white plastic box. She set it on the table, pulled out one of the chairs and sat down heavily.

"My feet seem to get tired earlier than they used to."

She laughed a little, pulled open a drawer in the box, and took out a very red flower impaled on green florist wire. "They take a while to make so I'm starting now. Came out pretty, don't you think?"

It was pretty. But it wasn't what I wanted.

"Doesn't she do a great job? Pastillage is hard because it dries so quickly. Just like your gum does when you stick it on the bedpost. You have to work fast. That's why the little sculpture tool. You can shape them with it. You can also slice your finger."

The voice was right behind me and so unexpected, I jumped. It was the young woman I'd seen. She was peering over my left shoulder, admiring the flower Rose held up.

Rose beamed at her. "I'm teaching Gina how to do this. She's already good at it." She rummaged in the box and brought up a pale pink rosebud. The color was soft and lovely, the tiny petals layered perfectly.

I reached out for it. "I love this."

"I can make the other ones, also. Rose's hands … it's getting harder for her to do all of this."

I looked more closely at the hand that held the red flower. I had never noticed before, but the knuckles were enlarged, and the fingers had the crooked look that indicates arthritis. The skin had developed brown spots and was beginning to take on the thinness of parchment. I looked down at Rose's face. Plumpness filled in the folds, but all the signs were there. I realized, suddenly, that Rose must be pretty darn close to seventy. She was getting old! Only, she sure didn't act like it.

"I'll put this back." Gina gently took the flower from Rose's hand and carefully laid it back in the plastic drawer before she looked back at me. "I think it's so romantic, getting married on New Year's Eve. And the cake is going to be beautiful."

What was so romantic about New Year's Eve? It was practical. Dan would never forget our anniversary. Neither would I. And the cake! The rosebuds were retreating, and I could see red poinsettias coming at me.

"And, Ellen ..." Rose was flipping pages in the catalog. "You're going to need at least two sheet cakes. Mary gave me the head count, and this cake won't feed all those people. So, I thought these would be nice."

I looked down again at the picture of the towering cake. That wouldn't feed all the people who were coming? Was the whole damn world coming to my wedding? It was a fact that at least half of it was. Rose and Salvatore Ianelli were. Was this Gina, who obviously worked here but whom I had never seen before, coming also? I had no idea. I'd lost control of the guest list, mostly because my mother and Dan's mother kept adding to it and I couldn't make either of them stop. In frustration, I'd pushed it onto Aunt Mary to sort out. And now I needed more cake?

"Susannah told me ... "

"Susannah." Rose stopped flipping through the catalog, and a dreamy look came over her face. "Such a pretty girl. All that dark curly hair, those beautiful blue eyes. If it weren't for them, I'd swear she was Italian. She's going to make a beautiful bride, and she's so lucky. Neil Bennington is a good man."

Italian? And what did she mean—Susannah a bride? And Neil a man? He was only twenty-two and still in veterinary school. He was just a boy. Well, maybe not. But not old enough for marriage. All these thoughts kept me off guard, and the next thing I knew, I was staring at a flat version of the tiered wedding cake. Only this time there were little cherubs at each corner, their tiny feet firmly implanted in the green ivy.

"I wanted to make these cakes for my Gabrielle when she got married, but no, she had to get married in North Carolina where her husband's fancy relatives live. Oh, well, that was years ago. I've made these cakes for lots of other brides, and they've all loved them. And now, we will make them for you. Gina and me."

I had no idea what to say, but I could feel those red flowers getting closer.

"That's exactly the kind of cake I had when I got married."

Gina was still looking over my shoulder, but she wasn't looking at the pictures. She was smiling at Rose.

"With red poinsettias?" I hoped my tone wasn't too sour, but I really didn't want those cakes.

"Well, no. Mine had pale yellow roses with white doves. But now it's Christmas."

"The wedding is New Year's Eve."

"Same thing." Rose patted Gina on the arm and beamed at the cake. "It's going to be beautiful. Even Doctor Sadler thought so. Didn't he, Gina?"

Doctor Sadler? Old Doctor Sadler? What did he have to do with my wedding cake? I hardly knew the man. We'd gone to Doctor Miller, who used to let me hold his stethoscope and always had a bowl of suckers on his desk.

The bell on the front door rang. Trish Wilson must have come here fresh from the beauty shop. She pushed the door open with her arm and was waving her hands in the air, making sure her nail polish didn't touch anything.

"Hi." She looked around and walked over to where we all stood gathered around the wedding cake book. "Oh, Ellen. How beautiful they are! Which one are you getting?"

Trish is an old friend of my Aunt Mary's. Of course, so is everyone else in town. I started to say I wasn't getting any of them but was too late. Rose pointed to the sheet cakes with the holly and the cherubs, then flipped pages until she came to the poinsettia tower. "This one. Isn't it wonderful?"

"Oh." Trish looked from the cake picture to me, and then back to the book. "My. It certainly will be festive."

I could feel my face burn.

"I came for my order, Rose. For Harry's birthday dessert. I'm just so excited to see what you and Sal came up with. So, if it's ready ..."

Rose's face went blank. She blinked a couple of times and a look of panic crept into her eyes.

Trish started to look uncomfortable. "I called you yesterday; we talked about it, but if you don't have it, well, I'll just ..."

I hadn't heard Sal come in. But there he was, a scowl on his face, chocolate frosting on his apron. He glared at Rose from under bushy eyebrows before he turned back to Trish. "Mrs. Wilson, I'm sure it's ready. What did you order?"

"I left it up to Rose. I've always gotten Harry's birthday dessert here, and I just knew you'd come up with something wonderful." Trish had started to back toward the door. "But if you didn't have time, that's fine. I can ..."

Sal walked back behind the counter and reached for a heavy spike that had a whole stack of small pieces of paper speared on it. He took off a couple before he found what he wanted. "Yes. It's right here. In Rose's writing."

Gina spoke up. "Sal, the Baba au Rhum, remember? The special order? That was for the Wilson's. I'm so sorry. I thought you knew that." She stepped in front of Trish and somehow maneuvered her so that her back was to Sal.

"Baba au Rhum? That was for Harry? I thought—"

"Sal doesn't make them much anymore, but they're all ready, and wait until you see them. I could hardly keep my fingers out of them. I'll go get them right now."

She disappeared into the back room before Sal could explode. And explode he did. "She should have told me," he kept saying. "Special order was all she said. If I'd known ... she kept ... I told you not to hire her," he yelled at Rose, who stood staring down at the wedding cake book, saying nothing.

"But you made them." Trish's enthusiasm was a little forced and her eyes never left Rose. "That's wonderful. They're Harry's favorite and I don't know how to make them." She let that trail off a little and transferred her gaze to the kitchen door.

Sal stopped and the expression on his face changed. The fury that had turned his face red faded. The look that replaced it was almost crafty. The smile below his gray mustache looked fake, the expression in his eyes calculating. "Of course I made them. It's just that … she should have told me. For you, I always make something extra special. It's fine, don't worry."

Trish had beamed with pleasure when Gina told her what she was getting, but that pleasure had faded away fast under Sal's unreasonable tirade. Now she just looked confused and uncomfortable.

Gina appeared again, carrying a sack and a pink box tied up with string. She didn't look at Sal. Instead, she gave Trish a wide smile. "Do you have whipping cream?"

"I have some of the squirt kind."

Gina frowned. "Oh, for something as special as this you need real whipping cream. Get the heavy kind and whip it yourself. Add two teaspoons of vanilla and a couple tablespoons or so of sugar. No more or it will be too sweet." She set the pink box down on the table, pushing aside some of the catalogs, and undid the string. "Here. Look."

We all looked. Six perfect little cakes sat in the box, swollen with rum sauce, currents peeking out of the apricot glaze that encased them.

"They came out nice, didn't they?" Gina looked into the box and smiled with satisfaction.

"They're beautiful." Rose nodded approval. "Sal outdid himself."

Sal grunted. He barely glanced in the box. Instead, he studied Gina appraisingly.

"Oh," I heard Trish say. "Oh. Whipping cream. Oh, yes. I can do that."

Gina closed the box and refastened the string. She handed it to Trish but kept the bag. "Sal made potato rolls this morning. I thought you might like a dozen. They're still warm." She opened the bag and took out one roll with a little piece of paper. It lay in her hand, round, brown with a light coating of white on top, giving off the delicious aroma that only warm, fresh bread can. "See?"

"Potato rolls. Oh, yes. Why, these look like … why, we haven't had these … Thank you. Yes, I would like them."

Trish looked curiously at Gina, glanced at Rose out of the corner of her eye, and turned to Sal. "You're wonderful. I can't thank you enough. Can you put it on my bill?"

"Of course." He was all smiles, beaming at Trish, but those dark eyes kept going back and forth between Gina and Rose. Sal was still not pleased about something. "You tell Harry that Rose and I wish him a happy birthday."

"I'll do that, and thanks again." Trish headed for the door, still beaming, pushed it open and was gone. Sal waited until the door closed, then he turned to Gina and glared. She pretended not to notice. Instead she walked over to Rose and stood very close to her.

What was all that about? What had Gina done other than put the special dessert in a box and offer a customer rolls? I wondered if Sal had made more. I loved Baba au Rhum. I glanced at my watch. Damn. I was going to be late. I started for the door as well, but Rose's voice stopped me. "Ellen, you really like the cake?"

I turned, grateful for the opening, fully intending to say, "No, we need to change it." But I didn't. I couldn't. She looked so hopeful and, somehow, fearful. "It's going to be wonderful. Just like you said. Have an appointment, have to run." And I did. Right out the door.

I sat in my car, staring out the windshield, wondering what had just happened. Somehow I had ended up with a wedding cake that was everything that I didn't want, and I was getting sheet cakes that I wasn't one bit sure we needed. It was time to have a conference with Aunt Mary about our guest list. Then I would have another talk with Rose. A very tactful but firm talk. For some reason Rose seemed to be in love with that cake. I wasn't. But it would take more time than I had right now to ease her into doing what I wanted without hurting her feelings. There were some advantages to the supermarket bakery. I didn't know anyone there, they'd never given me cookies when I was little or gone to bat for me when I wanted a Barbie cake, and they could care less what kind of cake I wanted for my wedding. Damn. Oh well. I'd figure it out. I'd go back. Later. In a day or so. There was still plenty of time. Maybe I could talk Sal into making more Baba au Rhum.

Chapter Four

I had arranged to meet Anne Kennedy at Grace House. I needed to see it so that I could establish a reasonable sales price. Anne had told me that the mortgage had long since been paid off, so the proceeds would go a long way toward the purchase of another, larger home. However, she had been adamant that they needed to find a new house before I could put it on the market. The residents had all been through bad times and didn't need prospective buyers who might be more curious about them than about the features of the house poking around. I gladly agreed, for a different reason. I was fairly certain that a house filled with people in transition to someplace else wouldn't show well. Usually we encouraged owners to "stage" their homes, putting out their prettiest things, packing up the rest, and storing them in a garage made newly neat, but in this case, empty would be better. We might—most likely would—have to do a few things to get it in shape to sell. I just hoped the job wouldn't involve much more than cleaning and painting.

Grace House was right in the middle of a quiet residential district. Modest three to four bedroom family homes lined both sides of the street, the sidewalks littered with bright plastic bikes, scooters, and skates. None of the homes was especially well kept, but none was in really bad shape. Mostly, they looked tired.

The house I was looking for was in the middle of the block. I pulled up in front and spent a moment studying it. Placed farther back on the lot than its neighbors, the front door was covered with a heavy metal screen door that looked new; the front windows were large, light, and clean.

The lawn was free of toys and landscaping. The house looked bare, unadorned, but the paint was fresh. On each side of the house was a high front fence, on one side a gate secured by a chain. The garage door was down and didn't have a handle, indicating it could only be worked by an automatic opener. I looked around. The house on one side had more trees, more bushes, but they weren't trimmed, and the paint was peeling off the rafters. The house on the opposite side had an even higher backyard fence and, judging from the growls behind it, more than one unfriendly dog. That garage door was also firmly shut. The only indication that this house was different from its neighbors was the small plaque above the mailbox that said "Grace House."

I walked up to the front door and rang the bell. "Ellen." Anne Kennedy opened the front door. "Your timing's perfect. I just got here myself." She fumbled for a second, but the screen door stayed shut. "Sorry. We have a new door and the lock's tricky. I'm not too good at it yet." There was a snap and the heavy screen opened. "There. Come in."

I stepped into a surprising room. I don't know what I'd expected, something depressing I guess, but this room was anything but. Bright flowered slipcovers on the two sofas, a rocking chair, and a deep red upholstered chair with an ottoman, all clustered around a low round coffee table that held a red bowl filled with pinecones and greenery. There was a Christmas tree in the corner, ablaze with lights, decorated with strings of cranberry, popcorn, and paper ornaments made by small hands. A fireplace sat in the middle of a long wall, scenting the room with last night's fire. It was flanked by bookcases overflowing with books, games, and DVDs, many of them Disney. Two shelves had been removed to make room for a TV. Windows filled the wall that faced the street. They were all covered with louvered blinds, open to let in the sparse winter light.

"It came out pretty well, didn't it?" Anne grinned at me.

I grinned back. It was hard not to. How this slightly plump, past middle age, grandmotherly looking woman could deal with the problems she must see day in and day out and still remain so cheerful, I didn't know. It made my bad temper over a ridiculous wedding dress and a garish wedding cake seem trivial. Well, almost trivial.

"It's great," I assured her. "Better than lots of the other houses I've seen in this neighborhood."

"I wanted it to be as cheerful as possible." She looked around the room. "These women and their kids have gone through bad times. They need something a little uplifting, even if it's only slipcovers." Then she laughed. "Besides, they wash. Come on, I'll show you the rest of it."

The house had three bedrooms, two with multiple beds, and they were all obviously occupied. "Many of these women come with their kids." Anne waved at the Spiderman pajamas and the Cinderella nightgown neatly folded on the dresser in one of the rooms. The only other sign of the presence of children was the Disney backpack propped up in the corner. "They have to stay in one room because of the lack of space, but also because these kids need to stay close to their moms. Lots of these women are newly divorced, or in the process. Often the husband won't provide support, and the woman isn't trained to do anything that comes close to making a living, or she's been out of the work force so long she can't go back to her old job. That's where we come in. But we do a lot more than job training. Counseling, help with child care, money management, and most important, we give them time to get back on their feet. We give them hope." She laughed and led the way to the next room. "Sounds a little pompous, maybe, but lots of times we can make the difference between a woman starting a successful new life or ending up on the streets."

The rooms were spartan in their furnishings, and in their neatness. Except for the last one. It had twin beds, one neatly made. The other was heaped with a blanket and bedspread tangled together. Clothes spilled out of the suitcase in the corner and a sweatshirt in obvious need of washing had been thrown on the low dresser along with a brush, hairspray, and what looked like an open pot of face cream. Clothing that smelled faintly of smoke and was hopefully also destined for the washing machine was piled in front of the dresser.

Anne looked at the mess and sighed. "Sometimes we can't pair up the women. That's another factor that makes us hard-up for space."

As we went through the bedrooms and bathrooms, I made notes on my legal pad. The shower dripped in one and the toilet wobbled in the other. One of the bedroom windows refused to open and a closet door wouldn't stay closed. Easy fixes. My home inspector would tell me if there were others. These are the repairs I like to have made before we put the house on the market. If left undone, buyers will always use them as bargaining chips to get a lower price.

We entered the kitchen, a corridor style with a door at the end that opened into the garage. A chipped Formica counter— topped with open shelves filled with mismatched plates, bowls, and coffee mugs—evidently doubled as a breakfast and lunch area. Two women sat on stools, one making circles with a wet glass on the countertop, the other pulling on a cigarette, waving the smoke away from her companion with her free hand as she puffed. Both had plates in front of them with the remains of what looked and smelled like tuna salad sandwiches. Behind them was a long table surrounded by an assortment of chairs. A blue and white crockery rooster sat in the middle of the table, a look of perpetual surprise on its face. A sliding glass door opened onto a good-sized backyard surrounded by the same high fence I had seen across the front. The lawn was piled high with decaying leaves and fringed with dormant untrimmed bushes. A single swing, hanging from the bare branch of a large tree, rocked all alone, pushed by the early winter breeze.

The older of the two women looked up as we entered and hurriedly ground her cigarette out in a saucer. Her blond hair showed dark brown at the roots; her face was long and thin. So was the rest of her. Her glance at me was cursory and dismissive. It was Anne who had her attention. Waving at the lingering smoke, she pushed the saucer farther away. She looked up at Anne but immediately dropped her eyes, like a child caught in the act of stealing a forbidden cookie.

"Leona." Anne said the woman's name like she was throwing a dart at a corkboard. She marched across the kitchen, also waving at the smoke. "This is a smoke- free house. You know that. If you can't ..." She glanced at me, and the fury in her voice subsided a little. "I've told you before not to smoke in here, and I've told you the consequences. We have rules ..." She looked at me again, then snapped at the woman, "Why aren't you at work?"

Leona turned slightly and looked at me again before she answered. She took in my baggy but warm sweater, my somewhat scuffed running shoes, and my lack of makeup and evidently decided I was—what. A new resident? At any rate, I was someone Anne didn't mind talking in front of so she nodded at me slightly before she answered. "Ruthie said it was slow. I could go home."

Ruthie? The Yum Yum's Ruthie?

"I've never been there at lunch hour when it was slow."

Had to be the Yum Yum, and Anne was right. People always had to wait for tables at lunch hour. The waitresses were all as highly charged as Ruthie herself. She wouldn't stand for anything else. This woman looked like a study in slow motion. Even the hand she used to wave away the smoke was slow, lazy. She must be driving Ruthie crazy. I wondered why she'd hired her.

"Leona, I had to move heaven and earth to get you that job."

That was why.

"You've got to …" She broke off and gave an exasperated sigh. It sounded as if Anne had a lot of practice being exasperated with Leona. But there was something else in Anne's voice. Anger. Boiling, roiling anger. Well controlled, but there. Our sweet-faced, patient Anne had quite a temper.

"He's been doin' it again." Leona's announcement was made in a raspy habitual smoker's voice and the words came out rushed. It sounded a lot like subject-changing to me. "You've got to do something, or Marilee here's"—this time she waved at the girl sitting beside her—"goin' to have a nervous collapse."

Leona's subject change worked. Anne turned her attention to the girl sitting beside Leona. She looked to be about eighteen or so and was as pretty as her companion was plain. Clouds of strawberry blond hair caught up in a clip, an oval face that reminded me of my grandmother's cameo, a tiny upturned nose, and eyes more green than blue framed by thick lashes. Her delicate prettiness was spoiled only by the fact she was in the last stage of pregnancy. There was no happy glow of expectation on her face. Not that there should have been. The last few weeks before a baby comes are downright miserable. This girl looked not only miserable but lost. What had happened to her? She should have been in school, worrying about college classes, sororities—well, maybe—but at least football games and other college things, like passing her classes. She should not be sitting in Grace House with red-rimmed eyes, swollen huge with child.

"Who's been doing what again? Not Doctor Sadler?" Anne studied Marilee closely, anger replaced with worry.

"Yeah. He was back here this morning telling Marilee how she had to give up her baby, sayin' there's no way she can raise it. Sayin' a baby needs two parents. Marilee kept telling him Grady kicked her out. All the more reason to put the kid up for adoption. Wouldn't let up."

The anger was back "That …" she said softly. I watched, fascinated, as she dug her fingernails into the palms of her hands and clenched her teeth firmly over whatever it was she wanted to say. After a second, she took a deep breath and walked over to stand beside the girl. Anne slid her hand gently around the girl's shoulder and gave it a small squeeze. "Tell me what happened. Did you tell him you didn't want to give it up?"

The girl kept her eyes on the counter, still moving the glass around, although it no longer made wet circles. "I tried to." Her voice was so low it was almost inaudible. Anne leaned in closer, and I found myself straining to hear as well.

"What happened then?"

"He didn't listen. Just said he'd bring by some paperwork for me to sign and left."

"Oh, Lord." This time Anne didn't look angry. She looked stricken. "I'm so sorry I wasn't here. What did you do? Call Leona?"

Marilee looked surprised. "No. I called Gina. At the bakery." She ducked her head, and her voice got even softer, if that were possible. "I was crying. Gina said I shouldn't be alone in case he came back. She couldn't come right then because Rose was out someplace, but Leona could."

Anne let her arm drop and turned slowly to look at Leona. "You were at the bakery?"

Leona flushed. "Well, since I wasn't needed at the Yum Yum, I thought I'd stop in and see what Gina was doing."

Gina? Ianelli's Bakery? That Gina? How did these people know her? Could she be a resident of Grace House? She sure hadn't impressed me as a woman who needed rescuing. Come to think of it, she'd talked about her wedding cake, but I hadn't seen a wedding ring. At least, I didn't remember one. So, maybe …

I didn't have long to ponder Gina's marital or mental state. Anne gave Leona one of those "we're going to talk later and you probably won't like it" looks and returned to

Marilee. "Honey, we've talked about this before. This is your baby. The decision is yours, not Doctor Sadler's, not Grady's. Do you want to change your mind and give it up for adoption?"

Marilee looked up for the first time. Her eyes gleamed with unshed tears, but there was a tightening around her mouth that just might be determination. She looked Anne full in the face, then back down at her swollen belly. Very softly she lifted a hand and dropped it down to caress the bulge. "No."

Anne nodded. "I'll talk to him. Again. Now, let's get this kitchen cleaned up. You two ate lunch late today and Nathan will be here any minute. It's almost time for group."

Both Leona and Marilee got up. Leona picked up her saucer, looked at it, glanced at Anne, emptied it in the trash, and stood, holding it, looking around. Marilee took it from her, rinsed it off, picked up the other dishes, put them all in the dishwasher, and wiped down the counter where she and Leona had been sitting. She sniffed the air, glanced at Anne, and picked up a can of air spray. The artificial smell of spring flowers mixed with the oppressive smell of smoke.

No one paid attention when the front door opened. The heavy screen clanged, and the sound of footsteps was only partially muffled by the thin carpet. A young man entered. Tall, pleasant looking, dressed in Chino's and a Land's Ends V-neck blue sweater over a turtleneck, he looked as if he should be teaching math in an Ivy League college instead of standing in the kitchen of a home for distressed women. But he obviously belonged because he shifted a pile of files he carried and beamed a greeting at everyone.

"You forgot to lock the front door again." He said it in an offhand way, as if it were a regular occurrence, then he also sniffed the air. "Who's been smoking? Oh." He frowned as he looked at Leona, who ignored him, then at Anne, who shrugged slightly. "Leona, second- hand smoke is not good for the baby. Or Marilee. You know the rules."

"Yeah, I know. I forgot. Won't happen again." Leona dropped her eyes and stared at the Formica countertop. Her hands were clenched fists.

The young man—I assumed this was the expected Nathan—looked as though he wanted to say a lot more about the smoking but didn't.

"Good news. I think I've got a line on another computer we can use and ..." He stopped, looking at me as if just noticing my presence. He nodded and gave me an encouraging smile. I wondered if he, too, thought I was a new resident. Well, the way I was dressed, maybe he did. Aunt Mary was right. I should have worn pantyhose.

"Where is everyone? Has Janice gone? Is she all right?" He looked closer at Marilee. "What's been going on?" Cheerfulness was replaced by anxiety.

"Doctor Sadler paid us another visit this morning." Anne's tone seemed deliberately mild.

"Damn." He sat the files down on the table and walked over to Marilee, who was still standing at the sink. He took the dishtowel out of her hand and hung it on a hook shaped like a cow's head before he touched her on the arm. "Are you all right?"

Marilee put one hand on her back and retreated a little, not meeting his eyes. "Fine. I'm fine."

Nathan turned to Anne, who gave an almost infinitesimal shrug. He turned back to Marilee. "He was at you again to put the baby up for adoption?"

"Yeah." If Marilee pushed herself any farther back into the counter she'd end up in the sink. Evidently Nathan noticed, because he stepped away from her.

"One of these days, I'm going to kill that old man," he muttered.

"Nathan," Anne said in a warning tone. "Marilee's going to do just what she planned. We'll talk about it later. And, no, Janice isn't gone. They won't have room for her until tomorrow. But Ian had a slight fever, and Margaret—" Anne paused and glanced over at me, "she's one of our volunteers—drove them to the doctor. They should be back soon. But we have to complete our plans to move them. We're not set up to … oh, Gina. There you are."

It was the Ianelli's Bakery Gina. She stood in the doorway, holding a large pink bakery box and a sack of what might have been rolls, looking from one to the other of us. Her eyes lingered on me longest, the surprise in them not hidden. "Why, hi." She smiled at me and then walked over to the counter, where she set down the pink bakery box and the sack. "I brought some potato rolls that … uh … Sal made today and a fudge cake for dinner. I thought the kids would like some."

This was addressed to Anne, but then she turned to me. "I didn't expect to see you here. I thought—"

"I am. And no, I'm not. I'm here to see Anne. About real estate."

Gina blinked a couple of times. "What?"

Anne started to laugh. "Oh, did you think … Ellen's not … she's our real estate agent. She's going to find us a bigger house and then sell this one."

"Ellen and I already met."

"Really? Where?"

"Over her wedding cake."

"She's getting married?" Leona looked appalled.

"Well, yes." Anne had a "what does that have to do with anything" look.

"Not a good idea." Leona really looked at me for the first time.

"To the police chief," Gina went on.

"*Really* not a good idea," Leona stated. "Cops are notorious for beating up their wives. I oughta know. My first husband was a cop. He even stole my kids."

"What did your second husband do?" Marilee's words came out soft and didn't sound as if she cared much.

36

Leona didn't say anything for a moment. "He drank. And when he finished drinking, he beat me up. Oh, you mean what did he do for a living? Construction. He ran all the heavy equipment. Then one day he'd had too much beer with lunch. He dropped the crane on someone. Broke the guy's back. Killed him." She paused, her hand creeping toward a pocket where a package of cigarettes bulged. Her fingers touched them, but she left them where they were. "They fired him. Now, there's a no-brainer. Only he didn't think so. He came home and tried to break mine. Went to jail for that one. Got ten years. For the guy he dropped the crane on. Not for what he did to me." There was a whole lot of bitterness in that statement. It didn't sound as if Leona's life had been much fun. And it showed. I took another quick look. She probably had been pretty once. But not now. She looked dour and unkempt. And sad.

"Leona, Nathan's time is short." Anne glanced at me and then at Nathan. "And so is Ellen's. Why don't you all go into the living room and get your group started? Ellen and I need to talk about houses."

"Good idea." Nathan immediately made sweeping gathering gestures, propelling the three women toward the living room. Blurting out personal histories to anyone but your counselor evidently wasn't encouraged.

Gina took Marilee by the arm. "You okay, sweetie?"

Marilee tried a smile. It wasn't very successful. "Yeah. I guess so." She reached down and patted her tummy. Gina reached over and patted it also.

"You're going to be fine, and so is this little one. Come on. Let's go make sure Nathan earns his salary."

Leona slowly followed them, a scowl on her face. Nathan picked up his files, rolled his eyes at Anne, and also disappeared into the living room.

I must have looked confused, because Anne started to explain. "Nathan is our counselor. He comes three afternoons a week, twice to do group counseling sessions, the other time for career counseling, which is a fancy way of saying we need to get them some kind of job that may eventually pay a living wage. We've established quite a list of businesses where we can place our women. They get training and a small salary. It's a bit like an apprentice program. Then, as they get stronger emotionally and acquire life skills, they also have job skills. This is an open house, but we do have some rules, and group sessions are required."

I looked at the battered oak desk jammed into the corner next to the sliding door. It held, barely, an antique computer and a printer made about the time of Ben Franklin. The keyboard sat on top with almost no room left to maneuver the mouse. I thought about the bookshelves in the living room that were overflowing with books, videos, and board games, and how the furniture was clustered tightly around the low table. Some of those books must be textbooks, but where did anyone go in this cramped house to study? Not in one of the dormitory style bedrooms, and there was no place else in the house that was any better. "I see why you need more space. But, don't they rotate or something? I mean, you must have a time limit on how long they can stay, don't you?"

"Yes, but it's flexible. Usually we say no more than one hundred twenty days, but sometimes that's not enough, and sometimes they're ready to move on sooner. We always have more women in need than we can take. I wouldn't have taken Janice—she really doesn't fit our program—but she was an emergency. She'll be gone tomorrow. The other three are fairly typical and we're working on programs for them. Now, what have you brought me?"

I moved the rooster down to the end of the table and spread out the papers. For the first time I was getting excited about this project. I might be pushed for time and in danger of running out of energy, but Grace House was a good idea, doing some really valuable work, and I wanted to be a part of it.

Anne needed to know how much money we would have to work with after all the costs of the sale had been deducted. I needed to know if she agreed with my suggested sales price. I put the graphs, showing comparable closed sales and similar homes currently offered for sale, in front of her. I had also prepared a net sheet, estimating the costs of the sale and what the final check to Grace House was likely to be. She barely glanced at any of it. "I'll take this to the board, but I'm sure you're right and that they'll agree. Did you bring any information on houses that might work?"

Okay. So Anne wasn't quite the businesswoman Aunt Mary thought she was. The board could handle that end of it. Anne's energies seemed to be focused entirely on the women and what programs she wanted to offer. And why not? That's what she was there for. I handed her a stack of listings I thought might work. She immediately started to look through them.

I got up and wandered around the kitchen, making notes as I went. "Are you leaving the refrigerator?"

"If I can. That thing belongs on the Antiques Roadshow."

I laughed and made another note on my sheet. "You talked about classrooms. For the women or for their children? The more you can tell me about what you do and how you set it up, the more time I can save by not dragging you out to look at things that won't work."

Anne stopped shuffling through the pile of listings and nodded. "I want to start a daycare in the new house. I'll need room for it, away from the living area of the residents. It would be a real win/win. Some of our women could work toward being licensed preschool employees, and the children of our residents would have a safe place to stay while their mothers work or go to school. We also need an area where the women can study or get on the computer. In addition to working, they're encouraged to enroll in classes that will help them, and we often have older children who need a place where they can do their homework. It doesn't have to be big, but we need a quiet area, separate from the living room."

"What a great idea," I said. "And the daycare sounds wonderful. Then someone like Marilee would have a place to leave her baby." Marilee had captured my imagination. Where were her parents? Where was the father of her baby? "Will she be staying long?" I asked.

Anne's face sort of closed up and she looked down at the sheets she had spread out all over the table. "She'll stay here for a while. As you heard, she wants to keep her baby. We'll do everything we can to help her do that."

"She seems so young." About Susannah's age.

"Yes. Look at this one. It comes closest. But I'd like more bedrooms and maybe a dining room." It was clear there would be no more discussion about the residents.

The house she had picked out was charming, or could be. It was in the old part of town, convenient to everything, but it needed work. Thousands of dollars of work. I told her so. Anne put it face down on the rest of them and sighed. "I'm sure you'll come up with something."

I gathered up the pile of rejected listings, slipped all of the information she would need to take to the board in a folder, handed it to her, and prepared to leave. "I have a much better idea of what you need. I'll call you tomorrow with what else I've found."

She nodded and started to get to her feet.

I hesitated. I wanted to ask one more question but wasn't sure how to phrase it tactfully. Maybe there wasn't a way.

"What does Doctor Sadler have to do with you? I mean, his wife founded Grace House. Does he have a say about what we buy, or how we price this place?"

"He's on the board, if that's what you mean, and is a major financial contributor." It took Anne a minute. She opened and closed her mouth a couple of times and cleared her throat before going on. "Do you know Doctor Sadler?"

"Not really. I know who he is, of course. I remember he was in Rotary with my father. My mother didn't like him."

Anne smiled at that. "A lot of women in this town don't like him. He's bossy. So he'll probably try to tell us all what to do, explain why we're so misguided, and refuse to listen to any opinion but his own. But Owen has only one vote, even if he'd like you to believe he runs the whole thing. The rest of the board is much easier to deal with."

"Even though his wife started Grace House?"

"Francis was a smart woman. I think she loved Owen, but she wasn't under any illusions. She wanted Grace House to work."

Wasn't that interesting? But it didn't entirely erase my concern that Doctor Sadler wouldn't try to sabotage any transaction the board decided to make if he didn't agree with it. I would have to count on Anne to make sure that didn't happen. No, actually I wouldn't. My Aunt Mary was on that board. I had nothing to worry about.

I said goodbye, thinking I had my work cut out for me on this one, and had turned to leave when the garage door groaned and started up.

Anne's head snapped around, and her body stiffened. "That's Margaret. She never uses the garage. Why is she coming in the garage? Something's wrong."

Chapter Five

A car pulled in. The garage door sounded a protest and started down again before the engine shut off. Anne was at the kitchen door, pulling it open as a woman came through, a small girl in her arms. The child's legs were wound around her mother's waist, pushing down her gray sweatpants. Her arms were tight around her mother's neck, her head buried in her shoulders. A boy, about five, clung to her free arm, his eyes huge and scared.

"What happened?" Anne's tone was grim. She took the boy's free arm and pulled them all into the kitchen. "Where's Margaret?"

A brisk looking woman of about fifty came into the room. Her hands shook as she slipped a set of car keys into a huge purse. "I'm right here. He saw us."

"Damn!" The expletive almost exploded out of Anne's mouth. "What happened?"

"Someone from the doctor's office must have tipped him off."

This had to be Janice. But who had seen them, and why did that make her go pale and give her voice a tremor?

"Emily, get down. Ian, let go. We're fine now." She tried unsuccessfully to detach the little girl from her hip. Her sweatpants slid down a little farther, revealing a pair of bright blue underpants. She flushed, shifted the child, and pulled her sweats back up. The boy just moved his grip from her hand to her arm.

"He was waiting for us when we came out." Margaret tried hard to act calm and controlled, but her voice trembled and the look on her face was a combination of fury and fear.

She put her purse down on the counter and went to the refrigerator. "Ian, how about some juice? The doctor said you needed lots of fluids. Look, orange juice." She took a glass from the cupboard and filled it. "Come on, let's sit here at the counter. Mommy will sit right beside you."

Ian detached himself from his mother, climbed up on one of the stools, and started to devour the cookies Margaret had put beside the juice. Janice sat down beside him, still holding the little girl, offering her a cookie and a sip from the second glass Margaret set in front of them. Her hand shook so badly the juice spilled onto the counter.

During all of this Anne waited, anxiety showing through the veneer of her patience. Margaret put the juice carton back into the refrigerator and walked around the counter toward the table. Anne followed. So did I. Margaret raised one eyebrow. Anne glanced my way as if about to ask me to leave. She didn't. "Did he follow you?"

"He sure tried," Margaret said grimly. A grin broke over her face but immediately faded. "He was no match for Nascar Margaret, though. I saw him about the same time he saw us and managed to leave him behind at that long light on Main and Chestnut. I thought he was going to run it. Maybe he did, but he hesitated too long. I made a couple of quick turns and lost him."

"Are you sure?"

Margaret's grim look was back. "No."

Neither said anything for a moment. "Okay." Anne looked at Janice, who still clutched the little girl tightly. "Janice, what will he do now? I mean, he saw you. He knows you're someplace close. What will he do?"

"Try and find us." She looked down at the child on her lap and stroked her hair. "That's why I asked Margaret to park the car in the garage. He'll remember it. He'll be driving around right now, trying to locate it."

Driving around? Trying to find them? Could she mean ... I'd read Anna Quinlan's *Black and Blue*. I'd seen *The*

Burning Bed on TV. Could this be … surely not.

Anne thought for a moment, her mouth set in a grim line. "I think our timetable just got moved up. It's time to get you out of here. Margaret, can you help them pack?" She turned to me. "Ellen, would you go tell Nathan I need him? Now. I'm going to make a couple of phone calls."

Janice had been watching us with hooded eyes. "We can't take Margaret's car."

"I know." Anne already had the phone and was dialing. "Go get ready to leave."

Janice slid off the stool, shifted the child to her hip, handed her the one remaining cookie, helped the boy off the stool, and started for the hallway that led to the bedrooms. No one said a word, not even the children. Margaret looked at Anne, shook her head, sighed, and hurried after them. I watched them go. The sense of danger, impending danger, was heavy in the air, making it difficult to breathe. Or maybe that was fear. Those books, the movie, were just stories, horrible … but stories. This was real, and I was having a hard time believing it. After all, this was just some guy looking for his wife and kids. How dangerous could that be?

Anne was already talking to someone, so I started for the living room. I met Nathan head on.

"What's happened?"

"I don't know," I said. "At least I don't understand. Janice's husband saw her and the kids at the doctor's and evidently tried to follow them. Now everyone is panicking."

"Oh, Lord." Nathan's good-natured grin faded. "Where's Anne?"

"In the kitchen making phone calls. What's going on?"

He stopped, opened his mouth, closed it, and shook his head. "You might have to help, so you'd better understand."

"Understand what?" I really wished he wouldn't look so grim. I was trying to convince myself that whatever was going on wasn't serious, or dangerous, and he wasn't helping.

"We take women who need help to get to the next stage of their lives, but we're not equipped for women who need protection. Only sometimes… Well, we took Janice and her kids because if we didn't, something really ugly might have happened. Janice's husband has threatened to kill her and, given his track record, it seemed a good idea to pay attention. If he's seen her, or has any idea of where she is, then we have to get her out of here. San Luis Obispo will just have to make room."

He turned to go into the kitchen, leaving me speechless. All of this was real. I followed, wondering with growing unease what was going to happen next, and how I could possibly help. It didn't take long to find out.

Anne was on the phone, talking in low, urgent tones. "Yes, we need to get them moved today. Nathan will have them. Where can he meet you?" She looked up as I came in. "Ellen, can you hand me a pad of paper? And a pen? They're right … thanks. Okay. Where? Got it. What time? No. They can't leave right now. I have to find out where he is and make sure … yes, I'll call you. No more than thirty minutes. Okay. Thanks."

She hung up and turned to Nathan. "Can you do it?"

"Of course. I don't think he knows my car. But how are we going to get them in it? I'm parked on the street, and if he's driving around, looking, we can't chance taking them out the front. And since he saw Margaret's car … we better leave it in the garage unless we're sure he's not around."

"How can you be sure?" Anne ran fingers through her hair. It was starting to look as if this wasn't the first time.

The tension was building, but I didn't want to believe that this woman, Janice, was truly in danger. "So what if he does see them? He can't do anything, can he? Not with everyone here. I mean, just tell him to go away."

Nathan looked at me as if I had lost my mind.

Anne said, "If only it worked that way. This man has threatened to kill Janice. He came close to doing it last year.

She stayed because she was afraid to leave, afraid for herself and for the kids. But a couple of days ago, she walked in on him with the little girl. He was ... he had her ... It's a good thing she found them when she did. The next day, when he was out of the house, she called us." She paused, as if trying to emphasize what she was going to say next. "The most dangerous time for an abused woman and her kids is when she's trying to leave. More women are killed then than any other time in these rotten relationships. Janice knows that. But when she saw how close her daughter came to ... when she realized what he was going to do to her, and that he'd try again, somehow the courage was there. She's still just one step away from not being able to function, but she's gotten this far."

"We don't normally take women like Janice, but this time we had to." Nathan's voice was grim, his expression angry and worried. "If he finds her before she gets a chance to get a restraining order and at least temporary custody of the kids, it's entirely possible he could take them away from her. And if that happens, she'll go back also. I don't think I have to tell you what might happen then. So, we need to get them down to San Luis Obispo. They're making room."

I felt a little sick. And I thought I'd had it bad. Brian was nothing like this man. A cheater, yes. Verbal abuse, he was an expert. But he'd never hit me or made me fear for my life. And he'd never touched Susannah. If he had ...

"How about a traffic stop? By the cops."

Nathan and Anne looked at each other, and then they both stared at me. "A traffic stop would be perfect. That way we'd know where he was." Nathan exchanged another look with Anne. "I could make sure we went another way, only ... how can we do that?"

"I have an idea." Janice and her children were going to get to San Luis Obispo. Safely. "It happens that I know the police chief." I grinned, and suddenly Anne looked hopeful. "Which means I know some of the staff. I could give Ida a call and see if something could be arranged."

"Who's Ida?" Nathan asked.

"The dispatcher. She's great, and she adores Dan."

Anne gave a short laugh. "Let's hope she adores you also. You're willing to try this?"

"Sure." I gulped, wondering just how much I was overstepping my boundaries. I didn't care. The vision of the child clinging to her mother, the spilled orange juice as the woman tried to hold the glass steady, the look in the eyes of those children, the smell of real fear, overwhelmed any reservations I had. Ida was getting a phone call.

"Okay, but you'll need some information. First, his name is Hamilton Winter." Anne stopped and waited, evidently to see if I reacted. I did.

"*The* Hamilton Winter? The local weatherman?"

"Unfortunately, the very one." She studied my face. "Surprised? Don't be. You never know who's going to be an abuser, just like you never know who's going to leave his family high and dry. Not supporting your wife and kids is just as abusive, in its own way, as beating them to a pulp. It just kills them more slowly. Now, how about that phone call?"

"I'll need more than his name. Can you find out what kind of car he drives? And his license number would come in handy."

Anne gave a grim little smile. "Would save some time, wouldn't it?" She turned to Nathan, who nodded and left the kitchen. He was back almost immediately, dragging a navy blue duffel bag filled to more than capacity. Judging by the knobby lumps, clothes were not its only contents. Margaret followed, carrying a Mickey Mouse backpack, equally overstuffed. I wondered how it would feel to have everything you owned, your whole life and your children's, reduced to one overstuffed duffel bag and a backpack advertising Disneyland.

Janice appeared, Emily on her hip and Ian hanging

from her arm. She clutched a slip of paper. "Here. This is the license number. He drives a Lincoln Town Car. What are you going to do?" Her eyes were large and round with anxiety, the lines in her face too deep for a woman her age. But her expression held a faint glimmer of hope as she handed Anne the paper.

"See if we can get you out of here in one piece." Anne took the paper, read it, and handed it to me. "Okay. I think this is all you'll need."

Gina walked into the room before I could pick up the phone. "What's going on?"

"Janice's husband saw them when they left the doctor's office," Nathan said. "We're trying to get them out of here and down to the safe house in San Luis Obispo."

"What kind of car does he drive?"

"A Lincoln Town Car," Anne said. "Why?"

I watched Gina take a deep breath. I think we all knew what she was about to say. "A Lincoln just passed here going slow. A sort of tan colored one. "

I thought Janice was going to pass out. Gina grabbed Emily and, with her other hand, lowered Janice onto one of the stools. The child started to howl. Janice reached out for her. The child knelt on her mother's knees and immediately buried her head in her neck.

"Mom?" Ian pushed up close to his mother. "Is Dad going to come in here?" His eyes were blinking, as if he were fighting tears. "Does he know we're in here?"

"No." Anne knelt down in front of Ian and took his hand. "No, Ian. He doesn't know. But just to make sure, we're going to send you to another house, one your Dad doesn't know anything about. Nathan will take you. You're going to be fine, and so is your Mom." She gave him a hug then looked up at us. "Gina, go back in the living room and see if he comes around again. Ellen, make your phone call."

Everyone in the room watched as I flipped open my cell— Nathan and Anne with expectancy and hope, Janice with what appeared to be a mixture of dread and resignation. Three rings later Ida picked up.

"You want me to do what? What will Dan say?"

"Nothing until he knows. Don't worry, Ida, I'll take full responsibility. Ask Gary to go. He's on duty, isn't he? Tell him this guy's a wife beater first, a VIP second. And Ida," I lowered my voice, hopefully enough so that the children couldn't hear. "He tried to … abuse his daughter. They need to leave, *now*. In the next ten minutes. Gary'll do it."

There was a pause. "My first husband hit me. Just once. I picked up my baby and got out. Fast. Don't worry, Ellen. Gary will stop this guy. A routine taillight check works pretty well, and, of course, he'll need to call it in, talk a while, you know. I'll call you when I know where he is. Tell this creep's wife good luck. Oh, and tell her I'm watching channel five from now on." The line went dead.

"She's setting it up. She'll call back with his location as soon as they've made the traffic stop. And he just lost one perfectly good viewer. Probably more."

"Good job." Anne nodded at me. "Okay. Here's what we're going to do. Margaret, you're going to get into your car and go home. Nathan, as soon as she's gone, pull your car into the garage and lower the door. We'll make sure they are in, and just as soon as Ellen gets the call that he's been stopped, you can leave."

Margaret looked stricken. "What if he's out there and sees me? This guy is dangerous."

"Not to you, he's not. If he does see you, he'll also see that your car is empty. And, if he tries to stop you, make sure he sees you're on your cell. Besides, Ellen is going to go out on the front porch with her cell phone and keep watch."

I was? Margaret looked at me speculatively. She didn't seem convinced that would make it safe to leave. It didn't convince me either. Keep watch? What was I supposed to do if he did drive by? However, Margaret had started rummaging in her bag for her keys. Evidently she had decided going was preferable to staying. From the look on her face, I was pretty sure Anne had just lost a volunteer. Briefly, I wondered if I could make that two. One look at Janice and her kids, huddled by their duffel bag, erased that thought. I was headed for the front porch.

Margaret walked over to Janice and gave her a hug. "Good luck." She ran her hand over Emily's hair and dropped a quick kiss on it before kneeling down in front of Ian. She took his hand in hers. "You're a good boy, Ian. Take care of your mom and sister, okay?"

The little boy looked at her with huge eyes and nodded.

"Let's do it." Nathan followed her into the garage, leaving the kitchen door open. He stood in the doorway and turned back to me. "Let me know as soon as you hear where he is."

Anne grabbed Janice's hand and squeezed. "They'll take good care of you down there." She turned to me and gave me what I'm sure she thought was a reassuring smile. "Stand on the front porch and act like you're talking to someone. You have a view down the street in both directions from there. If you see his car, wave your hand like you're trying to make a point and don't look at the car."

"What if Ida calls?"

"Take the call. Then we'll know they have him stopped. If he comes back by again, call out to Gina. She'll be right behind the front door. Then call—is it Ida?—and tell her his location."

There was silence in the kitchen. Margaret was already in her car, waiting. Nathan stood in the kitchen door, his car keys in his hand, also waiting. Anne looked at me expectantly. Janice just stood there, with her kids and her duffel bag, giving an occasional little shiver. Unfortunately, Anne's plan made sense. I tried not to let anyone see how scared I was as I picked up my cell phone and headed for the living room. I gave myself a little pep talk. After all, this guy wasn't after me. He didn't even know I existed. It was Janice and the kids he wanted. All I had to do was stand on the front porch and see if he drove by. Somehow, it didn't help.

"What's going on?" Marilee sat on the sofa, pillows stuffed behind her back. Leona sat upright in the red chair, the ottoman pushed to one side, watching everyone closely. The expression on her face was grave, but I got the impression that it was a front, a mask. Leona was excited by all the drama, the tension. Marilee, on the other hand, looked pasty white, her eyes huge, her mouth pinched. The poor kid was scared to death.

"Is it Grady? Gina, is that who you saw driving around out there?"

"No, sweetie. It was Janice's husband. We're going to move them. Now."

"Does he know they're in here?"

"No. And he's not going to find out. We're going to whisk Janice and those babies off to San Luis Obispo right under his nose. So don't you worry."

I didn't think it was Janice's husband Marilee was worried about. As soon as she heard that Grady—whoever he was— wasn't patrolling the street she relaxed. "This is so awful. Poor Janice. And those children." Marilee dropped her hand onto her stomach again and stroked it, as if comforting her unborn child. "At least Grady never hit me. Well, only when he was drunk, and he never tried to kill me. Even when he learned I was pregnant."

Grady? Her husband? Probably. Father of her baby, in any case. How nice he didn't hit her when he was sober. I wondered, briefly, how often he got drunk.

"Ellen, you better get out there. Where's your cell?"

I held it up and gave an audible gulp. Gina grinned at me. I couldn't make myself grin back.

"You'll be fine." She turned to the other two with much too much enthusiasm. "Ellen's going to be our lookout."

"Yeah?"

Leona looked at me as if she didn't share that

enthusiasm. I couldn't have agreed with her more. But Gina was at the door, holding it open. I went through it.

I've never wanted to be an actress, but never as badly as at that moment. What on earth was I supposed to do? I stood on the porch, very aware of the closed front door, held my cell phone to my ear, leaned up against a skinny pillar and tried to look natural. My mouth was so dry I couldn't even croak.

Nothing happened. Finally a green Honda Van turned into the street. It pulled into the driveway of the house across the street. A woman got out and opened the back door. Two kids and a dog jumped out. They all trooped into the house without a glance in my direction. After a few minutes the woman came back out, removed two bags of groceries from the van, glanced in my direction, and nodded. I nodded back. She went into the house.

What seemed like hours passed. I shifted my weight from foot to foot, let my head swivel from right to left, all the while pretending to talk. My hand and arm were starting to protest. I was tempted to give in and drop my arm down when a car turned the corner. A tan colored Lincoln Town Car was headed slowly my way. I could see the driver clearly, checking each house, each parked car. There was no mistaking that head of silver hair, that leading-man profile. It appeared nightly on the six o'clock news. He slowed a little when he saw me on the porch. I could see him lean over to get a better look, and the driver's window started to slide down.

It was panic, not acting ability, that made me believable. I started to talk into the dead cell phone as if my life depended on it. "Gina, it's him," I said between clenched teeth. I started to walk back and forth on the porch, ignoring the car, waving my arm as if I were having a madly important conversation. I was. "Gina, he's trying to talk to me." I turned my back to the car and kept pacing and waving. "Damn, he's calling out something." I kept pacing and waving. After a minute the engine picked up and the car slowly moved off. I kept talking and waving but got up enough courage to sneak a look. The car had turned the corner headed west.

The door of the house opened, and I bolted through it.

"Which way did he turn?"

"To the right."

"Should Margaret start?"

"No. Not yet." I dialed 911. "Ida, he's cruised by Grace House twice. He was just here and turned the corner going toward Cherry." I listened for a moment then hung up.

Anne appeared, looking a question at me. I was finally able to smile. "Gary's on his way. Ida will call just as soon as they stop him. Margaret can start, but she needs to go toward Elm."

"Come tell Nathan."

I followed Anne back to the kitchen. Janice was standing by the counter. Emily was sitting on it, her arms wrapped around her mother, her head still buried in her mother's neck. Ian stood by her side, his arms around her hips. I gave her a "thumbs up" as I came in. Her smile was tight-lipped, her face pinched and white, her eyes huge, but she kept patting her kids, first one, then the other, murmuring to them the whole time that things were going to be "fine, just fine." She had more courage than I would ever have.

Nathan stood by the kitchen door, keys in his hand. "Have they stopped him yet?"

"Not yet, but they know where he is."

"Where?"

"Over on Cherry."

"Okay."

He leaned down and said something to Margaret, then straightened up and hit the button on the garage door opener. The door started its slow ascent. We heard Margaret's engine start and she was backing down the driveway as the door settled itself on the garage ceiling. Her tires squealed a little as she turned into the street, the engine roared, then silence. But not for long. More engine noise as Nathan pulled his car into the garage. The door groaned in protest once more and clanged against the concrete as it closed.

"We did it." Nathan came through the door with a large grin on his face. "I'm putting Margaret up for Driver of the Year. You should have seen her take that corner." No one smiled with him. It just wasn't a smiling moment.

Gina came back into the kitchen, followed closely by Marilee and Leona. "Are they ready to leave?"

Anne barely glanced at them. "Just as soon as we know he's stopped. We're not taking any chances. But I'm alerting their ride. Ellen, can I borrow your cell phone? I've run my battery down." I handed it to her, and she dialed. "They'll be leaving in a few minutes." She listened a moment. "Good. And good luck. Yes. I'll talk to you tomorrow."

She snapped the phone shut and turned toward us. "Okay. Let's get that duffel in the car, then Janice and the kids. You have to be ready to roll as soon as we get that phone call."

Emily started to wail. "Not without my kitty."

She had a cat? I hadn't known they allowed pets, but it made sense. Pets were important. I thought of Jake, my big, lazy, yellow tomcat. He was the only thing, besides Susannah, I'd really cared about when I left Brian, or rather when he'd thrown me out. I'd taken stuff, mostly because his new girlfriend, who was moving in, wanted everything new, but only Susannah and Jake had really mattered. How horrible for this little girl to have to leave her cat behind. And I was sure she would have to. There was no room in that duffel bag for it.

Janice was trying to comfort the child while looking around with wild eyes; Nathan was lugging the duffel bag toward the kitchen door, saying they had to go. The child's cries got louder and more hysterical, and the boy's face was crumbling as well. Any second there would be two hysterical children, and the way I felt, an adult just might join them.

Leona walked over to Janice and reached out for the child. "Your poor mom's back's gonna give out. Want me to hold you for a while?"

The child buried her face deeper in her mother's shoulder and cried harder.

"Not now, Leona." Anne sounded as if she were barely holding on. "For God's sake, the child is under enough stress. Let's concentrate on getting them out of here. Doesn't anyone know where that damned cat is?"

"Look." Marilee stood in the doorway, holding a white, fluffy, stuffed cat in one hand. The other held the small of her back. "You left him on the coffee table." She handed the toy to the child, who grabbed it with one hand, never loosening her grip on her mother's neck. She buried her face in the soft fur, let loose another couple of sobs, and quieted. Her brother edged a little closer and patted his sister on the leg, still clinging tightly to his mother's arm. The frantic look that had been building eased, but the worry in his eyes didn't.

My cell phone rang.

"Hello?" Anne answered on the second ring. "Yes, she's right here." She handed it to me.

"Ida?" Talk about timing. "Gary's got him stopped? Yeah, I bet he is furious. They're checking his taillights? How long will that take? Well, stretch it out as long as you can. Where is he? Okay, got it. Tell Gary he's wonderful, and Ida, thanks."

I handed Anne the slip of paper where I'd written the location of the traffic stop.

"Oh, Lord, he's only a couple of blocks from here." Anne's face was pinched and white. So was Janice's.

"Yeah." Somehow that fact, even more than seeing him from the porch, gave me the shivers.

"Lets move, everybody. Janice, get your kids into the car. Nathan, is their stuff in?"

Nathan nodded and opened the kitchen door, practically pushing Janice and the kids through. "Get into the backseat, all of you. Kids, you're on the floor. Janice, duck down on the seat as soon as we're clear of the garage. Just in case."

They obeyed. Nathan slid into the front seat and hit the clicker. The door groaned again and started its slow ascent. The engine started.

"Wish us luck." Nathan's window slid up.

The rest of us were crammed into the kitchen, waiting as the door finally made it up all the way. No one waved as the car backed out, hit the end of the driveway, and turned left. We stepped out into the garage and watched until it turned the corner and was gone. As we returned to the kitchen, Anne paused, reached back and pushed the button. The door protested again and started its slow slide down.

Chapter Six

I drove home slowly, trying to make sense out of what had happened. I'd felt a little uneasy at first, meeting those women whose lives were in so much turmoil. It hadn't been so long since mine had also been turned upside down. Maybe that was why I was uneasy. Their problems made me remember that time—the pain, humiliation, and confusion of being rejected by my husband. I didn't want to be reminded.

Our marriage had effectively been over years before Brian had asked—demanded—a divorce. I'd known that, known I had to do something, but had let it go on, had avoided making those painful decisions until they were thrust on me. Unlike the women at Grace House, I got lucky. Brenda Ferrell was the best attorney a woman could have. She looked like a Newport Beach trophy wife with her designer suits, perfect makeup, thin to the point of emaciation figure, but she had a tongue made out of razor blades and a passion for going after men who tire of their families and no longer want to pay the bills for them after they've found a young playmate. When she was finished with Brian, Susannah had a very generous trust fund and I had … Well, I was in no danger of starving. I wasn't so sure Brian wasn't. I also had a brand new real estate license and a job in Santa Louisa where I'd grown up and where I was more than happy to reestablish my roots. I had Susannah—at least when she wasn't at college—and I had my Aunt Mary, the most grounded person I knew, who made sure I was grounded as well.

And I had Dan. I smiled at the thought. It hadn't been

easy to let myself love him. Twenty years of alternating between neglect and criticism do things to you. They leave wounds, and mine weren't entirely healed. But they were getting better. My foot rested a little heavier on the gas pedal. I could hardly wait to get home. I'd prepare dinner, Dan would have a beer; I'd have wine, and I'd tell him everything that had happened. He already knew about the traffic stop, I was sure. There wasn't much that happened in his police department he didn't know about. But the rest! The threat Hamilton Winter was to his wife, the terror in her eyes, the fear I had felt … and the other women. Marilee, so young, her life in shambles. Maybe Doctor Sadler was right. Maybe she should put the baby up for adoption. But yet, the look in her eyes, the determined set to her chin, the way she touched her tummy … maybe … And Leona. I didn't know what to think about her. Whatever "making it" meant, I didn't think it included Leona. And then there was Gina. There was a sadness about the girl I didn't understand. It had nothing to do with competence or even self-assurance. She seemed at home in the bakery, especially for someone who was learning. She was certainly attractive, and she was nice to other people. Thoughtful. She'd been tender with Rose and she'd brought home a cake for the children. I wondered if they'd taken it. Of course they hadn't. Who cared about cake when you were running for your life? The thought made me shiver. I wondered where Janice and her kids were now. In the safe house in San Luis Obispo, I hoped.

I could hardly wait to hear what Dan thought when I told him. I couldn't believe it. I was going to tell him. Everything. And he would listen and tell me what he thought and then we'd … It would never have occurred to me to tell Brian anything except what time we were due for cocktails at the next fundraiser we were to attend. That brought me back to tonight's dinner. Did I have to stop at the store? No, and I wasn't going by the office either. I could pick up my messages from home, which meant I could swing by the cemetery and avoid the traffic on the main bridge

I was so deep in thought that I almost didn't see her.

The old woman was at the cemetery gates, waving her arms, staggering to keep upright. I braked and backed up.

"What's the matter?" I got to her just as she collapsed. Her face was gray, her breathing coming in labored gasps.

"I think he's dead."

I looked up the drive. What was she talking about? They were all dead. Weren't they?

"Is it your husband?" I asked. "Where is he?"

"Up there." She pointed toward a hill where the graves were littered with statues and granite monuments. "His grave is up there." She paused and took a deep breath. This time her words came out stronger. "It isn't him. It's Doctor Sadler. He's got blood all over him. Someone's killed him. Do something!"

Doctor Sadler? Up there? Blood? Why would he be ... no. This couldn't be happening. I looked down at the frail little thing. Her breathing seemed a little better, but her color was still terrible. Shock. She was in shock. I couldn't remember what you did for shock, but I knew there was something. Mouth to mouth? No. Lie her down flat? Elevate her feet?

"Aren't you going to do something? Go up there?"

She was imagining it. She must be. Only, she'd seen something and it didn't seem I had much choice but to find out what. First, though, I needed to get her to my car. I had a little trouble with that; she didn't bend very well but finally made it. She leaned back against the seat. "Well? Get going."

"I am. Just sit back and try to relax." I wanted to sound soothing. Instead I sounded as unnerved as she. "Where did you say he is? If he's hurt ... I have my cell phone." I wasn't at all sure what this frail little woman had seen, but it was certainly possible Doctor Sadler, or someone, had had an accident and needed help. However, I wasn't so unnerved that I was going to call anyone before I knew what I was calling about.

I followed her directions and drove into a parking area that contained only one very old, very large car. Its back passenger door was open, and a mat lay on the gravel.

"Up there." She pointed up a path that wound peacefully between old monuments. A huge oak reigned sedately at the top of the rise. The dead slept here, but in peace and tranquility. Violence and blood seemed to have no place.

I started up the small hill, convincing myself with every step that there was nothing to find. I was wrong.

At least I knew enough not to go too close. In any event, it wasn't necessary. Even at a distance, I could tell that the elderly man who lay across the grave would soon be in one of his own. I felt my knees give way and came to rest on a fat marble bench at the foot of a grave. I didn't know whose it was but sent him or her a thank you anyway. It took a little fumbling before I was able to get my cell phone out of my pocket and another minute before my fingers would dial 911. My eyes never left the body. I don't know if I thought I could will him to move, or what, but I couldn't seem to see anything else.

"Ida." I hardly recognized my own voice. "It's Ellen. Listen—"

"Did you get that poor woman away safely?" she interrupted. "That kind of thing just makes me sick. Gary said he was so rude, I—"

"Ida, listen. I'll tell you about her later. I have another problem." She was silent for a few seconds after I finished telling her what I had found, then immediately went into dispatcher mode. "Did you touch him?"

"No." Touch him? I shuddered. "I know better than that. I'm just sitting here, on someone's bench, looking at him. Can you get … uh … you know, the right people out here?"

"Stay on the line, Ellen. I'm making the calls right now. Don't move."

As if I could. "Ida, there's an old lady in my car. She was the one who found him. Make sure the ambulance people take a look at her."

"Will do. Who is she?"

"I've no idea. But if she's feeling like I am, she's going to need a little help."

"Oh oh. Are you going to be sick? Put your head between your legs."

I thought that was for fainting but didn't bother to say so. "I'm fine. Just get the troops here."

I wasn't fine. Not one bit. I'd seen dead people before, but this! My head was swimming, and Ida's advice seemed pretty good. At least I wouldn't have to look at what remained of what I supposed was Dr. Sadler.

Sirens. Screaming loudly and getting closer. Help was on the way. I couldn't see the front gates from where I sat, but I could see the road. It filled up fast with police cars, fire trucks, and an ambulance. I rose to my feet, vowing I wouldn't get sick on what might be crime scene grass, and walked down the trail toward the parking lot.

Two black and whites pulled into the lot, followed by an ambulance. My friend Gary was in the first car.

"You've had a busy day," he observed. "Where's this body?"

"Up there." I pointed up the hill. "Right under that oak tree, on the grave by the fallen angel."

The officer who unwound himself from behind the wheel of the second car was new to me. Young, tall, very serious, he looked appalled at my description. "You can't have a fallen angel in this cemetery. It's ... sacrilegious."

"It's a statue. Of an angel. It's fallen over," I explained. "The ... victim is right beside it."

"I knew that." He started up the hill right behind the paramedics. Gary watched him go. "He's new," he said, as if that explained everything. "You all right, Ellen? You look kind of white. I've got some coffee. Would that help?"

Before I answered him, I glanced over at my car. My old lady seemed to be leaning back against the seat, her mouth hanging open. Wonderful. She was probably having a stroke or something. No. Her color looked okay. But coffee might help. It would sure help me.

"Thanks. Coffee would be wonderful. Do you have two cups? Bring it over to my car. I think I'd better go sit with that lady. She's the one who found him, and I'm not real sure how she's doing."

Gary looked at her curiously. "Who is she?"

"Haven't got a clue." But it was time to find out. "And, Gary, after the paramedics get through up there, could you have them check her out?"

I climbed into the driver's seat and leaned over my passenger, prepared to do whatever was necessary to help this sweet, helpless old lady. I hoped that didn't include a mad dash to the emergency room.

"You woke me up!" Her eyes opened, and her mouth snapped shut. "I sleep every day at this time. Pretty darned uncomfortable car you got. Couldn't get the seat back. Police here yet? Took them long enough."

My own mouth flapped open and closed a couple of times. Before I could say anything, Gary was at my window, a coffee flask in one hand, a slightly dented Styrofoam cup and a faded green plastic mug in the other. "I hope you both don't mind black."

Silently, I passed the Styrofoam cup to her and took the plastic mug. Luckily it was partway full, so I couldn't see what probably resided on the bottom. My grumpy friend took a sip. "Dear God in heaven, what is this stuff? Tastes like dirty socks."

I sniffed mine. She was right. "How long has this been in there?"

Gary's face got red. "Don't rightly remember. A couple

of days?"

"More like a week," the old lady grumbled. "You got any water?"

Gary took off, fast. I didn't know if he went for water or just to get out of there. I could hardly blame him. I wondered if she was always like this, or if shock had made her irritable. I quit wondering.

"Was it Doctor Sadler? Roll this window down."

I did as she asked, or rather commanded. "I don't know. I didn't get very close to it … the dead … him, and I don't really know Doctor Sadler."

"Humph. Lucky you. Meddlesome old fart. Thinks he knows everything, what's best for everyone. Donates his time to the home and drives us all crazy. Calls us all old. What in tarnation does he think he is?" She paused to lean out the window and dumped her coffee on the gravel. "If that's him up there, and I'd be willing to bet cash money it is, he won't get any older."

What a lovely day this was turning out to be. First my wedding cake was about to grow bright red poinsettias, then all the drama at Grace House, a corpse in the cemetery, and as an added extra bonus, I was sitting next to one of the most foul tempered old ladies I'd ever come up against.

"You mentioned a home." I poured my own coffee out the window, crime scene or no crime scene. "Are you at Shady Meadows?"

"Do you know another old folks' home in this godforsaken excuse for a town?"

I wasn't sure which part of that to respond to. Maybe none of it, but if I didn't, I wouldn't find out who she was or how she got here.

"Ah." Now there was a real conversation starter. "I'm Ellen McKenzie. My family's been here a long time. The Pages. Maybe you know my …" It would have to be my grandmother. My mother was way too young to have ever hung out with this old lady.

"Miriam Page. I knew her. You don't look a thing like her."

Okay. We'd made some progress. "I didn't get your name."

"Probably because I didn't give it."

"You might want to now. We'll need it for our records, you know, because you found the body and all that."

I whirled around, banging my elbow on the steering wheel. Dan was standing at the window, a faint smile on his face.

"Ouch. Do you have to sneak up like that?"

"Who are you?" The old lady peered at him, distrust and suspicion blaring from her rheumy little eyes.

"This is Dan Dunham, chief of police of this God forsaken town." It just slipped out. My elbow hurt, the day had been horrible, and I was rapidly getting as grumpy as my wizened companion.

Dan glanced at me, obviously surprised. He looked suspiciously as if he was going to laugh. I glared at him. He smiled back and turned his attention to the occupant of the passenger seat. "Can you tell us your name, ma'am? And what you were doing when you … uh … found the—"

"The body?" She seemed to relish being blunt. "I'd come to put flowers on my late husband's grave. He was a mean old goat, but I like to visit him. Rub it in that I'm still here and he's not."

Dan and I looked at each other. This time I thought he was going to laugh out loud. I didn't think it was so funny. Her poor late husband had probably died in self-defense.

"That darn fool bus, Dial-a-something, dropped me off at the gate, wouldn't take me inside," she continued. "Took me awhile to climb that hill, and when I got up there, I saw the angel on the ground. Went over to have a look, and there he was, Doctor Sadler. All dead and bloody."

"Did you see anyone else?" Dan was waving over one of his uniformed officers while he talked to her. "Anyone driving away, walking around?"

"Not a living soul." She evidently thought this was funny, because she started to cackle.

Dan seemed to have lost his inclination to laugh. He looked pinched around the mouth. "Your name, ma'am?"

"Eloise Hudson. Mrs. Hudson to you youngsters."

"You live ... where, Mrs. Hudson?"

"Shady Acres, of course. Not that it's so damned shady. Mowed down all the trees when they built the place and now there's nothing but twigs. Not a leaf on any of them."

I started to say something about December, natural for trees to lose their leaves in the winter. Instead, I let my head drop on the back of the seat. Let Dan deal with her. I wasn't up to it.

"I gotta pee."

For the first time, Dan seemed out of his depth. He looked around a little wildly, evidently in search of a facility, but there wasn't one. He no longer depended on hand gestures. He hollered. "Jennifer, get over here." A red-haired uniformed policewoman came running. "Mrs. Hudson," he pointed— unnecessarily I thought—at the old lady, "found our victim. Now she needs to find a ladies room. Can you help her?"

"Take me home." Mrs. Hudson's tone left no room for argument. "It's not that far." I took another look at her, and for the first time, agreed. She had turned a rather alarming shade of gray, and her mouth looked tight and colorless. Did they have a nurse at the home? I sure hoped so.

"Take her home, Jennifer. Do you have a car?"

"I came with Gary."

"I'll take care of Gary. Take the black and white and get her to the home. After she uses the bathroom, you might ask for a little more information on what she saw today. What time she got here, all that."

If Jennifer had been assigned a thirty-page essay on the history of ancient Greece, complete with footnotes and due tomorrow, she couldn't have looked more appalled. She glanced at the old woman, then back at Dan. His face was pure stone. She sighed, went around the other side of the car, opened the door, and helped her charge to her feet. "Okay, Mrs. Hudson. My car is right over here."

"Can we turn on the siren?" Head up, wispy white hair floating in the breeze, she started for the squad car almost at a trot. Poor Jennifer.

We watched them go. "Jen's a good girl," Dan finally said. "Hated to do that to her, but she's a lot more likely to get something out of the old ... *dear* than anybody else."

I laughed for the first time all day. "You don't have to pretend with me. She's awful. Can you imagine having her as your grandmother?" A thought struck me. "She's not coming to our wedding, is she?"

That brought Dan's attention back to me. Fast. "Good God, I hope not. Why? Do you know her?"

"No, but she knew my grandmother and, well, you know my mother. She's invited everyone else in town." I paused, wondering why mothers of the bride got so carried away with weddings. Would I be like that? Grooms' mothers were just as bad. Dan's mother was. "Whoever my mother missed, your mother found."

"Yeah." Dan watched the car disappear down the drive. "They're out of control." He paused, taking the threat of Mrs. Hudson attending our wedding seriously. "I don't think my mother knows the Hudsons. And even your mother wouldn't invite someone your grandmother ... would she?"

"I don't think so." The back of my neck began to prickle. "Unless she sent out a blanket invitation to everyone in Shady Acres?"

Dan's smile was back. "Mary would stop her. Go home. I have a lot of questions to ask you, but I'd much rather get answers over a beer and some dinner. Get out of here."

I didn't need a second invitation. Dan stepped away

from the car. I put it in gear and moved it slowly through the maze of emergency vehicles. The old Cadillac was wedged between an ambulance and a black and white, its back door still open, the mat still on the gravel. Waiting. I shuddered and headed for the gate and home.

Chapter Seven

I pulled the car into my driveway and turned off the engine. The effort of opening the door and getting out seemed too much. Instead I sat, staring at the closed garage door. I'd had some emotionally racking days before, but this one made them seem almost joyful.

Susannah appeared on the steps. "Why are you sitting there?"

I rallied enough to open the door. My feet rested on the driveway but the rest of me didn't want to move. I finally reached for my purse and made it out of the car. The briefcase could stay where it was.

"Oh oh. It hasn't been a good day." Susannah walked down the rest of the steps, a can of soda in her hand, reached around me, and grabbed my briefcase. "What happened?"

"I'll tell you in a minute. First, I need to get rid of these shoes and drink a glass of wine. Maybe not in that order."

She preceded me into the kitchen and set my briefcase down beside the hutch. "Red or white?" she said as she slid a glass off of the rack. She guided me onto one of the kitchen chairs and turned to the wine.

"White. There's a bottle chilling in the refrigerator."

It wasn't until there was a glass in front of me that Susannah pulled out her chair and sat down opposite. "Give."

So I did. I started with the bakery, meeting Gina, then the surreptitious removal of Janice and her kids to a new safe house. I wasn't sure I'd adequately described the fear that had gripped me, that had gripped everyone, but she seemed to get it.

"How awful." Susannah's eyes were wide, her face drawn. "We've been talking about this kind of thing in our sociology class. How women enter into these relationships and why they don't seem to be able to get out. It destroys their confidence, for one thing. It's hard to believe. Although, maybe not for you."

I didn't know if she was referring to this afternoon or my marriage to her father. I decided not to ask. "That's only half of it."

"There's more?"

"Oh, yes." I told her about the old woman and finding Doctor Sadler's body in the cemetery.

She didn't say anything for a while, just kept staring at me, twirling the soda can between her fingers. "You sure know how to fill up a day."

I laughed. It was tinged slightly with hysteria, but still, it felt good. "Luckily, most of them aren't quite this full."

The screen door on the back porch slammed. "Okay, tell me what's going on." Aunt Mary marched into the room, glaring first at me, then at Susannah. "What's all this about you finding Owen Sadler dead in the cemetery, ordering traffic stops on our local TV weatherman, and generally creating havoc in this town?"

The information age started in small towns. We don't need the Internet; we have the phone. Even though the party line is history, information spreads faster than a California wildfire. So I didn't bother to ask how she knew all this. I only asked where she wanted me to start.

"With Owen Sadler. Then you can tell me about the rest."

So, once again, I went through my story. Aunt Mary listened intently until I told her the old woman's name.

"Eloise Hudson? Is she still alive? Last I heard, she was taking up her oldest daughter's spare bedroom and her son-in-law and granddaughter were threatening to move to Alaska."

"I guess they won, because she now terrorizes Shady Acres."

Aunt Mary laughed. "That I can believe. Mother used to hide when she saw her coming up the walk." Immediately she sobered. "That's horrible about Owen. Do you have any idea what happened?"

"No. Only that it wasn't an accident. Someone bashed his head in with the arm of an angel."

"What?" Aunt Mary exclaimed.

"You're kidding," Susannah said.

The screen door slammed, and Neil—Pat Bennington's son and Susannah's reigning candidate for husband—walked in. He hung his Stetson on the back of a chair, bent down, and gave Susannah a peck on the cheek. "You hear about old Doctor Sadler? Someone bashed in his head with the arm of an angel. Can I have a beer?"

I nodded and he headed for the refrigerator. "The angel was one of those grave marker things. It had fallen over, and the arm was off. Someone picked it up and swung it at him. It was lying right beside him, covered with …" I shivered, remembering the gory condition of the angel arm.

"Oh, yuck." Susannah put down her soda can and stared at me. "And you had to see all that? Poor Mom."

"Poor Owen," Aunt Mary said.

"Did I know him?" Susannah asked.

"No."

"I did." Neil closed the refrigerator door and popped open the top of his beer can. "He scared me when I was a kid. But I think he was a good doctor. Pretty opinionated though. Must have pushed someone a little too hard."

"Oh." I hadn't thought of who had killed him or why. I hadn't had time. "He was an old man. Why would someone do that deliberately? Robbery makes more sense."

"You didn't know Doctor Sadler." Neil took a big swallow of the beer, came up for air, and grinned.

"What does Dan say?" Aunt Mary eyed my glass of

wine. Susannah got up, took another glass off the hanging rack, filled it, and put it in front of her. Aunt Mary smiled at her and took a sip.

"Dan hasn't said anything. He didn't get a chance. Except that he'd be home for dinner."

I thought about that. Home. Not "coming over," but home. It sounded good. Getting dinner didn't. I groaned.

"I'll get dinner."

I looked up, surprised. Susannah had many interests, but kitchen chores of any kind had never been among them. She smiled brightly at Neil. Hmmm. However, my energy level was at zero, so, since she had offered ... "Okay," I said. "You're on."

She looked a little startled. "What do we have?"

We might as well make this easy. And edible. "There's Marinara sauce in the freezer, and some rolls. Pasta in the pantry. There must be something around here for salad. That should do it."

"Should I take the sauce out now?"

"If we're going to eat tonight, yes."

Susannah pushed back her chair and headed for the freezer on the back porch. Neil watched her proudly, then pushed back his own chair and followed.

"He won't be so darned pleased with her when he finds out she has no idea how to fill a freezer with anything but ice cream," I muttered.

Aunt Mary smothered a laugh and watched Susannah carry a large carton into the kitchen, clearly marked Marinara sauce.

"Is this it?"

I sighed and took another sip of wine. "That's it. Put it in the sink and let the hot water run on it. It'll never defrost in time if you don't."

"Really? Okay. Tell Aunt Mary about the woman who escaped from her husband."

"Does this have anything to do with your traffic stop?"

71

"I'm afraid so." I told my story once more.

After I finished, Neil stared at me, open mouthed. Aunt Mary's lips made a tight straight line.

"I never did like that man," she said. "What did Anne say?"

"Not much. We talked about what kind of house she needs and how much I can get for the one they're in, but she's leaving the financing up to the board."

Aunt Mary grimaced. "I have no idea how you do something like that. Maybe some of the others know."

"You'd better find out. We're going to have to buy it before we sell the old one. I can see why Anne wants a bigger house so badly. She has a lot of great ideas, and she can't carry them out where they are now. I was just leaving when we had our little drama."

"Don't be flip."

"I'm not. Really. It's just that I've had about as much horror as I can absorb for one day."

Aunt Mary examined me closely. "You do look pretty undone. What time will Dan be home?"

She was doing it, too. Dan. Home. Here. It sounded so natural it was a little unnerving. It had taken me more than a year to decide Dan wasn't my ex-husband, Brian, and that he wouldn't dump me as Brian had. I loved Dan, *really* loved him, as a friend and as a lover. Moreover, I trusted him. A remarkably comfortable and surprising feeling.

"Hopefully, pretty soon."

"Why don't you go upstairs and get freshened up? I'll help Susannah get dinner ready."

A nice, tactful way of saying my hair was a mess and my makeup was smeared. But a washcloth, maybe even a shower, sounded wonderful. I reached for the wine bottle, poured a little more in my glass, and stood up.

"There's fresh Parmesan cheese in the refrigerator but it needs to be grated." I said. "The rolls are frozen, so they should go into foil, and the sauce needs—"

"We're on it. Get."

I was halfway up the stairs when I remembered I'd forgotten to tell them about the wedding cake. Doctor Sadler had been in the bakery earlier, and then he'd shown up at Grace House. Or had it been the other way around? Either way, he'd ended up at the cemetery. I paused. How odd. I hadn't thought about Doctor Sadler in years. There had been no reason I should. And yet today he had turned up three times. I shivered again at the thought of him, dead on that grave. It was going to take a long time to get over the sight of him, lying there, bloody and bashed … Poor old guy. Whoever had done that had either been full of rage or completely panicked. And poor Dan. He was the one who was going to have to find the person who did it. I sent up a quick "thank you" that I didn't have to get involved in any of it and climbed the rest of the stairs on my way to the shower. I planned on standing under very hot water for as long as I could. Maybe I could wash away some of the tragedy that had weighted down this day.

Chapter Eight

I was one of the few in town who didn't attend Doctor Sadler's funeral. It wasn't that I forgot. That wasn't possible with Dan mumbling about no fingerprints on the angel arm when there should have been and Aunt Mary making pointed comments about flowers. It was simply that I hadn't known the man; finding him dead didn't change that and I had way too many things to do. I'd spent the last couple of days looking for a suitable replacement for Grace House, had found a couple, and had an appointment to show them to Anne. I also had several escrows that needed attention if they were to close on time, a couple of other sellers who kept wanting to know why their overpriced houses hadn't sold, Christmas presents to buy and wrap and, of course, a wedding to finish planning.

I still hadn't booked a caterer. It seemed that Christmas and New Year's were their busy seasons, especially New Year's Eve. One harassed sounding woman actually laughed at me. "Why didn't you start planning this a year ago?" she'd asked before hanging up on me. *Because I didn't know I was getting married a year ago* I wanted to yell back, but it was too late, and it didn't matter anyway. I wouldn't have hired her if she had won the year's best chef award on one of those reality shows. But I was beginning to get nervous. I had to have something besides wine at the reception. Wine and wedding cake. Lots of each. Most of Santa Louisa would be greeting the New Year with first class hangovers unless I did better than that. So, with the forlorn hope that Sal or Rose might know someone, I decided to stop by the bakery on the chance that one of them had not gone to the funeral. I hoped

Rose was the one who had stayed behind. In which case, I planned to bring the conversation around to the wedding cake as well. Tactfully and carefully, but firmly.

No one was behind the counter. I took a deep breath and let myself bask in the heady aroma of fresh baked bread and warm pastries before I looked around. The glass case was filled with trays of Danish—cherry, blueberry, cheese—and there were turnovers on the next shelf down, warm apple slices peeking out of the corners. Placed beside them were small tarts filled with lemon or chocolate, topped with delicate little swirls of whipped cream. I walked closer. Those looked different. The crust was thin and flaky looking. The lemon looked smooth and creamy, the chocolate light enough to take off and fly. I peered back at the turnovers. Their crust was thick, heavy. The Danish looked heavy. But the tarts ...

Layer cakes were on the top shelf, most of them the same kind I had seen a few days ago, suspiciously similar to those that filled the shelves at Marketland. But there was one ... Could it be? The little sign in front of it said it was. Lemon Semolina Cake. There it sat, fat and round, drenched in the lemon sugar sauce traditionally poured over the hot cake. I didn't know Sal had ever made them. The only one I had ever tasted came from an Italian bakery and deli in Newport Beach. It was expensive; everything in Newport Beach was expensive, but the pastries and breads that came out of that shop were worth the price. This cake looked just as moist, as light, as wonderful as the Newport one. I could feel my mouth water. And pucker, just thinking about that lemon tang.

I wasn't going home without that cake. But where was everyone? Someone had to be here. The front door was unlocked and the little bell had rung. I walked over to the low part of the counter where the cash register was and leaned over.

"Is anyone here?"

No answer. Just a blackboard hung on the back wall, silently advertising the specials of the day. Orange cranberry muffins, sourdough bread, and Boston cream pie. No mention of the Lemon Semolina Cake.

"Oh." Gina appeared from the back room. "I'm sorry. I didn't hear the bell." She was wrapped in a smudged white apron that somehow managed to exaggerate the curves of her more than shapely figure. Her mane of dark hair was pulled back in a severe ponytail, but tendrils had escaped to lightly curl around her face. She wore no makeup, so perhaps it was the heat from the bakery ovens that gave her skin that fine sheen and her cheeks that rose-colored glow.

"No problem. I was looking at the things in the case. That Lemon Semolina Cake is mine."

Gina actually smiled. "I'll get it out for you now. You know, not too many people know what it is."

"We had an Italian bakery and deli close to where I lived in Newport Beach. I went there a lot. They used to make them." I grinned a little sheepishly. "I became addicted."

"It's easy to do. The Greeks also make this cake. A slightly different version, but great." A buzzer sounded and Gina jumped. "I'll get your cake in a minute. I have to get … Do you mind? I'm here alone and I have to get the bread … Come on in back."

I walked around the counter and followed her into the back room, the heart of the bakery. It wasn't very large. In fact, it looked downright cramped. There was a double oven against the back wall. Next to it was a stainless steel rolling rack that contained trays, small loaves of what smelled like cinnamon bread on some of them. There were Boston cream pies on another tray, but they looked flat and the chocolate icing waxy. Another wall had a stainless steel sink and drain board piled high with metal bowls. A dishwasher sat next to the drain board. There was a rack above it that held an assortment of wooden rolling pins. They ranged from tiny to really big. The largest one had a chunk out of its handle, revealing the steel rod that ran through it. A large refrigerator/freezer took up the rest of the wall. Frosted cakes, some with decorations, and several cream pies sat on the shelves of the refrigerator, clearly seen through the glass doors. Two white layers rested on a large, mobile cart that sat in the middle of the room, waiting to be put together.

Gina pulled a baking sheet full of bread loaves out of the oven. "Raisin cinnamon." She hadn't needed to say that. The aroma drifted through the air, making me salivate. She proceeded to place them on cooling racks, then turned back to take another full tray out of the lower oven.

"But those aren't done." The loaves were high and tender-looking but very white. Doughy white.

"Of course not." Gina opened the door of the upper oven and slid in the tray. "They just came out of the proofer."

"The what?"

"Proofer." She turned to look at me. "Oh. I'm sorry. That bottom thing isn't an oven. It's used for the bread and lots of the pastries. Anything with yeast. They rise faster and more evenly in there. The top is a convection oven. We can bake a whole lot more than a home kitchen can, and do it in a lot less time."

"Maybe so, but you still have to be here at five o'clock in the morning. I'm going to skip the baking and stick to buying. Especially if Sal keeps going back to Baba au Rhum and Semolina cakes."

Gina smiled. "It's true, we do get here early. But not as early as when bakers really did bake."

"What do you mean? You don't bake all this? Then, who does?"

"We buy a lot of it frozen. We thaw it out, let it rise in the proofer, stick it in the oven, and what do you know? We have bread. Or cinnamon rolls. Or Danish."

"What about the cakes?"

"Cake mix." Gina smiled at the look on my face. "Not all of them. But this whole operation is pretty streamlined. I don't think Sal could do it anymore if he couldn't rely on some shortcuts."

"He still makes some things from scratch. Like the Baba au Rhum. That was no mix."

"No." Gina had finished putting the bread on the rolling tray rack and had gone over to the half finished cake. "That was no mix. And this Christmas, the Panettone won't be made from one either." She spread what looked like strawberry filling on the bottom layer and placed the top one over it. Another bowl held frosting, which she started to spread on the sides. It didn't look too different from what I did. Well, what I had watched Aunt Mary do. I haven't baked many layer cakes. Almost none. Maybe one. "What's Panettone?"

Gina stopped spreading and looked up at me as if she couldn't believe what she was hearing. "You've never had Panettone? Not even at the bakery you were telling me about?"

"Well, no. I thought it was some kind of fruit cake, and we don't especially like …"

Her expression of disbelief deepened. "You mean the kind someone gives you for Christmas and you finally throw out at Easter? This one's different. It's an ancient cake recipe, made with yeast and baked in a dome shape. It originated in Milan and there's a sort of folktale about how it was created. There are several versions, but they all agree that a young man named Tony, Antonio, invented it to impress the Duke and to win his daughter's hand in marriage. It seems a lot to ask of a cake, but evidently it worked. It's become an Italian household tradition to serve it on Christmas Eve."

"Why?"

"Why Christmas Eve? I don't know. Why Plum Pudding? Plums aren't even in season at Christmas. All I know is, it's a wonderful cake." She waved her spatula around a little, emphasizing each point with great enthusiasm. Strawberry jam flew off. Some landed on her apron, more ended on the table.

"Oops." She looked at the mess, then at me. "Did I get any on you?"

"No. You missed me. But you got yourself pretty good."

She looked down at her apron and laughed. "Guess I'd better not get so carried away. But, Ellen, you have to have a Panettone this year."

"Are those the ones you see boxed in the stores? Big yellow boxes?"

The scorn in her voice was magnificent. "That's what they call them. But they're poor imitations at best. See this?" Gina whirled around on her stool and picked up a ceramic bowl partially covered with a large dishtowel. She whipped it off to show me a gray gluey looking mass. It gave off a strong yeasty smell.

"This is the 'mother.' You've heard of sourdough starter? Well, this is the base for the cake. I ... Sal and I will bake a test cake to make sure we have this right. A new batch will be made about a week before Christmas. The cakes have to rest at least a day before being eaten, so we'll make them a couple of days before, ready to be picked up Christmas Eve. They're going to be by special order only. Want me to put your name on the list?"

Did I? I had no idea. But I thought of all the people who would be in town for Christmas this year. "Yes. They sound wonderful." I wasn't sure they did, but you can't have too much dessert at Christmas.

Gina must have known what I was thinking because she laughed. "Don't worry. It also makes wonderful French toast. I'll give you the recipe when you pick yours up, but I doubt you'll have enough left."

Gina seemed pretty familiar with Italian baking for someone who had only been working in a bakery a couple of weeks. "Are you going to make them?"

Gina nodded, her concentration on her careful strokes. "Probably." Then her hand jerked. "Damn. Oh. Am I going to make them? No. Sal will. I'll just … help. After all, that's what I'm here for. To learn how to do it all." She paused and looked up at me, chocolate frosting dripping from her spatula. "I love doing this. I've always loved baking. There's something fundamental about it. References to bread are spread liberally throughout the Bible and the whole history of mankind. It makes me feel … connected." The serious look vanished and she grinned. "Besides, I'm good at it." She dumped more frosting on the top and started gently moving it around. It didn't look like the waxy frosting on the other cakes. I wondered why this was so glossy and spread so nicely.

"Do you make the fillings or do you buy those also?" The strawberry filling that remained in the stainless steel bowl didn't have the dull thick sheen of most of the jams I used. This was thinner but somehow not runny, and the color was that of fresh strawberries. So was the scent.

"No, Rose makes all the fillings. At least for now. Want to taste?" She gestured toward the bowl. "Go ahead, use your finger. That bowl is going directly into the dishwasher." She watched me dip my finger into the small pool of filling left at the bottom of the bowl. "Wonderful."

She smiled, a real smile, full of satisfaction, but it faded quickly. "I hope you don't mind if I finish this. It's a special order, a birthday cake. I've only got an hour before Mrs. Bing comes to pick it up." She picked up a package that was half pushed under the frosting bowl. "Look. Disney Princesses. Melissa Bing is going to be five and I guess she's in love with the whole princess thing. Also chocolate and strawberries." She went back to frosting the cake. "Melissa is going to have a wonderful birthday."

There was wistfulness in her tone. It made me wonder what Gina's birthdays had been like.

"Okay. I'm going to put this in the refrigerator for a few

minutes before I decorate it. That way the frosting will set a little, and I won't be in as much danger of wrecking it." She stared down at the cake for a moment, then at the pastry tube laying on the table and the small bowls of pale frosting, waiting for a dab of color from the half-squeezed plastic tubes lying haphazardly beside them. "You know, Sal didn't want me to do this. He doesn't want me to do anything but stand and watch and wait on the next customer." Her smile was small and not meant for me. "However, he had no choice but to trust me. Well, maybe not *trust*, but he had to let me do it. I hope Mrs. Bing gets here before Sal. Now, let's go get your Semolina Cake."

It didn't take long. And, since I was there, I added a half dozen of the cranberry orange muffins, a loaf of the just-out-of-the-oven cinnamon raisin bread, and, a further testament to my lack of will power, a cream cheese Danish. I'd give Pat and Susannah my review later. When it was all gone.

Gina tied up the pink box that contained the cake and piled the smaller box containing the muffins on top and handed them to me. "How are you going to carry all this? Wait." She slipped the bread into a paper bag and tucked it under my right arm. I had the Danish, partially wrapped in a piece of paper, in the other hand but that wasn't a problem. It wouldn't last until I got home. And home was where I was going, if I had enough time. I didn't want my precious cake bouncing around in the backseat while I showed Anne houses.

"Did Rose go to the funeral?"

Gina looked a little surprised. "Yes, they both went. They'd known Doctor Sadler a long time."

"When will they be back?"

"I don't know," she said. "I think they are going to go to the cemetery and then there's the reception, or the gathering, or whatever they call it, at the church hall. I sent over a couple of cakes for it."

"You did?" Why that surprised me I didn't know. "I

really need to talk to Rose."

"About your wedding cake?"

"Well, yes, that's one thing. I also wondered if they knew any caterers. I thought maybe they worked with one they could recommend. One that's still not completely booked for New Year's Eve."

"Doesn't the Inn have a chef?"

"Yes. He's been booked for months. I'm getting so desperate I may go back to the guy who wanted to barbecue tri-tip. Not that I don't like tri-tip, or barbecue, but it wasn't what I had in mind for my wedding reception."

Gina smiled. "I'll bet his idea for hors d'oeuvres was the little flakey pastry things filled with spinach. The ones you can buy frozen at the wholesale market."

"How did you know?"

"I think I've run into him before. I wonder … Look. I'm going to talk to Marilee. Maybe she can help."

"Marilee?" I pictured her as I had seen her last. Huge with child, white-faced with fright. What on earth could she do?

"Marilee worked for a catering company part-time her last two years in high school, and they loved her." Gina smiled at my surprise. "You'd never suspect, would you. Poor, scared Marilee. And she has plenty to be scared about right now. But she loved the catering business. After this baby is born, she's going to go back to it, maybe even train as a chef. Not a cook, a *chef*. I'll get her to ask Central Coast Catering if they can do it. If anyone can get you a caterer, one you'll like, it's Marilee."

I just stared at Gina for a minute, trying to balance this version of Marilee with the one I'd seen. It didn't fit, but then, I'd only seen the girl under the worst of circumstances. I'd never heard of Central Coast Catering, but if they offered something besides tri-tip and fried potatoes, I was in. "Okay. Ask her. She can't do any worse than I've done. But, when Rose gets back, could you ask her also?"

"I can. And, Ellen, I'll do something else. Let me talk to Rose about the cake. I think I can convince her that the one you want is best."

I thought I might kiss her. Or hug her, or something. "How can you do that?"

"You liked her strawberry filling, right?"

I nodded, puzzled.

"We'll get Rose to make several different kinds of her special fillings and each layer will feature one of them. That should make her forget the poinsettias.

"Do you really think so?"

"Sure. She wants to make something special for you, so we'll substitute red flowers for fillings. I'll call you … later today?"

"Great. I'll be back in the office … oh … in a couple of hours. I have an appointment with Anne and I'd better get going or I won't have enough time to drop all this stuff off at home."

I handed Gina a twenty dollar bill. She rang everything up and handed me a small handful of coins and a couple of ones. I looked at them and thought maybe I'd better reconsider my no baking rule. I thanked her and headed for the door.

"Ellen, wait."

She walked ahead of me and opened the door. The little bell sounded, but she ignored it. "Ellen, does Chief Dunham have any idea who killed Doctor Sadler?"

Did she really think I'd answer that, even if I knew? "Dan won't talk about ongoing investigations." I hoped it didn't sound as pompous to her as it did to me. "Why?"

"Because … well … you know Grady Wilcox? Marilee's husband?"

"No. I'd never even heard of him until yesterday."

"Oh. Well, he's been looking for Marilee. Hard."

I waited. There had to be more.

"He's such a hothead, no one wants to tell him where

she is, but I guess he's furious for some reason and determined to find her."

"I thought he threw her out." I remembered the look on Marilee's face when she asked who it was driving by the house the other day and how relieved she had been to find out it was Janice's husband. Not hers. Not again, I thought. Not another poor woman about to become a victim of her husband.

"He did throw her out. And after she left, he had a great time. He and his buddies got drunk and high; they pretty much trashed the mobile home they'd been renting."

"So why all of a sudden does he want her back? To do the dishes?"

That got a small smile. "I doubt if Grady even notices them. No. And I'm not sure he wants her back. He wants to find her for some other reason entirely."

"What reason?"

"I don't know. But Anne's daughter, Kate," she looked at me expectantly, as if she thought I should know her but I shook my head, "works weekends at Smitty's Barbecue, and she says Grady's half frantic he wants to find her so bad."

I stood in the open doorway, my arms filled with baked goods, more than a little confused. I felt bad for Marilee but this was information I didn't need. I wondered where Gina was going with it.

"Does Marilee know he's trying to find her? Does she know why?"

"She knows he's looking for her and she's scared of him. I asked her what he wants. She says she doesn't know, but I don't think that's true."

"Well, that's too bad, but I really have to go. I have an appointment with Anne and …"

"Grady drove by here the day Doctor Sadler was killed," Gina said hurriedly. "He was headed in the direction of the cemetery."

It was more confusion than quality of information that

stopped me again. "Are you suggesting that Grady killed Doctor Sadler?" Surely that wasn't what she meant. "Why?"

"Doctor Sadler knew where Marilee was staying. Grady knew that because Doctor Sadler called him trying to get him to agree to the adoption. He even got Grady to sign the papers giving up all his parental rights."

"What?" I couldn't believe what she had just said. My appointment with Anne momentarily forgotten, I pressed on. "He went behind Marilee's back to get the father's permission? When he knew she wanted to keep the baby?"

"Doctor Sadler is … was … the kind of guy who thought he knew best. And I have to admit, the baby would be a lot better off with some other father than Grady."

"Still …"

"I know." Gina looked very uncomfortable. "It was a reprehensible thing to do. It was all I could do to keep my mouth shut the day he came in here, bragging that all he had to do now was put pressure on Marilee to sign and the kid would have a great new home."

I was clutching my cake box so hard I was in danger of squishing it. And, I had to go. I was going to be late, but I had to ask Gina one more question. "And you think Grady followed him to the cemetery, asked him where he could find Marilee, and when Doctor Sadler wouldn't tell him, killed him?"

"I think … Yes, something like that."

I stared at her, trying to think of something to say. My opinion of Dr. Sadler had just sunk to a new low, but this was about the most far-fetched theory I'd ever heard, or even read about. The cemetery was on the other side of the main bridge in town and several thousand people went over that bridge every day. The fact that one person with a very tentative tie to the murder victim had also crossed it was not my idea of proof of murder. It didn't even make him a suspect. "How could Grady have known where Doctor Sadler had gone?"

The expression on Gina's face was grim. "Every Tuesday and Saturday Doctor Sadler visited his wife's grave. He always went at the same time. You could set your watch by those visits. Everyone in town knew. All Grady Wilcox had to do was drive out there and wait for him. And, I think he did."

"And you want me to do ... what?"

"Mention it to Chief Dunham. Tell him to ... think about it. Grady Wilcox is an out of control idiot and he wants to find Marilee. Bad." She looked at me intently, no trace of the smile that had been on her face while she worked on the cake. "I'm worried, Ellen. Tell Chief Dunham. Please."

She let go of the door, which started to close. I moved out of the way and stood on the sidewalk for a moment. I watched Gina through the glass door as she walked toward the back of the bakery, I assumed to finish decorating the Princess cake. She wanted me to tell Dan... Exactly what? That Marilee's husband was a hothead and had been seen driving in the general direction of the cemetery on the same day Doctor Sadler had been killed? Dan would be really impressed. However, I would tell him that Marilee might be in some kind of danger from him. Or was she? Maybe I was still traumatized by Janice and her terrible ordeal. I'd pass all this on to Dan anyway. He was the chief of police. Let him deal with it. I had pressing concerns of my own. I turned and walked toward my car. I still had time to stop at home, but only if I hurried.

Chapter Nine

I left the muffins on the kitchen table and hid the Lemon Semolina Cake in the hutch. I had no idea who might turn up—Dan, Susannah, and if she came home, Neil was bound to follow. I hoped the muffins would distract the perennially hungry members of my family and they wouldn't go hunting for something more. I really wanted at least one piece of that cake. Which brought me back to Gina. How wonderful it would be if she could talk Rose out of the poinsettia tower. I didn't want to hurt her feelings, for some reason she seemed to take such pride in that cake, but I didn't want it. This wedding was turning out to be everyone's but Dan's and mine. My dress, the caterer, the guest list ... I'd lost control of all of them. If I could just get my cake back, or not get the one I didn't want, I would be forever in Gina's debt.

Weddings, it was turning out, were a lot more work and a whole lot more emotional turmoil than I had realized. I'd heard all the jokes about them—nervous brides, awful mothers and mothers-in-law, drunk grooms—and knew that lots of them were staged like Broadway productions. I wanted to avoid all of that. I had envisioned a small wedding, just family and a few close friends. I would be in a simple but elegant gown and Dan would look handsome in a traditional tux. The reception dinner would be tasteful and the wines would be remarkable. Instead I had a guest list that kept getting longer, a wedding dress that was being transformed into I didn't know what, and no caterer. Actually, I had one. I just didn't want him. No wonder I was frustrated and grumpy.

I drove over the bridge toward Grace House. The closer

we got to the big day, the more convinced I was that Dan and I should have eloped. I was having a recurring dream that I was walking down the aisle wearing that Scarlet O'Hara getup, veil trailing behind the huge hat. My mother was beaming at me while everyone else rolled around in the pews, laughing. At the end of the church aisle, where an altar should have been, was a giant wedding cake with bright red flowers all over it. Rev. Forester stood behind it, grinning at me, a knife in one hand, a plate in the other.

Grace House's front door was closed against the early winter chill, but I could still hear raised voices. I hesitated a moment, not wanting to intrude on some personal trauma, not wanting to intrude on any kind of trauma, but I had an appointment. I breathed deeply and rang the bell. It took a moment before it was answered.

"Ellen. I'm so sorry. Did I keep you waiting? We're sort of … uh … having a discussion."

Anne held the door wide and I walked into a room vibrating with tension and hostility.

Leona and Nathan stood in the middle of the living room, staring at each other like the Gingham Dog and the Calico Cat. Marilee huddled on the couch, one hand holding her back, the other dabbing at tearstained eyes with a flaking tissue.

"Oh," I said, lamely." I didn't mean to interrupt. Are you having one of your group things?"

"No, not exactly." Nathan never took his eyes off Leona

"Let's ask her." Leona jumped toward me, grabbed my hand, and dragged me into the middle of the room. "She doesn't give a flying fuck what happens around here. She's got problems of her own, so she'll be a neutral party. So, Ellen, what do you think?"

What I thought was I'd landed myself in something I wanted nothing to do with. I wanted out, and quick, but as Leona still held my arm and all the others were staring at me, I figured I'd better say something. I settled for the obvious.

"My opinion on what?"

Anne sighed deeply and extricated my arm from Leona's strong grasp. "Let's all sit down, shall we?"

Everyone slowly choose a chair. Nathan pulled a kitchen chair up beside the sofa, as close to Marilee as he could get. He reached over as if to take her hand but quickly pulled back. Leona chose the sofa. She sat so close she was almost in Marilee's lap, what was left of it. The poor kid was so squished she could barely raise her arm to dab at her eyes.

I took the chair closest to the door.

"Ellen, Leona wants to leave Grace House," Anne began. She shook her head at the chair Nathan had dragged up to the sofa for her, choosing instead to pace up and down. She paused to look at me expectantly.

I nodded sagely, wondering why anyone would object to that.

"And she wants to take Marilee with her."

Oh, oh. That didn't sound like such a great idea. Evidently Nathan didn't think so either because he spoke up passionately. "They can't do that. Marilee will need lots of counseling after the baby's born. And she's got plans. That job with Central Coast Catering is waiting for her and later she wants to go to the Culinary Institute. That's going to take money. She'll need to save and she'll need help with the baby while she's in school and while she's studying. It'll be months before she can move out."

"Months!" Anne whipped around to stare at Nathan. "We're not equipped to …"

"See? " Leona spat at him. "I'll take care of the baby. I had two kids of my own. I took care of them just fine, and I can take care of this one. I've got a job at the Yum Yum. I'm startin' to get tips. We'll make out great."

"I've talked to Ruthie." Anne returned her attention to Leona. She ran her fingers through her short gray hair, making some strands stand on end. There were a lot of emotions in her voice, but the chief one was exasperation.

Or frustration. "Leona, if you don't start showing up on time and stop taking so many cigarette breaks, you won't have one much longer."

"I'll get another job."

Another? That might take a bit of doing. If Ruthie fired her, it wouldn't be likely anyone in the food business would hire her. Of course, she could always try to get on as a greeter at Wal-Mart.

"Leona, you've been in and out of Grace House … how many times? And how many times have you gotten an apartment, a job, and started to drink again?"

"Yeah," Leona mumbled. "But this time it's different. This time I'm done for good. And I'd stay sober if I had them to look after. The baby'd take up a lot of time. I only drink because I get bored. Besides, Ruthie hasn't fired me. She just sorta—"

"Warned you?" I could have sworn Anne gritted her teeth. Maybe not, but I sure felt like doing it. "Leona, you still need help. Part of the deal we made with you when you came back this time was that you attend AA meetings on a regular basis. How many have you gone to?"

Leona's voice was so low the only word I caught sounded like "transportation."

Anne ignored that. "Not one. Not one! And you've been here over two weeks. Homer Taylor isn't going to rent you that mobile home any more. No one else will rent to you either unless you can prove you've got a stable job. If Ruthie fires you, getting another one isn't going to be easy. And how are you going to help Marilee take care of the baby if you're working every day?" She dropped into the vacant chair, as if her argument had zapped every last ounce of energy, and stared at Leona.

We all watched Leona struggle, trying to find a way out of what was so obviously true. Her eyes shifted from side to side, not really looking at any of us, giving the impression of a cornered animal.

Someone hiccupped. I looked around. Marilee's tissue was nothing more than a ball of fuzz. Her eyes were red but the tears had dried. She turned her head and looked directly at Leona. "I'm not going to get an apartment, Leona, with you or anyone else. At least not right now."

"That's right." Nathan sounded almost triumphant. "You need to stay right here and … You'll be safe here."

What made him think she wouldn't be safe in an apartment? I thought about Gina, how she had said Marilee's husband was hunting for her. Did Nathan think he might … do something? What? Why?

"Of course you're going to stay here." Anne leaned forward over the coffee table, pushed aside the bowl of pinecones and took one of Marilee's hands in hers. "We already discussed that. And after the baby's born, we'll figure out daycare so you can go back to work."

Anne didn't look as if she could figure out how to get to the front door. She looked exhausted. And no wonder. I'd only known her a few days but everyone had presented another of someone else's horrendous problems for her to solve. Now she was practically guaranteeing Marilee and her unborn child a place to stay for an indefinite period, and she was throwing in babysitting. How was she going to do that and accommodate all of the other women standing in line, needing help?

"I'll keep the baby. We'll both stay right here. I only work the lunch hour. I'll have plenty of time."

Leona sounded on the verge of hysteria, as though not getting an apartment with Marilee or sharing living quarters with her would mean her life was over. Why, I wondered. What was so important about living with Marilee? Surely she could find another roommate. But … maybe she couldn't find one with a baby.

Anne let go of Marilee's hand and threw herself back in her chair. "Leona …"

That was as far as she got.

"No." Marilee struggled to sit up straight, her face white.

"That's not a good idea." Nathan's voice was loud and clear, loaded with alarm.

"Why not?" Leona reacted as if physically attacked. She shrank back on the sofa, pushing back into the cushions and raising her arms as if to protect herself. The reaction seemed almost involuntary, as if she reacted that way often, because she immediately sat up straight again, belligerence in her tone and the stiffness of her body. "Why can't I help? You afraid I'll drop it or something? Or maybe you were listening to that old know-it-all Sadler." She twisted around a little, maneuvering into the middle of the sofa until she could face Marilee. "Is that it? Did he tell you not to go in with me?" Her tone was shrill and her eyes narrowed with rage.

"What on earth do you mean?" Anne asked.

"He turned you against me." She glared at Marilee, then turned to include the rest of us. There was more than rage, more than frustration on Leona's face. There was despair. She had a corner of her sweatshirt in her hand and was twisting it, round and round, faster and faster, as she talked, words matching her hands, faster and faster. "He told me I was a fool to even think about taking Marilee away, and he didn't want me to take care of the baby. That he'd see to it I couldn't. Arrogant old bastard. Just like all of them, men, always think they know best. He told you, didn't he? And now you're going to try to stop me, too."

I could feel my mouth go dry. She'd told Doctor Sadler her idiotic scheme? Of course he had tried to talk her out of it. Only, coming from him, it was probably an order. I watched the corner of the sweatshirt, thought about strong hands and the arm of an angel. Leona had been at the bakery when Marilee had called Gina and walked back to Grace House. The cemetery was a short detour over the bridge. The angel arm must have been lying conveniently on the ground, just waiting to be picked up and swung. And I remembered something else. Tuna sandwiches and a late lunch. A very late lunch. What was it you always looked for in mystery novels and, I was sure, in solving real crimes? Motive, means, and opportunity. I wondered if Leona knew she had just cast herself in the role of murder suspect.

Chapter Ten

CSI ended, and Dan turned the TV off before the commercials started, leaned back, and yawned. "I'm beat." He picked up Jake, who had been lying across both of us, put him on the floor, gathered up the empty ice cream bowls and headed for the kitchen. I put aside the pile of presents I hadn't finished wrapping, shoved paper and tape into a bag, and followed with cups and saucers.

"There's no room in this thing." He stared into the dishwasher.

"Sure there is. Just move those plates over and—"

"You do it."

He moved aside. I did. He stood in the middle of the kitchen and watched me.

"How's your wedding dress coming along?" he asked. "Are you going to be happy with it?"

I added soap, closed the door, and flipped the switch. "No idea. Pat won't let me see it until she gets it together, and frankly, with all I have to do, I'm grateful. My list gets longer, not shorter. What are we going to give your parents for Christmas?"

"The chance to come to our wedding." He grinned.

"Be serious."

"I'm perfectly serious. The inn ballroom is putting a huge dent in our savings and we still don't know how much the florist is going to cost. Or the caterer. Do we have any idea how many people are coming?"

I shook my head, wondering if Dan was going to explode. He didn't. He sighed. "Somehow we're going to have to reign in both of our mothers. We won't have any savings left at this rate."

Our savings. Twice, he'd said "*our* savings." Brian, my ex, had never referred to anything we had as "ours." Only *his*.

"As for a Christmas present, get my Mom a potholder or something," Dan went on gloomily. "She'll love it."

Now there was a good way to impress an impending mother-in-law, even one I'd known all my life. Maybe that sweater I'd seen when I was in San Luis Obispo last week. It was really pretty and it was the kind of thing Georgie always wore. It shouldn't take more than—let's see. A couple of hours should do it. Oh, well. Maybe I could check off some other people on my list while I was there. I didn't have anything for Dan's fourteen-year-old niece, his sister-in-law, or his father.

I followed him out of the kitchen and toward the staircase. He paused to pick up Jake. "How this cat gets so limp, I'll never know." He yawned again.

"Dan." I paused on the first step.

He turned to look at me and smiled. "Charlie Rose doesn't come on until midnight. I can't stay up that long."

I had to laugh. "Watching him wasn't what I had in mind. I was thinking—"

"Good," he interrupted. "It wasn't what I had in mind, either." He reached down the staircase and took my hand. "I was thinking—perhaps something a little more physical? Marriage should have a few special—perks. I have one or two I was going to save for our honeymoon, but since that won't be until May, maybe tonight's the night." His grin was downright evil. My shudder was pure pleasure.

Dan went down the hall into the bathroom, and I sat on the bed, thinking about perks. I smiled and stretched, ready to pull the sweatshirt over my head, but stopped.

"Dan," I called out. The water wasn't running. He should be able to hear me.

"Hmmn?" was the muffled reply.

"Do you know yet who killed Doctor Sadler?"

He walked back in wearing nothing but his shorts. Navy blue shorts. Oh my, I thought, my my my. For a man in his forties, he certainly looked … I finished pulling off the sweatshirt and reached around to undo my bra.

"Let me do that."

I let him.

"Well, do you?" My question was a bit muffled, but I needed to ask before I got too distracted.

"No." He was pretty distracted himself. "And I don't want you playing detective. Last time you almost got killed. The wedding just wouldn't be the same without you."

"Dan." I tried to sit up, but that didn't quite work out. "Listen one second. Okay?"

"One second." Only he didn't stop doing what he was doing.

"Grady Wilcox was seen going toward the cemetery the day Doctor Sadler was killed. Gina said—"

"We've already talked to him, Ellie, and to everyone who is remotely connected with Grace House and all the other charities, clubs, and organizations old Doctor Sadler honored with his presence, and, of course, his advice." He paused, pulled me around to face him, and laughed. "Got it in before you could ask, didn't I?"

I laughed, too. Sort of. "So you know he's looking for Marilee?"

"He's not making it a secret."

"But, Marilee's scared to death of him. Could he …"

"Quit worrying. She's fine. Grady's got a meth problem but so far he's destroyed no one but himself. However, we're keeping on eye on him. And, before you say anything, I don't think he killed the good doctor. And I do plan on finding who did before the wedding. In the meantime, like this meantime, let's forget it. Hmm?"

We did. At least, I did. Dan's "perks" were better than advertised, and the next half hour was most pleasant.

However, once Jake had been let back onto the bed, the lights were out, and Dan was softly snoring, I lay awake for a while. The police were aware that Grady Wilcox wanted to find Marilee, and I doubted they were interested because they thought Grady wanted to apologize. Dan had refused to say anything more. True, he had other things on his mind, but at the best of times he said very little about what the police thought or did. Maybe, just *maybe*, Gina was onto something. At any rate, it sounded as if Marilee needed to stay hidden for a while. Marilee. I replayed the scene from this afternoon— Leona's determination to set up housekeeping with her, Nathan and Anne's equally determined opposition to that plan—and wondered some more. Where were her parents? No one had suggested she go home or even that she call them. What kind of parents would abandon their barely more than teenage daughter to the mercy of a wacko husband and impending childbirth? I sighed. My ex, for one.

And then there was Leona. Again, Leona. Was her hatred of Doctor Sadler so great she could have killed him? Considering the look on her face, the answer was a large "maybe." She could easily have gone to the cemetery, possibly to talk to him one more time, and become so incensed she picked up the angel arm and killed him. I could picture it—him refusing to listen to her, Leona becoming more and more agitated, him more stubborn, until finally, she loses it. Only, there was no proof. No fingerprints and no bloody clothes. I almost sat up in bed. Bloody clothes. Surely whoever killed Doctor Sadler ended up with bloody clothing. There was enough on everything else. Some had to have gotten on the murderer. So, what had happened to the clothes? I tried to remember what Leona was wearing when I met her in the kitchen. Whatever it was, it hadn't been bloody. I looked over at Dan. He was sound asleep, snoring gently. He wouldn't be too happy if I woke him up to ask about bloody clothing. I pushed Jake off my pillow and snuggled down beside him. I'd ask him tomorrow. I planned on asking a lot of questions tomorrow.

The drama generated by Leona the afternoon before had continued for a while. By the time things had calmed down, neither Anne Kennedy nor I had the time or the energy to look at houses, so we had scheduled another appointment. For tomorrow. Maybe, just maybe, I'd ask her a few questions unrelated to real estate. Like, did Leona have a jacket that was no longer hanging in the entry hall closet?

Chapter Eleven

The next morning we both had meetings, so, of course, the coffee took forever to brew and Dan took half a century in the shower. I was wandering around in my bathrobe and furry slippers, trying to get the antiquated furnace to give up a little more heat and wondering how soon I could convince a plumber to come fix the shower in the bathroom my father had put in off the service porch when my sister and I were teenagers. I had ignored the problem when it was just Susannah and me. Now, when she was home from school, there would be three of us. This morning's juggling of shower and teeth brushing made me painfully aware of the need to get it up and running. I had to call that plumber. I glanced once more at the clock. Five minutes more, that was all Dan was getting. Then I'd start banging on the bathroom door.

He walked into the kitchen shaved, pressed, and looking wonderful.

"You look beautiful." His kiss was much more than perfunctory.

Wonderful I did not look, but I liked hearing it anyway. It sure beat what Brian would have said. I returned the kiss with enthusiasm before pouring him coffee.

"I've given notice on my condo." He reached for the sugar and heaped two spoonfuls into his mug before I could stop him. "I have to be out January First. As that's the day after the wedding, besides being some other kind of holiday, I thought we might as well start moving my stuff over here this weekend." He took a bite of the orange cranberry muffin I put in front of him, ignoring the bowl of oatmeal alongside.

"This is good. Did Mary make these?"

I noticed he hadn't asked if I'd made them. Oh, well. "No. I got it at Ianelli's Bakery. Why?"

"It's better than usual. Not so … it's sort of … it tastes better. What's this?"

"Oatmeal."

"I haven't had that since I was a kid." He picked up his spoon and gingerly poked at it.

"It doesn't bite and it doesn't explode. Try it."

He stared into the bowl, then picked up the cream pitcher and inspected its contents with suspicion. "This isn't cream. It's not even milk. It's blue."

"It's not blue. It's just … not very white."

"It's skim milk, isn't it."

"I'm worried about your arteries. You eat way too many eggs, you take cream in your coffee, you like bacon, all that stuff. I have visions of your arteries clogging up like the drain in that blasted shower, full of black yucky stuff, keeping the blood from flowing. I'm just trying to make sure don't you have a heart attack."

"I don't think skim milk's going to do the trick. A nice calm life might. And so far, my love, life with you hasn't come close. However," he looked at me over his mug and grinned, "I'm willing to take my chances. But, Ellie, I really do like cream, or at least milk that's white, in my coffee."

Marriage is all about compromise. It had never worked that way while I was married to Brian. "How about that creamer stuff? The nonfat kind?"

Dan frowned. I held my breath. "Get the Irish Cream flavor."

Wow. The butterflies that had started fluttering around in my midsection retreated. Maybe this marriage was going to work after all. "This weekend? What are we going to move? Stuff like what? Books? Dishes? That old recliner?" I'd been wondering about that chair. I hated it.

"The chair can wait. I thought we'd pack up some of

the other stuff. My beer mugs, that kind of thing."

I started to say something about the chair but stopped. Marriage is all about compromise.

Dan pushed his oatmeal bowl away and downed his coffee. "I'll eat some tomorrow," he said, sneaking a look at me. "Promise." He snatched the other half of his orange cranberry muffin and looked as if he were heading for the front door.

"Wait." I followed him into the living room. "Something happened yesterday I didn't tell you about last night."

"Something more about Grady Wilcox? I said we'd already questioned him." Dan frowned as he pulled his coat off the peg.

"Did he tell you that he'd signed release papers so Marilee's baby could be adopted? Without her knowledge? And that Doctor Sadler got him to do it?"

Dan froze, one arm in his jacket, the other in the air, fishing for the empty sleeve. "Doctor Sadler got him to do that? And the mother didn't know about it?"

"She still might not know."

"Somehow he avoided mentioning that fact." He slid his other arm into his coat, settled it over his shoulder holster and buttoned the bottom button. "It doesn't really change anything. And it hardly gives Grady a motive for murder."

"But it might give Leona one."

"Who?"

"I tried to tell you last night."

"You did?"

"Well, before we … I started to—"

"Before we got distracted?" Dan laughed. I grinned back at him.

"Right. Before then. But Dan, something happened when I was at Grace House yesterday." I relayed what Leona had said, trying to describe her anger, but Dan didn't seem

101

impressed.

"Ellie, we agreed you'd stay out of this one. I'm pretty sure Leona, whoever she is, didn't beat poor old Doctor Sadler to death."

"Then who did?"

"We're looking into that."

"Dan, listen."

"Ellie, I have a meeting. So do you."

"I know. But they can't start without you, and I still have a little time. I've been thinking."

Dan groaned then grinned at me. I didn't think it was that funny so I ignored it and went on.

"Doctor Sadler was an old man. He wasn't a threat to anybody, except maybe someone at Grace House. Grady Wilcox is looking for Marilee. It's possible he tried to get Doctor Sadler to tell him where she was, and when he wouldn't, he might have hit him in frustration. But Leona had a real motive. She wants that baby. Doctor Sadler was determined she wasn't going to get it. I think she needs to be …"

"Looked at?" Dan quit grinning and thought for a moment. "Why would you think Leona had a chance at the baby? It doesn't belong to her. And if the mother doesn't want to share an apartment, let alone her baby, then where's the motive?"

I opened my mouth to protest, to tell him he was making this too simple, that Leona wanted to live with Marilee and her baby and was violently bitter against Doctor Sadler for trying to stop her. Only Dan wasn't waiting to hear all that.

"I'll give Anne a call and talk to her about Leona, but, short of asking her if she thinks she's capable of murder, I'm not sure I'll learn much."

"Ask her if Leona has a jacket or coat that has gone missing."

"What?" That stopped him. "Why?"

"There was a lot of blood around there. It doesn't seem possible whoever did it got away without some of it on their hands and clothes. There was a lot on that angel arm, also. Why didn't you get fingerprints?"

Dan looked at me for what seemed like a long time. "From here on, we're only watching the Disney channel. All we got off that angel arm were smudges. The killer must have worn gloves. And, yes. Whoever it was must have gotten blood on them."

"So you are looking for bloody clothes?"

He sighed. "I'll ask Anne." He dropped a kiss on my forehead. "See you tonight. And, please, try not to find any more bodies, okay? It's going to be a busy enough day."

He left. I stuck my tongue out at the closed door and went upstairs to shower and dress. With luck, I'd make our office meeting on time.

Chapter Twelve

The office meeting had been blessedly short. I had an hour before I had to meet Anne. Just enough time to stop by Ianelli's Bakery. I hadn't heard from Gina about a possible caterer and my need was critical. Mother had left a message at my office. Why she didn't call me at home I had no idea, but the message had sent me into red alert. She had heard from Aunt Mary that I was having trouble finding a caterer, so would I like it if she came early? She, Aunt Mary, and I could make the dinner. Dinner for over three hundred people! My mother! If cooking skills are contained in some gene, mother didn't get one. She makes a mean meatloaf, and her fried chicken is really good. She soaks it in buttermilk. I don't know what that does, but it works. Everything else comes out of a box, the freezer, or the deli. The thought of her bustling around Aunt Mary's kitchen, or mine, trying to turn out hundreds of tiny shrimp canapés gave me heartburn. I was finding a caterer today. I no longer cared if tri-tip and canned salsa were on the menu.

I drove by slowly, looking for a parking place. There wasn't one. I turned right on Main, then right again. Nothing. It was getting harder and harder to find parking in our small town. That meant growth, people shopping, all good things for the town, but it was still frustrating. After three times around the block, I decided to try the alley.

There it was. An open parking spot, right outside the bakery's back door. I hesitated a minute, looking for a sign telling me not to park. I didn't see one. I parked the car as close to the door as I could get, hoping I wasn't completely blocking the alley. I got out and looked. Plenty of room. If the car was really small. Trucks? Probably not. As for SUVs, they used way too much gas and should say home anyway.

The screen door was closed but not locked. I let it slam behind me to announce my presence, but it didn't matter. The kitchen was empty. I took a deep breath, letting the aroma of warm bread caress me, and looked around. The rolling racks were full of bread and muffins—pumpkin muffins. With raisins. I sighed. I would once again leave with a little pink box. I glanced at the refrigerator, but it contained only a couple of whipped cream topped pies. I stepped closer. The crust of all of them had the same sort of thick look I'd noticed on the turnovers, but the chocolate pie filling looked like satin. Shiny, dark, rich, just itching to calm frazzled nerves at the end of a long day. Maybe … no. I refused to be tempted. Dan shouldn't eat whipped cream or extra rich chocolate. And, although I hated to admit it, neither should I. Besides, there were a couple of slices of Lemon Semolina Cake left. I made my way into the bakery, ready to find Gina. Instead I found Rose. She was standing with her back to me, studying something in her hand.

"Rose?"

She quickly stuffed whatever she was holding in her apron pocket and whirled around to face me.

"Oh, Ellen. It's only you." Relief was evident and a smile whipped away the alarm, but tears still pooled in her eyes.

"Only me." I wondered who she had been afraid was there. I took a closer look at her. "Are you all right?"

"Fine; I'm fine." She rummaged in her apron pocket and brought out a tissue and a photograph. She transferred the picture to her left hand and dabbed her eyes with her right one.

"You don't look fine." I took a step closer and peered at her. "Has something happened?"

"It happened years ago." There was bitterness in her voice I'd never heard before. "Usually I don't let myself remember, but today would have been her birthday."

"Whose birthday?"

"Gina's." She smiled slightly at the puzzled look on my face, glanced once more at the picture, and handed it to me.

I looked down at the radiantly smiling face of a young girl about sixteen or so. Huge brown eyes, long, thick dark brown hair, full red lips, and breasts that would have made Marilyn Monroe crazy with envy. The girl was lush, ripe, and ready for life.

I took another look. The clothes and long loose hair said "late seventies," and I knew who this was.

"Your daughter? The one who …?"

Rose nodded. "Gina."

Gina! The coincidence was unsettling. I remembered from somewhere that Sal and Rose had two daughters, one of whom had died. Had I ever heard their names? I couldn't remember. No wonder she was teary eyed. Having another Gina in her life, especially now, must have brought back all the old pain. I thought about Susannah and what losing her would mean. I couldn't even begin to imagine the suffering, the devastation.

"I'm so sorry." It seemed a little late for condolences. Her Gina must have died—I looked at the picture again— about thirty years ago.

"She was such a happy girl, always smiling, so friendly. You remember her, don't you? She used to give you a cookie when your mother brought you in. Everyone remembers her."

I didn't but wasn't about to tell Rose. I looked again at the picture of this laughing, beautiful, vivacious girl. I wondered what she had really been like. There was a devil dancing in her eyes and a stubborn tilt to her chin that made me think people might remember her for things Rose knew nothing about.

I handed back the picture. She looked at it once more before gently slipping it into her pocket. "It was the worst day of my life. Sal hates me to talk about it. So, around him, I don't. But that doesn't keep me from remembering."

Her eyes had lost focus, as though she was seeing a world lost long ago. Her usually smiling mouth was pinched, the lines around it deep. There was bitterness in her voice, mixed with a sorrow the years hadn't even dented. I didn't know what to say, but it probably didn't matter. I wasn't sure my presence registered. Rose was somewhere else, in another time, reliving a tragedy. Her shoulders started to shake, and tears welled up once more. I didn't know what to do but it didn't seem like a good time for words. I reached out and touched her on the shoulder, and she almost fell into my arms. I found myself patting her on the back as one would a small child, wishing I had a tissue as I felt hot tears soak into my blouse. I felt her take a gulp and then she pushed herself back away from me.

"I'm so sorry, Ellen. It's just that … sometimes …" She reached again into the pocket of her voluminous apron and pulled out a tissue tangled around a thin latex glove. She dropped the glove into the white trash can beside the counter and dabbed her eyes with the tissue. Shaking off the world of memories, she tried hard to smile. "That's why I took on the new Gina. She reminds me of all the good things about my daughter, and she makes me laugh."

There was a faint resemblance—the dark hair, the beautiful body—but the laughing part I didn't buy. No devil danced in the sad eyes of the Gina I knew, and no smile stayed for long on her serious face. As for her being funny, I'd met camels with a better sense of humor.

I glanced at my watch. It was time to change the subject. "I was in here the other day and asked Gina if you worked with any caterers. I'm getting desperate and thought maybe you could help me."

"Oh. Caterers?"

"For the wedding."

She looked as if she had never heard of the wedding.

"Mine and Dan's. New Year's Eve. At the Inn ballroom."

"Of course." She frowned at me. "Did you think I would forget?"

"No, of course not. It's just that the Inn caterer has been booked for months, and so has just about everyone else I've talked to. I thought maybe you might know someone—"

"Rose!"

There was no mistaking that roar. I watched Rose stiffen, fright flickering in her dark eyes. But it just as quickly disappeared. Her chin rose a little and she answered, "I'm in here."

Sal stalked into the bakery from the kitchen, fury staining his face bright red. "Some idiot woman's parked right in front of the door. I had to park down by Belle's Flowers. I told you to put up a sign. But no, you forgot, didn't you. Why can't … oh."

He forced a smile when it finally registered there was a customer in the bakery. It didn't reach his eyes.

"Ellen, I didn't know you were here. Is Rose helping you all right?"

He walked over to the catalog laden table, pulled out one of the chairs and dropped into it. "Rose. Is there any of that coffee left that's fit to drink? Make a new pot. Sit down, Ellen. Won't take a minute. Rose?" He rummaged in his jacket pocket, took out a red handkerchief, and mopped his face.

Rose hadn't moved. "What makes you think it's a woman?"

He looked at her with blank eyes. "What?"

"The car. Why do you think a woman parked it there?" There were a lot of emotions mixed up in Rose's voice. I couldn't even begin to sort them all out, but resentment came out loud and clear. Resentment and a little bit of fear.

Sal finally looked up at her. "Because it's a dumb place to park." There was only one way to describe his voice.

Belittling. The casual way he threw his little barb spoke of years of practice. I thought about Brian and thanked God one more time for my escape.

"Ellen, how about that coffee?"

"No, thanks. I have to leave. I just stopped by to see if you—either of you—could recommend a caterer. I talked to Gina, and she was going to ask Marilee, but I'm running out of time ... and Sal, I'm the idiot woman parked out there. I'm so sorry. I'll move my car right away."

I was furious, so furious I didn't care about caterers or even pumpkin muffins, except I would have gladly thrown one at Sal. Rude beyond belief to Rose, and then the whole Uriah Heep act with me. Who did he think he was? I looked at him again and had to sigh. He was an old man, old and cranky. I wondered why he was sweating on this chilly day. Was he sick? He really didn't look good. His hair was thin and what was left was white. His mustache was also liberally laced with white, unevenly trimmed and droopy. His face was deeply lined, his eyes faintly red-rimmed, and the knuckles on his hands were large and swollen. His feet hurt—I guessed that because he already had pushed off one of his shoes— and who knew what else. And I'd taken his parking space.

Rose reappeared with a small tray. Silently she put a white mug in front of him, along with a matching sugar bowl and cream pitcher. He poured the cream liberally and spooned several large helpings of sugar into the mug. I shuddered to think what his arteries looked like.

Finally he looked up. "Don't worry about the car, Ellen." The smile he gave me was as false as his teeth.

"I won't," I told him. My smile wasn't any more genuine, but I did try. After all, he was a tired old man. But Rose was a tired old woman. She deserved some consideration also. I turned to go, but what he said next stopped me.

"Rose, is this Marilee the girl who used to work for me?

The one you liked so much but who had the boyfriend who stole my cookies?"

"He didn't steal. I told him he could have a couple. They were day old."

"He didn't look like the kind who would eat cookies. Doesn't matter. He's no good. Neither is she."

Marilee had worked here? They knew her and her husband, Grady? Santa Louisa was, indeed, a small town.

"She's a good girl." There was a tightening around Rose's mouth as she defended Marilee but her voice was low, almost inaudible. "She went to work for Central Coast Catering after she left here and they loved her."

"Central Coast. Is that the—?" Sal's voice wasn't low.

"Yes. The one you cussed at. Too bad. I hear they're giving Bread and Butter Bakery a lot of business. Business we could have used."

"Who?" Sal looked blank.

"That new place in San Luis Obispo."

Sal's face started to get red. He slammed down his mug and sputtered. "That Central Coast kid was nothing but a smart mouth. Telling me how to make rolls, telling me they were dry. What does he know? Thinks he's some hotshot caterer, can go around giving me orders."

"The ones we sent him were too dry. And he knows enough to be making money."

I knew my mouth was gaping but I had never heard Rose talk back to Sal, not in the years I was growing up, nor in the year or so since I had returned. There was a glint in her eye, but her face remained expressionless as she watched Sal's get redder. He looked as if he was going to have a stroke. I started to wonder if I should grab the phone and call 911. But he glanced at me and took a deep breath, obviously trying to calm down. Rose set a glass of water in front of him and a pill. "Here," she said. "Take this."

He looked up at her, then back down at the pill. I waited for him to thank her, or argue, or complain about something. He didn't. He glanced back up at her again, grunted, picked up the pill, and swallowed it.

"Call Central Coast, Ellen. They're a good outfit." He paused, pushed the water aside, and took a swallow of coffee instead. "Better not say I recommended them. I don't think that guy likes me much." He smiled down into his coffee mug, a more than self-satisfied smile. I'd make sure I didn't mention Sal's name.

"Thanks. I'll call them right away." I started to move toward the door. "I have an appointment, so I'd better get going. Sorry about taking your parking place. See you later."

Sal waved his hand in a dismissive gesture. Rose walked over and gave me a hug. "Gina talked to me about the wedding cake. I'm so glad you like my fillings. I think a different one for each layer, don't you? And I'm so glad you chose the tiny little flowers. It's going to be beautiful. You'll see. Don't you worry about a thing." She was still smiling as I left.

I sat in my car for a moment, trying to pull myself together. I had a lead on a caterer and it sounded as if my cake was going to be the way I wanted. How that happened, I wasn't sure, but I was sure that Rose's easy abandonment of the poinsettia tower was due to Gina. I had to think of some special way to thank her. And I wasn't to worry. Of course not. What did I have to worry about? I didn't have enough fingers to tick them all off. But at least I was making progress. The caterer was getting a call right now, and the cake problem was no longer a problem—maybe. And I could tell my mother not to come prepared to cook. And—thanks to my niece and her winemaker husband—Dan had ordered a lot of truly wonderful champagne. I planned on making a huge dent in it. I might even start tonight.

Chapter Thirteen

"This one is perfect," Anne sighed happily. "Don't you think so, Mary?"

Aunt Mary beamed back at her. "I told you Ellen would find the perfect place."

"Six bedrooms! I can hardly believe it."

My enthusiasm was a little more tempered—by experience and by uneasiness about financing. But the house was perfect. "As soon as I saw this come up on the hot sheet, I knew it was the one. The house is good sized, but it's the street that's perfect. Large lots and a dead-end street." After what happened with Janice, I had become a big fan of dead-end streets. The only traffic was people who lived there, so a strange car, or truck, would be noticed. "You'll need a conditional use permit, but I don't think that will be a problem. We'll make getting it a condition of the offer."

We all stood in the living room of what was about to, hopefully, become the new Grace House, looking around, congratulating ourselves on what a wise choice this was.

"The kitchen is huge. Plenty of space for the girls to experiment with baking." Anne walked toward it again. "Look at all this storage and the laundry room! The set tub in the laundry should work for the cosmetology students. I can install a big mirror and—well, maybe not a mirror. We had one girl who never did learn to cut hair, and the result was—we finally got her a job as a nurse's aid." She looked around once more, her face all smiles. "The wallpaper has to go, but that's a small thing. This stove looks pretty old, though. Do you think it works?"

Aunt Mary, a woman who knows stoves, walked over

and started to fiddle with knobs. Flames lit and went out, the oven ignited, the broiler roared. "Seems to. Let's run the dishwasher."

I was busy taking notes, jotting down things I particularly wanted the home inspector to look at, if we got that far, wondering if the listing agent had a termite report yet, making a list of questions to ask her, all the while watching Anne and Aunt Mary mentally move in.

"That long dining room table will be wonderful right there." Anne waved her hand at the huge empty space by the French doors in the breakfast room. "This is much bigger than we have now. We'll need more chairs."

"I'll take that up with the board," Aunt Mary said, "and you'll need more beds and chests, more towels and bed linen. Hmm. I wonder—"

"Watch it," I told Anne, "she's about to raid one of her rummage sales."

"You could do worse," I was told tartly.

Anne smiled. "Most of our things are donated. I gave up years ago expecting anything to match. Room is what we need and the ability to provide a safe, clean environment for these women and their kids while they sort their lives out."

"Speaking of that," Aunt Mary said, "did you get Janice away safely?"

All traces of Anne's smile faded, and she shook her head. "They're safe for a while, but there's a whole lot of legal work ahead. This jerk's not going to shrug and walk away." She paused, a thoughtful look on her face. "You know, I don't think I could do a women's shelter. Dealing with the problems our women bring is just about as much as I can handle."

The picture of Janice's defeated eyes, the two children clinging to her the only thing that gave her the courage to try to escape, swam into my mind. "But you got them away. They're safe now."

"For the time being." She looked around the house and

started to smile, as if she could see the next wave of women and children who would make their home here while working their way out of the hopeless trap their lives had become. "This place seems perfect, don't you think, Mary?"

"Yes. I don't think we could do better. It's an old house but it looks in excellent condition and the price seems fair. Ellen, you did a good job of putting together those comparables. I've never seen that done before and it really helps. I'll present all your information to the board, but I'm sure they'll agree with me."

So was I. There wasn't one person on it who wouldn't bow to her wishes. The deal was as good as done. Well, not quite. We had to get the seller to take our offer, but I planned on writing one he couldn't refuse. At least, I hoped I could. I still had to find out where the money was coming from, and neither Anne nor Aunt Mary seemed to have a definitive answer.

"If you're sure, I'll start to draft an offer for both of you to approve, but I need more information before I can finish it."

"Like what?" Aunt Mary looked as if she had no idea what I was talking about. She probably didn't.

"Like, who has the authority to sign the offer? Can either of you or do you have to call a board meeting and get everyone's approval? And how are you going to take title? Is the board a corporation, a nonprofit, or what? And ... how about money? You have equity in Grace House but not enough to buy this one. Besides, the old one isn't sold yet. In this market, that could take awhile. Unless you have enough cash in the bank to buy this one, we're going to have to find some kind of financing. Do either of you know how we're going to do that?"

Aunt Mary and Anne looked at each other, equally blank faced.

"I thought you'd take care of all that," Aunt Mary said.

"I will, as soon as I know what to do."

"Can't we make the offer and find out about those things later?" Anne looked so disappointed I almost said "sure," but luckily some degree of professionalism took over. "Not if you want the seller to accept your offer. He's going to have to know how and when he's going to get his money, and he will want to know that whoever is making the offer is authorized to do it. Anne, if you sign it and you have no legal authority to do so, then if one of the board members or whoever legally represents Grace House in business transactions says they don't think this is a good deal, or you don't have the authority or can't get the money, the deal is off. No seller would take his house off the market for that kind of offer, especially not now, with prices dropping daily and buyers few and far between."

Aunt Mary and Anne looked at each other again, but this time they grinned.

"We need someone legal, who knows all the answers to your questions, right? I know just who to call. How about if I meet you at your office at say … four o'clock? Anne, can you make it then?"

Anne was beaming. "If you can get in touch with him by then."

"Who's 'him'?" There was a conspiratorial tone here I wasn't sure I liked.

"You'll see. Mary, I'll meet you at Ellen's office. Can I walk through one more time? I just want to make sure …"

"Of course. Take all the time you need." I took a quick peek at my watch and pushed away all thoughts of the mountain of paperwork stacked on my desk. It looked as if I was going to add one more file to that mound, at least if Aunt Mary got the right answers from whoever it was she was going to call.

One of them produced a tape measure and they went to work. "This dining room will make a great play area for our preschool. That eating area in the kitchen is so big I won't need this room to eat in. And look at this."

Anne flung open inside French doors to expose a small room whose function was not immediately obvious. There were open shelves above dark cupboards along two walls, a cabinet that contained a shallow sink on a third. Beside it was a swinging door that opened into the kitchen. I had one of those between my kitchen and dining room. I'd always liked the slightly old fashioned feel of it and the fact that you didn't have to look at dirty dishes in the sink when you had guests for dinner. The fourth wall had a large window that looked out on a neglected rose garden but it saved the room from being as dark as a cellar.

"This must have been the butler's pantry at one time." Anne circled the room, pulling out drawers, running her fingers over the shelves, peering into the cabinet under the sink. "I think it was two rooms. A butler's pantry and a storeroom. See? There was a wall there once."

Aunt Mary circled the room the other way. She stopped and examined the beam Anne had pointed out. "I think you're right. I'll bet that window was added later also; just look how different it is. These shelves and the sink are newer. I'll bet they held the good dishes and platters, serving dishes, that kind of thing." She pushed on the swinging door, confirming that it opened into the kitchen, and stopped to examine the chandelier. "This looks as old as the house."

I made another note on my list. Inspect wiring on chandelier. "As old as the house" meant about one hundred plus a few years.

Anne continued her tour. "I'll bet those drawers were for tablecloths. And these were for silverware. Look how shallow they are. They'll be great for computer paper and stuff like that." She handed Aunt Mary one end of the tape. "I think this is going to be our classroom. I can get a desk along that wall, and another over here … these shelves will hold tons of books and the computer. Where are the outlets?

I watched them, amused. They were both so excited, planning all the things this house could offer. It was like watching a couple of kids planning a new fort. Only what they were planning was no game. This house had to be many things to a lot of people. Each discovery they made, each new use they found room for, would make life just a little bit better for the women who would soon inhabit the house. I looked at my "things we needed to inspect" list and added "outlets."

Anne's cell phone rang. Her "hi" was bright, but it changed quickly. "Is she all right? He's doing what?" She listened for a moment, face pale with anxiety. That didn't last long either. "He didn't." Anger replaced anxiety, staining her cheeks red, compressing her mouth into a narrow straight line.

Aunt Mary and I looked at each other and strained to hear whom Anne was talking to and what was happening. Whatever was going on, it didn't sound good.

"Where is she now? Good. Is anyone else hurt? All right. I'll be there as soon as I can."

She snapped her cell phone shut and turned to face us, eyes bright with anger. "Marilee's gone into labor. She's at the hospital now." Her hand was shaking a little as she pushed the phone into her purse.

"Is she all right?" Aunt Mary looked a little puzzled. "This is her first. She's got a long way to go, so unless—"

"Is who hurt?" Marilee's labor pains weren't going to hurt anybody but her. Something else was happening, something that had calm, collected, Anne completely unnerved.

"Marilee's fine. At least, she would be if … it's Grady. Somehow he found out she was being admitted and he showed up, demanding to see her. He's there right now, threatening to beat up anyone who gets in his way. He's already punched a male nurse."

"Where's Marilee?" This was beginning to seem all too familiar.

"They got her into an elevator and upstairs right about

the time Grady was attacking the nurse. So far they've kept him from storming up the stairs and the police are on the way. Poor kid. She's scared to death. That was Gina on the phone. She sounds pretty scared as well. She says Marilee's having mild hysterics in between pains. They're trying to sedate her but she's having none of it."

She probably wanted to make sure she didn't doze off and wake up to find Grady in her room. Under the circumstances, a good decision but, even though it had been almost twenty years since I'd had Susannah, I remembered vividly how wonderful even a little bit of painkiller felt. Or kept me from feeling. I'd never met Grady, but he'd just earned one more black mark in my book.

"And, just to make everything perfect, Leona's there. She wants to be in the labor room with Marilee. So far, Gina's been able to keep her out, but she says for me to hurry. So I'd better … Where are my car keys? I know … oh." She gave an embarrassed laugh. "I came with you. Ellen, would you mind?"

"Taking you to the hospital? Of course not. But, where's her mother?"

I knew that was none of my business, but I couldn't help it. My mother had been with me, feeding me ice and telling me to push. She might be a little flighty and a rotten cook, but she'd never let me down when it counted. Brian had. He'd stuck his head in a couple of times, told me I was doing fine, and went off to "do rounds." I never knew "rounds" took twelve hours.

"Marilee doesn't want either of them there. She told us not to call them." Anne's face was closed. There would be no discussion about Marilee's parents. But she must have seen how upset I was, because her face softened. "She's not alone, Ellen. Gina's there and I'm on my way. We won't leave her."

She wouldn't either. She'd stay with her the whole time, and she wouldn't let Grady, or Leona, near her. Marilee might just be in luck after all.

"You two go get in the car. I'll finish locking up."

"We'll help."

Aunt Mary started checking windows, doors, the stove, with Anne right behind her. I gathered up the papers still on the kitchen drain board, locked the back door, made sure I had all of the keys ready to go back into the lockbox, and followed them both out to the car. I watched Anne crawl into the backseat and thought, once more, how lucky Grace House was to have her. Every moment since I'd met her had been fraught with turmoil of some sort. She'd been great with Janice, keeping the children calm, keeping us all calm as she made sure their escape was organized and orderly. I was certain she was still overseeing their new life even though they were now out of range. She had been firm when Leona had her tantrum over whisking Marilee off to an apartment, but she'd also been kind. I would have hit her. If not for her, Leona just might have bullied Marilee into accepting her idiotic plan. Now Leona was trying to worm her way into the labor room, Grady Wilcox right behind her. Neither was there to hold Marilee's hand and tell her to breathe. How was Anne going to deal with them? It was obvious she wasn't going to be at my office this afternoon. But maybe that was just as well. Somebody needed to tell me how they planned to pay for this new house. I'd find out soon enough, but first, we were going to have a baby. I climbed in the driver's seat and started the engine.

"Hold on," I told them.

"Ellen, not too fast. That baby's not …"

Whatever else Aunt Mary said was lost in the roar of the engine as I took off, tires squealing as I headed for the freeway. Nascar Margaret? Haw! She was nothing compared to Indy Ellen.

Chapter Fourteen

"So you just drove away and left Anne there?" Dan wiped the last bite of pizza off his mouth and reached for his beer mug.

"There wasn't much else I could do. Two of your cars were there. Then someone ran out of the emergency exit to grab Anne. She kept telling me to leave, take Aunt Mary and leave. That she'd call as soon as she knew something."

"She was right. Grady made quite a scene."

"How do you know? Were you there?"

"I do get reports."

Dan smiled down on me. We were half-sitting, half-lying on his living room carpet. Boxes, some packed, some half full, were clustered around us. An empty pizza box sat on the coffee table along with an empty beer can and an almost empty wineglass. It wasn't until we sat down to eat that we started to talk about something other than what went into storage, what went to my house, and what got thrown out. Not much got thrown out. Not even his chipped beer mugs. I hoped they would be happy living next to my mismatched wineglasses.

"So, what happened?" I sat up a little and reached for my wine glass.

"You mean after Grady punched the nurse? Dropped the guy like a stone. One of the other nurses and a security guy jumped Grady and held him down until my guys got there. Grady went to jail, the nurse went into one of those little rooms and got two stitches in his lip, and Marilee went upstairs to the labor room. Last I heard she was still there, but no baby."

"What about Leona? Did you arrest her also?"

"You don't arrest someone just because they want to be with a friend."

"There's a lot more to it than that. Leona wants the baby."

"That's what you keep saying. My guys said she was worried about her friend, kept saying she didn't have anyone to be with her, she needed someone."

"Anne was the someone she wanted, not Leona."

"And when they explained that to this Leona—does she have a last name?—she backed right off."

"Really?" Somehow that was not what I would have expected. "Last name? I think it's Wilson, but I'm not sure. Listen, I've heard her in action. I can't imagine her just smiling at everybody and saying … what did she say?"

"Not much, I guess. She went down the hall to the waiting room with that other woman from Grace House. They never saw her again."

"That must be Gina. Remember? I told you about her. She works for Sal and Rose at the bakery. I wonder if they'll spend the night there. According to Aunt Mary, it's going to be a long one. Poor Marilee." I thought back to Susannah's birth. Most of that very long ordeal was a blur, but the part I wouldn't mind forgetting, wasn't. I took a big sip of my wine. "How long can you keep Grady in jail?"

"Long enough to keep him out of the labor room." Dan stretched. "If she hurries up. He'll be out by morning, if he can make bail. We charged him with aggravated assault and got a restraining order forbidding him to come within one hundred feet of her or the hospital, but once he's bailed out, he'll go back." Dan picked up his beer can, shook it gently, then crumpled it in his hand. "I don't know why he's so determined to see that girl, but he's half wild to get at her. A little thing like a restraining order won't keep him out of the hospital. If all he'd done was make a damn fool nuisance of himself, he'd already be out, but assault's a lot more serious than disturbing the peace. We managed to throw in interfering with a police officer and a couple of other things. Raises the ante a little."

"But why did he show up? He doesn't want the baby; that's supposedly why he kicked Marilee out. Why all this sudden need to find her, be with her?"

"He's not saying. But he sure said a lot of other things. Over and over. His vocabulary of four letter words isn't extensive, but it's colorful. Let's go home."

Home. We were sitting in Dan's condo, surrounded by all his stuff, and he talked about going *home*. Our collective home. This was taking some getting used to, but I liked it.

He yawned. "I'm bushed. Let's go. Here." He hauled me to my feet. "If you'll clean up all this," he waved vaguely at the pizza box, napkins, and the crushed beer can, "I'll carry the boxes out to the car."

I'd finished stuffing the trash into a large black trash bag, putting the dishes in the dishwasher, and was doing a little yawning of my own, when I felt arms slide around my waist. A mustache brushed my ear. Warm breath was on my neck. "Good thing you had the foresight to get a king-sized bed."

"I got it so Jake would have lots of room." I was somewhat distracted. Dan's bed in the condo was only a double and the mattress was hard. I had to get undistracted or we wouldn't make it to my—our—king-size bed. "Let's go."

"You got it for a cat? Funny. All this time I thought it was because you were waiting for me."

"I got it before I had any idea you, too, had returned to our mutual hometown. At the time, the cat was the only being I planned on letting sleep on—or in—my bed."

"And now?" One eyebrow went up and the grin was more like a leer.

"And now, sharing seems like a good idea."

"But selectively."

"Definitely, selectively."

The leer got bigger. "Let's get a move on."

I tucked my purse under my arm and turned off the light on the lamp table in front of the window. A phone sat on it, silent. I stared at it for a moment.

"Dan."

"Umm? Come on, Ellie, let's go."

"Wait. As chief of police, you're always on call, aren't you?"

"Sort of. If something big happens, like a murder, I get called. You know that. I've always turned up when you've found a body. A habit I hope you discontinue after we're married."

"It's not like I plan on finding them. They find me. But that's not what I wanted to … Dan, do you give dispatch the phone number of where you'll be? You know, at night?"

He looked at me for a minute, as if he had no idea of what I was talking about, and then he got it. Laughter started in his eyes, spread down his face, and ended up coming out in great waves. He didn't stop until tears ran down his face.

"Are you asking if I gave dispatch your phone number? If they know that's where I spend my nights? I didn't have to. If they want me, they'll call my cell, but Ellie, they all know where I am. And no one seemed the least bit surprised." He laughed some more then gathered me to him. "Good thing I'm making an honest woman of you, isn't it."

I kicked him on the shin. "It's not funny."

"Ouch." He let me go and rubbed his shin. "You kick hard for a girl."

"Don't forget it. Honest woman, my foot. How about, I'm making an honest man of you?"

"I've never heard it put quite like that before, but I guess it does work both ways. Can we go home now and be … honest?" The grin I got was irresistible.

"You do sometimes come up with good ideas." I looked around the darkened room at the phone sitting so innocently on the lamp table. At least the one beside my bed wasn't ringing off the hook, looking for Dan Dunham, Chief of Police, in a place he was not officially supposed to be, but where everyone in town knew he was. Did I care? I thought about it for a second. No. Not one bit. "Let's go home."

Chapter Fifteen

"What kind of flowers did you order for the church?" Susannah asked through a mouthful of pancakes.

The four of us—Dan, Susannah, Jake, and I—were in the kitchen having breakfast. Susannah was home for a couple of days supposedly to work on a paper. It was probably just a coincidence that Neil was also home.

Dan and Susannah were at the table eating pancakes and sausage. Jake, on the floor, was having sausage. I leaned against the sink, slowly sipping a Slim Fast. I had no idea what Pat had in mind for my wedding dress, but I was determined to be ready.

"White poinsettias," I said. "There will be small fir trees around the altar, with those tiny white lights, and the flowers will sit around them. I wonder why Aunt Mary doesn't call? I'm worried about Marilee."

"You said it was going to be long." Dan drowned his pancakes in syrup. "Do we have eggs?"

"No. I'll get some today. I wonder if I should call the hospital?"

"You did that already. An hour ago. She'll call when she has news."

He went back to reading his newspaper. I sipped my Slim Fast.

"Sounds like the altar is going to be pretty. Did you have poinsettias planned for anywhere else? Red ones maybe?"

"I already told you. No red ones. This is going to be all white with … Why are you grinning like that?"

"Hmmm?"

"Susannah. You know something I'm not going to like. Give."

"I think your flowers are going to be red." She was barely able to control her grin. "Just like on your cake. It's nice they're going to match, don't you think?"

My mouth went dry and my stomach lurched. I looked down at the half-finished can and put it down on the drain board. No. This wasn't funny. I'd put my flower order into a commercial nursery in Santa Maria weeks ago. They were famous for their beautiful, double white poinsettias. They sold out every Christmas. If you didn't order way in advance you were out of luck. I had, and I'd checked with them again only last week. They'd promised me white.

"I'm sorry, Mom." There was a trace of sympathy under her grin. "Something happened to the white ones. They got blight, or something. They're all dying."

"Dying." This wasn't possible. I didn't want red *anything*. I wanted white. Green fir trees on the altar and green dresses on the attendants. And white flowers.

Dan put his newspaper down and stared at her also. "How do you know?"

"Valerie Kirkpatrick told me." She poured syrup over her remaining pancakes and proceeded to calmly cut them into pieces.

"Who's Valerie Kirkpatrick, and what does she have to do with our flowers?"

I was glad Dan could still talk. I could feel my mouth hanging open but seemed incapable of closing it or making speech come out of it.

Susannah chewed, swallowed, and reached for her glass of milk.

"I think your mother is going to have a stroke if you don't explain." His tone left no room for more excuses.

"Okay." Susannah stuck one last bite in her mouth and pushed her plate away. "I'm sorry I teased you, Mom, but I'm not joking about the flowers. It's just that it's so ironic.

First the cake and now this."

"I'm not getting white?" It came out a bit squeaky, but it was all I was capable of.

"Valerie's one of the horticultural students at Cal Poly. She works part-time for a commercial grower in Santa Maria. I know her because her boyfriend and Neil rodeo together. We were at a party last night. We were talking, and I said I thought my mom had ordered her wedding flowers from the place where she worked. She said, oh no. Is she the one who … and I said yes and she said … I'm really sorry, Mom. I know it's not funny, only …"

"Sorry," I repeated. "Red poinsettias on my cake, red poinsettias on the altar, I wonder if Pat plans on sewing a few on my dress."

Dan pushed his paper away. "I thought you got rid of the flowers on the cake."

"I thought so, too, but who knows."

Susannah slipped another bite of sausage in Jake's dish before she looked up at me. "You're upset."

How astute of her to notice. "This is my second wedding. The first was in a grubby little chapel in Las Vegas. A fat lady played the organ, only she couldn't remember what key she was in, and the Justice of the Peace smelled like a brewery and kept calling me Eleanor. I really don't want a third one, so I thought it would be nice if this one was … oh, you know … perfect. Only it's not shaping up that way. Yes, I'm upset."

I stormed around the kitchen, taking aim at the trash can with my Slim Fast can. I missed. Fake strawberry milkshake slowly seeped out to pool on the floor. I stared at it. Dan and Susannah stared at me. Jake started toward the mess on the floor.

"Don't even think about it," I snarled at him. He looked at the sticky glop, then up at me, grabbed what was left of his sausage and took it and himself to safety on top of the refrigerator.

Susannah wadded up a handful of paper towels, wet them, and started to mop up the Slim Fast mess. "Maybe the florist can find them some place else." She didn't look at me as she carefully placed the soggy paper towels in the trash can. "I've got to go. Neil and I are meeting for coffee. Maybe he'll have an idea."

"He's a veterinary student. What does he know about flowers?"

"Not much, but he sure knows a lot of people. We can ask around." She rolled her eyes at Dan, came over, and gave me a hug and a quick kiss on the cheek, then exited out the back door. It slammed behind her.

"Damn. Double damn. Now what do we do?" I poured myself a cup of coffee and waved the pot in Dan's direction. He shook his head. I set the pot back down with a bang and plopped down in the chair vacated by Susannah.

"We could elope." Dan pushed his chair back, stood up, and carried his plate to the sink.

"Don't tempt me. But even if the whole town forgave us for running out on their party, my mother never would."

"I don't think mine would either." He walked behind my chair and started to massage the back of my neck. "Relax. You're all full of knots. We'll think of something."

"Like what?"

His hands stopped. "Don't they have a two-toned one? Sort of pink and white?"

Two-toned? Pink and white? I twisted around to look at him, wondering if he was kidding, and it hit me. The blush ones. I'd had them last year, and they'd been lovely. Maybe we could …

"See?" Dan laughed at me. He nuzzled my cheek, letting his mustache tickle me a little. "If you just relax, things will work out."

"Oh yeah? They haven't worked out yet." I pushed my own chair back.

"Where are you going?"

"To get the phone book. I need to call the florist. She hasn't called me back about any of the rest of the flowers, but maybe she'll think this is a challenge. Go to work. Go catch some bad guys or something."

Dan caught me by the arm and pulled me back against him. Tight against him. "We still could elope," he whispered in my ear. "No worries about cakes, flowers, caterers, guest lists. Sound good?" His lips nibbled my earlobe, and his breath tickled the hairs on the back of my neck. "You know what else sounds good?" He let his hands slip underneath my bathrobe, tugging at the knot on the tie. "I have some time. I'm the chief. There's no one to complain if I'm late."

I started to push him away, then thought, why? The florist wasn't open this early anyway.

Chapter Sixteen

I sat at my desk trying to put the finishing touches on Anne's offer. I had called the listing agent and gotten as much information from her as I could and, except for a couple of minor points like ownership and financing, I was ready for signatures. Only I still had no idea who had the authority to sign it. Grace House just about had to be a nonprofit, but since I wasn't the IRS, that didn't interest me. How they planned to pay for it did.

All of my favorite lenders were neatly filed on my computer under, would you believe it, *lenders*. I found the file and started slowly down the list. I stopped when I got to Jack McDonald. He was a loan broker and a good one. You would never guess it if you passed him on the street. Tall, thin with long legs always encased in jeans, he was the perfect picture of the Marlboro Man. He looked like the type who'd just parked his horse while he came into town for necessary provisions. That wasn't far from the truth. He parked his horse at the fairgrounds, where his team had recently been named state team roping champions. When he wasn't roping, he ran the most efficient loan office in town. I dialed his number and got the answering machine. I glanced at the clock. Lunchtime. I sighed and left a detailed message.

I dialed Anne's cell once more. No answer. I didn't leave another message. I had already left two and frustration was building. Surely Marilee had produced that child by now, and I needed someone to give me the rest of the information if I was going to put this offer together. That person came in the form of Aunt Mary, sinking heavily into the chair beside my desk.

"It's a boy. Nice, big healthy boy." Aunt Mary set a large shopping bag down beside her. "That feels good. My feet are killing me."

"Where have you been?"

That question was prompted partly by exasperation at having to wait so long for news about Marilee and not being able to find Anne to answer my questions, and partly by simple curiosity. Her shopping bag looked heavy.

"Everywhere." She sighed heavily. "I got nervous waiting, so decided to go to Michael's. By the time I got back to the hospital, she'd had the baby."

"You went shopping while you waited for the baby?"

"It beat sitting on one of those hard hospital chairs. Besides, Michael's had an early sale on Christmas decorations. Want to see what I got?"

"I want to know about Marilee and the baby. And did you call ... whoever you were going to call to get me the information I need?"

She beamed. "They're fine. When I left, she was sitting up in bed, trying to nurse him. He was screaming his lungs out. Poor kid, she looked terrified."

"She always looks terrified. How big is he?"

"Over nine pounds."

"No wonder it took so long. And she's all right?"

"Sore but fine."

"Where's Leona?"

"Leona." She shook her head. "Would you believe she made almost as much fuss as Grady? Insisted Marilee needed her. Of course, she waited to pitch her fit until the police left with Grady. When she finally realized she wasn't going into the labor room, she demanded a chair so she could sit up in the hall. The head nurse was so exasperated she threatened to call the police back. After that, Gina managed to drag her out of there."

"Good for Gina. And good for Marilee. I'm glad everything is fine. Now can we get on with this offer?

Where's Anne?"

"Delayed. That's why I'm here."

"Oh oh. Grady again? Dan said they were going to try to hold him a while longer."

"No, Sal."

"Sal. What was he doing at the hospital?" I wondered if I looked as confused as I felt.

"No, silly. At the bakery. He and Gina got into a squabble, and he tried to fire her. Anne went over to see if she could smooth it all out. And, of course, she did."

"What were they fighting about?"

"First because Gina was late. She spent most of the night at the hospital, making sure Leona didn't leave the waiting room, and I guess she fell asleep on toward morning. When she woke up Marilee still hadn't had the baby so Gina made Leona go back to Grace House to wait before she went to work. Then when she got there Sal was complaining they didn't have any early morning customers and Gina had the audacity to suggest they get a machine that makes those fancy coffees—what do you call them? The ones with all the whipped cream on top?"

"Cappuccino? Latté? Espresso?"

"I guess. She said they should put in tables, use all that extra floor space as a coffee house, play music, that kind of thing."

"Good idea. They could erect bright awnings and put little tables outside as well. There's no place like that downtown. It would bring in more customers." It would bring in me. Especially if they kept making more specialty things. The bakery in Newport Beach offered little corn cakes. What had he called them? Pan De Mei. They were wonderful. I got hungry just thinking about them.

"It probably would." Aunt Mary was plainly amused at the expression on my face. "I guess I'm going to have to try one of those coffees." Her smile left and she got serious. "Rose has told me often how hard it is competing with the new large markets. They all have in-house bakeries. They also buy a lot of their stuff frozen and just bake it as they need it. Did you know that?"

"Yes. But so does Sal. He needs to offer the things he used to make."

"Like?"

"Gingerbread. Didn't he make gingerbread?"

"No. I did. And you have the recipe somewhere."

"Oh. Anyway, something like what Gina suggested might really help. But Sal doesn't want to?"

Aunt Mary sighed and wiggled her toes. "I'm not so sure he doesn't want to. I think it's more it wasn't his idea. Gina's learning the business fast, and she's smart. Sal can't stand it."

I thought about that. "Sal and Gina don't like each other much, do they?"

"No." She picked up her shopping bag and started to rummage through it. "Look at this. We're going to have so many people in and out over the holidays, I thought I'd do a little extra decorating. See? Angel candles."

"Why?"

"Why what? Angel candles? I thought they'd be cute on the—"

"Why do Sal and Gina hate each other?"

She sighed and stuffed the candles back in the bag. "Besides the fact that Gina is turning out to be a good baker and has innovative ideas, she thinks Sal is too hard on Rose and tells him so."

"He is."

"I know. He always has been. He was hard on his girls, too. And on everyone who's ever worked there. Gina, for some reason, has appointed herself Rose's protector." She looked thoughtful and her tone changed. "Rose has been a little … vague … lately, so having someone run interference between them isn't a bad idea, but it's driving Sal nutty." She grinned. "Sal deserves it."

She reached into her purse and took out a slip of paper that she slid over to me. "Here."

"What's this?" I picked it up and looked at it. There was a name and phone number scrawled on it.

"That's who you talk to about Grace House."

Her face was blank, no expression in her voice either. That was not like her. I looked back down at the paper. I'd never heard of this person.

"Okay," I said slowly. "Who is this and why do I want to talk to him?"

"He's Grace House's attorney. I had a long talk with him and told him what we want to do. He's expecting your call. I'll see you tonight at my house for dinner." She pushed herself up out of the chair, claimed her shopping bag, and started to leave.

An attorney. I'd never yet dealt with a real estate attorney. California doesn't use them to complete transactions. We use escrow instead. The escrow officer acts as a neutral party between the buyer and seller. He—or more often *she*—does our title work, interfaces with the lender, goes over the loan documents with the buyer to make sure they reflect the terms of the contract, collects the funds, records deeds, and does a million other things. The only time an attorney gets involved is when there's a problem or when either the buyer or seller is a little out of the ordinary. Grace House qualified. But still …

"Don't look so put out. He's a nice man, and he'll have all the answers. Be there at six o'clock."

"Where?"

"I just told you. My house. For dinner. You're bringing dessert."

I was? "I didn't know we were invited to dinner."

"Well, now you do. I'm giving Susannah a cooking lesson, and you and Dan get the results. And Neil, of course. He might as well know early on what he's getting himself into."

I stared after her as she sailed through the office, smiling and nodding. Cooking lesson. Susannah. Neil. That all sounded way too domestic. Was it time to start worrying? Maybe it was past time. I gave myself a mental shake. If I needed to worry about something, it had better be about finishing this offer, which meant calling the attorney and making an appointment. I also needed to follow through on my existing escrows and find out what had happened to that nice young couple that had expressed interest in the cute house I listed on Cherry. I might even find time to track down that gingerbread recipe. Aunt Mary wasn't the only one in this family who could bake. Maybe.

Chapter Seventeen

"Why are we going in the front door?"

"Because this is hot."

Dan jabbed at Aunt Mary's doorbell while trying to juggle the gingerbread. I'd found the recipe. I actually had all of the ingredients, including the cup of hot coffee that went in last, and—crossing my fingers I wouldn't mess it up too badly—had gone to work. It looked and smelled wonderful. I'd wrapped the baking dish in a couple of dishtowels to keep it warm on the short trip over here. Evidently it was keeping Dan's hands warm also. Perhaps a little too warm, judging from the way he passed the dish back and forth between them.

"Why did you come in the front door?" Aunt Mary stood in the doorway, effectively blocking our entry.

"Because my hands are burning off. Move. Please."

She did. Dan hurried past her, on his way to the kitchen, to gain relief from the hot dish and most likely to get a beer.

She sniffed the air as Dan rushed by her. "Gingerbread?"

I nodded.

"My old recipe?"

I nodded again. She smiled. "It would have been faster to go in the back door. It's never locked."

"I know. But it's some kind of guy thing." I slipped out of my coat and headed for the front hall closet.

"Like not asking for directions?"

"I think so." I turned toward her and shrugged.

"Men." She turned and followed Dan toward her old,

warm, inviting kitchen. Generations of wonderful meals had come out of that room. I hoped that tonight, with a new generation cook, would be no exception.

Dan was leaning against the counter, top already off his beer bottle, talking to Neil, whose beer was half gone. Susannah was standing at the stove, hair damp around her forehead, looking lost. The gingerbread was on the kitchen table, still wrapped in the dishtowels.

"Is that pot roast I smell?" I headed for Aunt Mary's bottom cupboard, pulled out a cooling rack, unwrapped the gingerbread, and pushed it to the back of the counter, hopefully out of harm's way. "It smells wonderful."

"So does that." Neil walked over and inhaled deeply. "I love gingerbread. This one is darker than my mom's. Hers is sort of light brown."

"It's the coffee." Aunt Mary was a little distracted. I could tell she was having a hard time not taking the potholder out of Susannah's hand as she took the lid off of a large pot.

"How can you tell if these things are ready to mash?"

Aunt Mary shot me a glance that said, plainly, have you taught this child nothing? She got out a long-handled fork, handed it to Susannah who took it gingerly and proceeded to stab something in the pot. "It went in. Does that mean they're done?"

It seemed a good time to leave. "Dan, how would you like to pour me a glass of wine?" He looked at me, then back at Susannah, and smiled. He set his beer down and reached for the unopened red wine bottle sitting on the drain board.

"That's for dinner. There's an open bottle of white in the fridge." Aunt Mary carefully inserted a fork into the potatoes and then handed it back to Susannah. "Feel that? They're not done. Almost, but not quite. Check the green beans."

Poor Susannah. She looked helpless. I could almost hear her, "Check them for what?" If I didn't get out of there,

I'd either burst out laughing or do what Aunt Mary so obviously wanted to do, push her away from the stove and do it all myself. Aunt Mary had more self-control. "I'll be in the living room." I fled.

Dan followed me. "Here." He handed me a full glass with a questioning look.

I ignored the look but took the glass. "At least she's trying."

"Susannah's doing real good." Neil was right behind us. He eased his long body down on Aunt Mary's overstuffed chair. Dan and I lowered ourselves onto the sofa. "She's going to be a great cook, don't you think?"

I thought it was one of the best examples of wishful thinking I'd ever heard, but it didn't seem the time for a reality check. "She couldn't have a better teacher."

Dan examined his beer thoughtfully. Before he could comment on Susannah's kitchen skills, I decided to change the subject. "Have you heard the news about Marilee? She had a boy."

"I heard," Dan said. "So did Grady. We had to turn him loose this afternoon, but not before I made damn sure he knew about the restraining order. If he goes near that hospital, he'll land right back in jail."

"Who's Marilee?" asked Neil. "Oh. Grady Wilcox's wife?"

"Do you know Grady Wilcox?" I put my glass down on the coffee table and stared at Neil. They were about the same age, all of them. Neil and Grady could very well have gone to high school together. If Susannah had grown up here, she might have been one of Marilee's classmates. No, Susannah would have been a year or so ahead, but in a school the size of ours, they probably would have known each other. How differently they had all turned out. Neil going to veterinary school, Susannah to Cal Poly, Grady spending most of his time in jail or trying to avoid going back there, and Marilee—the youngest of them all—now a mother.

"Grady's not much good."

"So I've heard."

"He was a troublemaker all through high school, and I don't think he's changed. I heard he kicked his wife out when she got pregnant. Hard to party with a kid screaming in the other room. And that's all he's ever wanted to do—party and drink himself into oblivion and get high. I don't remember the girl he married. I guess she was behind us a couple of years."

"Probably. Poor Anne."

Neil looked blank. "Who's Anne?"

"Anne Kennedy." That didn't seem to clear things up. "She runs Grace House." Nothing.

"Never mind. Anyway, she stayed up all night with her. I don't know if it was because Marilee's family wasn't around or because she wanted to make sure Grady didn't stage an encore performance at the hospital."

"We made sure of that." Dan drained his beer.

"Do you want another?" Neil started up out of his chair.

"Thanks, no." Dan looked at me and grinned. "I'll wait and have a glass of that red wine with dinner. Ellen says red wine's good for my arteries."

Neil didn't look as if he was buying that one but was too polite to say so.

"Speaking of Anne, did you get a chance to show her any houses?" Dan tightened his arm around me and gave me a little squeeze.

"I did better than that. We're going to make an offer on one."

"I don't suppose you're going to tell me which one."

"It's that big old blue house on Filbert. It's really perfect. Now all I have to do is get the attorney to approve the offer and get it accepted. Next, I have to convince the city to give us a conditional use permit, and, of course, the house has to pass all the inspections. Because of what it will be used for, it's going to have to meet a higher standard than just a normal everyday sale. Oh, and I need the Grace House attorney to explain to me how we're going to finance it."

"Is that all?" He laughed. "You can do it. I have faith. Who's the attorney?"

"Somebody named Butler."

"Sam Butler?"

I nodded.

"He's a good man. And a good attorney."

Since Dan was in a position to know every attorney in town and pass firsthand judgment on them, his vote of confidence in Mr. Butler relieved a little of my anxiety. A little.

"Dinner."

As we all trouped into the dining room, Susannah stood in the doorway to the living room looking hot, sweaty, proud, and a little anxious.

Dishes were passed and conversation came to a halt while gravy was poured, meat cut, and potatoes consumed.

"Wonderful," Neil pronounced

Susannah beamed and everyone relaxed.

"Have you talked to Sam Butler?" Aunt Mary discreetly pushed a lump in her mashed potatoes aside and looked up at me.

"Yes, this afternoon. I faxed him the offer and have an appointment with him in the morning. If he approves and we can get all of the financing straightened out, I'll have it signed and then present it tomorrow, if possible. As president of the board, you may be the one who has to sign, so don't go anywhere without telling me. The listing agent is being really co-operative about all this, says the owner loves the idea that it will be the next Grace House. I think we'll get it."

"That will make Anne happy. She really wants that house." Aunt Mary frowned. I held my breath. Had she just thought of another problem? No. Just another lump. She hid it in the gravy and looked up. "She had quite a day. And night."

"Did something else happen besides the baby?" Dan tried to mash down a lump in his potatoes with his fork. It refused to give. He pushed it to one side, glanced at Susannah, then carefully tested the rest before taking a bite.

"You mean besides Leona trying to crash the labor room? The only person I can think of who had that many people wanting to witness a birth was Queen Victoria."

"Your history's a little shaky." Aunt Mary washed down some pot roast with a sip of wine and put down her fork. "It was common practice for a queen to have onlookers. That way all of the court could certify that the baby was born alive and that the child presented to the world as the next in line for the throne was the real deal." She looked as if she was about to continue her history lecture but I got there first.

"I wonder if the current Queen Elizabeth put up with a roomful when she had Prince Charles."

"How disgusting," Susannah said. Her fork was on her plate as well and she was eyeing her green beans with suspicion. They did look a little brown on the bottom.

Dan and Neil both looked uncomfortable at this very domestic turn in the conversation. I took pity on them and returned it to something they could handle. A fight. "There was some kind of spat at the bakery between Sal and Gina. Aunt Mary knows all about it."

All heads turned toward her. She had just taken a sip of wine and wasn't quite prepared so she swallowed too quickly. After a cough or two, she blotted her mouth with a napkin. "There's not much to tell. Nothing unusual happened. Gina was late getting in, she took Leona home and made sure she was going to stay there, and then she and Sal got into it over how to get more customers. I guess Rose said something and Sal started to yell. Gina tried to defend Rose and Sal started yelling at her. Tried to fire her but finally backed down." She pursed her lips in disapproval.

"Sal's always yelling at someone about something. I don't know how Rose has stood it all these years." After another sip of wine her expression changed. "Although Rose has been giving him reason lately. She seems … vague."

"Maybe she's getting Alzheimer's." Susannah was also pushing lumps around. She looked perplexed. "How do you get your potatoes so smooth? These look like they have white rocks in them."

"Practice," said Aunt Mary. "I don't know what's wrong with her, but it's a good thing she has Gina."

"Who's Gina?" Neil had been following the conversation, head going back and forth, like someone watching a ping pong game. He never got his answer. The phone rang.

"Who on earth could that be?" Aunt Mary pushed her chair back and picked up the phone that rested on the corner of the built-in hutch. She listened a minute. "Oh, my God." The color drained from her face and her hand shook a little as she handed the phone to Dan.

"It's for you."

"Chief Dunham." There was a pause. "Son of a … Okay. Right away." His face didn't look much better as he handed the phone back to Aunt Mary.

He threw his napkin on the table, oblivious to the fact that it landed squarely on his plate, where it immediately started to sop up gravy. His chair almost went over as he pushed it back. "Someone needs to take Ellen home. I'll be awhile."

"What's happened?" I put down my own fork and started to push my chair back.

"Grace House is on fire." He was already headed for the door, the information thrown over his shoulder as he went.

Aunt Mary was already gathering up napkins and picking up plates. "Is everyone out?"

"Everyone is out and accounted for, all except one."

"Who?" I asked.

"Leona." The door slammed, and he was gone.

Chapter Eighteen

We stood halfway down the block—Neil, Susannah, Aunt Mary, and I—watching the last few tongues of flames shoot into the sky before dying under the spray of water pouring on them. All that was left was charred, smoldering ruins where once had been a house. The metal screen door glowed with heat, the backyard swing, visible from where we stood through the ruins, hung from one rope. The other had burned through when the tree caught fire.

Dan had left immediately, but we stayed long enough to put away the food. "There will be hungry mouths to feed later," Aunt Mary had said with a grim set to her mouth.

"They think it was arson." Anne Kennedy walked out of the smoke to join us. She had on an old padded jacket over what looked like pajama bottoms, her sockless feet thrust into running shoes. Her eyes were red, I didn't think totally from smoke. "I've been talking to the fire captain. Arson. How could anyone? Think what we've lost."

"Think what you didn't lose." Aunt Mary put her arm around her and squeezed her tight. "Everyone got out alive." She stopped suddenly and let her arm drop. "Didn't they?"

"I don't know." Anne was ringing her hands, her eyes glued on the smoldering building. "Marilee and the baby are in that police car over there. So is Gina. Nathan is still talking to the police. I don't know where Leona is. No one has seen her."

"Marilee! Why isn't she in the hospital?" Aunt Mary wheeled around to stare at Anne. "That child just gave birth this morning. She has no business being anywhere but in bed."

"You're right." Anne looked on the verge of collapse. Not surprising. The last forty-eight hours would have felled Wonder Woman. "We decided, the doctor, Marilee, and me, that she—they—were safer here than at the hospital. Too many ways for Grady to sneak in if he wanted to, and he seemed determined to get to her. It didn't turn out to be a very good decision."

Grady. The fire was deliberate. Had he finally discovered she was staying at Grace House and set it on fire to … do what? Force her out?

Nathan joined us. His eyes were bloodshot, his face sooty. There was a burn mark on his cheek that looked raw and sore, and his eyebrows were gone. "We've …" He started to cough—a dry, raspy cough—and I could hear him wheeze as he tried to get it under control. That he'd been in the fire was obvious, but why?

"We've got to get Marilee and the baby out of this smoke. Someplace safe."

He had a good point. The smoke filled my lungs, too, making it hard to breathe without coughing. It had turned the night sky a dull, filthy gray or bright red, depending on what the slowly circulating lights from the emergency vehicles illuminated.

"Nathan." Anne clutched his arm, using it as much to hold herself up as to get his attention. "You were here? What happened? Look at it! It must have gone up like kindling wood."

"It exploded." I don't think he even felt Anne hanging from him. His eyes went from the last gasping flames to the police car, where Marilee evidently sat, and back. "I came over to make sure she was all right. I was so worried. When you told me what happened in the hospital, I had to make sure … She was lying on the sofa in the living room, holding the baby. Gina was going to get her some water from the kitchen. Only there was an explosion." He stopped, shook his head as if to clear it. "Thank God the kitchen door was closed. If it had been open … anyway, I got her up, grabbed the baby and stuck him in the car seat. Marilee couldn't move very fast, but we had to get out. I yelled at Gina to grab onto my belt, and I guess she did. I could feel the flames and the smoke—so thick I couldn't see. I couldn't find the door. I thought we weren't going to … the next thing I knew, we were all on the lawn across the street and the fire engines and police were coming from every direction. Someone put Marilee in that car over there. But a doctor needs to look at her."

"Explosion. Good God. Maybe it was that old gas stove." Anne didn't look as if she really believed that, but it was probably better than thinking someone had deliberately blown up the house.

Nathan turned to look at her. "The stove?" He shook his head, his lips pursed with what looked like anger. "Maybe. The fire department will find out what caused it. Right now we need to do something about Marilee and the baby."

"And Gina," Aunt Mary said softly. "Didn't you say Gina was also over there in that car?"

"Oh. Yes. Look, there's a paramedic. Finally." Nathan took off almost at a run. A couple of paramedics were kneeling beside the police car. They were on the opposite side from us. I couldn't see but could hear a baby cry. That was a good sign. Or was it? He must be gulping in tons of smoke. The crying stopped. Maybe they were giving him oxygen. I hoped so. I could use a little myself.

"Are they going to take them to the hospital?" Susannah's voice sounded small and scared. I'd forgotten she was there, standing behind me. I turned now to look at her, but she was fine, safely encased in Neil's arms.

Dan appeared beside her, face smudged with soot, eyes bloodshot from smoke, but his eyebrows were still intact. "They aren't going to the hospital. Medics say there's nothing wrong with any of them that a bath and a good bed won't cure."

"Oh." Anne suddenly emerged from her shock-induced trance. "Oh my God. Yes, we'll need someplace … but it's got to be safe … I can't have this … they have to be safe. The Good Night Motor Inn? No. That's way out on the freeway. How about the Heritage Inn here in town? I'll call them. Where's my cell phone?"

"They're coming to our house."

That was it. Just a flat statement that riveted all eyes on Dan. Especially mine. What did he mean, our house? All of them? Marilee and the baby? Gina? Leona? But where was Leona? Did anyone know? And what if Grady somehow found out Marilee was at my house? I wondered wildly if my insurance covered arson.

"Grady Wilcox was spotted cruising this area earlier this evening."

"Oh, Dan. Do you think he did this?" I wouldn't have believed Anne's face could get any whiter, but she paled another three shades. I was afraid she was going to pass out.

"He was around here; we know that. Nice of him to drive such a flamboyant truck. Makes it easier to keep track of him." Dan stooped down and took a better look at Anne. "Are you all right? You look—"

"I'm fine." Her voice rang with impatience, or maybe it was impending hysteria. "At any rate, as fine as I can be. Grace House is gone. My girls have nothing, except for one very new baby, and now you think the father of that baby tried to kill him and his mother by setting the house on fire. I'm responsible for these girls. I'm supposed to be keeping them safe. How can I do that …"

A bald, portly man I'd never seen before appeared out of the smoke and slid his arm around Anne, who had started to shake.

"Oh, Howard," she said as she leaned against him. "I'm so glad you're here. That damned City Council meeting …

No one would put me through, and these girls … Look at that!" She gestured wildly toward the house, tears spilling from her eyes.

"Hush, now. They're going to be fine, and so are you." He pulled her close while he looked around the group. His eyes stopped traveling when they got to Dan.

"Evening, Dan. This is just about the worst fire I've seen. You've got everyone out of those other houses?"

Dan nodded. "Evening, Mr. Major. The first thing my people did."

"They're doing their usual fine job." He paused a moment, watching the last tongues of flame die down under the onslaught of water. "You think this Grady person might be responsible for … that?" He waved his free hand toward the slowly smoldering house.

"Don't know. But he's been tearing the town apart looking for his wife. Made a huge scene at the hospital yesterday, punched out a nurse, but then, I'm sure Anne told you all that. I can't rule him out, so to be on the safe side, I think we'll take these girls home with us." Dan glanced over at me. "There's only two of them and they have to go somewhere."

Howard slowly nodded. He turned Anne so that she faced him. "That all right with you?"

"Two? Where's Leona? Where did she go? " It was as if Leona's absence had just sunk in. "She did go someplace, didn't she? She couldn't have been in ..." The possibility of where she might be, or might have been, was just beginning to sink in for the rest of us.

We all looked at one another.

"Nathan." Aunt Mary sounded breathless and a little sick. "If she'd been in the house, surely he would have seen her."

"Not if she was in her room." Anne didn't sound any better than Aunt Mary.

"Do the firemen know someone is missing?" I had

never seen Dan look so grim. With good reason. The thought of poor Leona, trapped in her room, not realizing that the house was on fire until it was too late, calling out for help with no one to hear, was almost more than I could bear. Behind me, Susannah sucked in a mouthful of air. I didn't hear her release it.

"You all stay here. I'd better check with the fire chief." Dan disappeared into the smoke once more.

"She couldn't have been in there. Could she?" I didn't know if Susannah was addressing me, Neil, or the world in general. No one had an answer. All we could do was wait for Dan to come back and hope for news. Good news. In the meantime, I wasn't sure what to do. It seemed we were going to have Gina, Marilee, and her new baby as houseguests. Should I try to round them up? Get my car? Where was I going to put them? Were the towels in the bathroom clean?

I tried to peer through the smoke, hoping to see Dan. Instead we got Nathan.

"Anne, Marilee is about to collapse, and I'm really worried about the baby. Gina's staying with them, but we need to move them. Only, where?"

Anne just stared at him. The idea that Leona might have been trapped in the house seemed to have been the one thing she couldn't deal with. It was her husband, Howard, who took charge.

"Chief Dunham has agreed to take them to his house— *their* house." He gestured vaguely in my direction. No wonder. If he knew my name, it had left him in the stress of the moment. And after all, we hadn't been formally introduced. "As soon as Dan gets back, we'll make arrangements."

"Where did he go? We need to get Marilee."

Anne finally came alive. "Nathan." She grabbed him by the arm, pulling him around so he had to look at her. "Was Leona in the house?"

"What?" Nathan stared at Anne for a moment, looked

into Howard's face, then from him to each of us before he turned to stare at the smoldering wreck. "No. She couldn't have been."

"You didn't see her?" Howard's voice was low but intense. "Did either of the girls say anything about her?"

"No." Nathan seemed unable to move, to do anything but stare at the house, which still threw white smoke and steam into the air. If Leona had been in there ... I saw Nathan shudder. A strong tremor ran through me as well.

"They'll start looking as soon as they can." Dan was back. He rested his hand on my arm and squeezed. "In the meantime, I put out an alert for her. If she isn't ... we'll find her."

"We need to move Marilee and her baby, Dan." I had never heard Aunt Mary's voice so shaky, but she was right. There was nothing we could do for Leona.

"We're going to, Mary, right now." He draped his other arm over her shoulders and gave her a light hug. She blinked a couple of times but managed to keep the gathering tears from falling. Dan turned to me. "Whose car did you bring?"

"Mine."

"Good. Can you take Marilee and the baby? Gina, too?"

I nodded, too stunned to speak. Leona. Like Nathan, I was having a hard time tearing my eyes off what was left of the house. Instead of tears, I felt my stomach lurch. Was she really ... I swallowed hard, forcing the bile that was collecting in my throat back down into my stomach where it belonged. I was not going to be sick. Not right now. I had people who depended on me and I had to concentrate on their needs. Like, where was I going to put them? Did I have enough beds? Sheets? Clean towels? Coffee?

Dan put his arm around me and pulled me close. "Are you all right with this?" His tone was low, for me only, and it was delivered with a soft kiss that landed on the side of my neck.

I nodded. "But, Dan," My voice was as soft as his had been. "Do you really think Grady might … is Marilee really in danger? Is that why …?"

"I think it's possible. But if you're scared, if you don't want to do this, I'll find someplace else. "

He studied my face, waiting for an answer. I knew, as sure as I had ever known anything, that if I said "no, I'm scared, I can't do it," he would make other arrangements and would never say he was disappointed in me or make me feel guilty. I looked over at the car where Marilee sat with her new baby. I looked at Anne, who smiled at me expectantly. Maybe Dan wouldn't be disappointed with me, but I would be. I took a deep breath and said, "Of course they're coming to our house."

"Did I ever tell you I love you?" That went into my ear. I barely heard it above all the noise, but I heard it. I whispered back, "I love you too." The words warmed me.

"See you at home later."

Home. Later. Probably much later, and home was going to be much more crowded.

"Okay." I did a little mental shoulder squaring and turned to face the group. "Nathan, go get the girls. I'm parked down the street; I'll pull the car up as far as I can. Let's get them out of here." I hoped he heard where I planned to park because he was already halfway to the squad car.

"You'll need food," Aunt Mary stated. Her voice didn't sound so thin; her chin came up and I could see her jaw set. She had started to plan. Leona would not be forgotten, but there was a task to be completed first, people to feed. "Susannah, you and Neil can take me home. We'll pack up the dinner leftovers and some blankets and things and bring it all back to your mother's."

"Good. Nathan can help me." Anne looked over at the squad car. Nathan had disappeared around the passenger side. "If I can tear him away from Marilee." She turned back to look once more at the house. "Everything's gone. Baby diapers, toothbrushes, clean clothes; there's nothing left for anyone. We're going to have to get on the phone and start collecting."

Everything gone. For all of them. They'd had little enough, but this! How would they even begin to rebuild? I took a look at Aunt Mary's face, listened to Anne's crisp voice, and got out my car keys. We'd start at my house, with pot roast and a bed.

"I've got to get back to the council meeting." Howard had released Anne. He gave her an approving nod before he turned to Dan. "We're having a heated argument over water fountains in the park. I'll try to change the subject to donations for these ladies." He lowered his voice and almost whispered to Dan. "Let me know about Leona. This doesn't sound one bit good."

"None of this sounds good." Dan's voice was also low, but I heard what he said. And what he didn't say.

"Nathan's going to follow Ellen home and stay there until I can get a squad car to sit in front of the house." Dan raised his voice so everyone could hear, but he looked directly at me. "Anne, he can help you after Neil brings Susannah and Mary back to our house, but I don't want Marilee alone. Or alone with just Ellen. I'll get a car over there as soon as I can."

He might just as well have come right out and said he thought Grady had set the fire but he hadn't gotten what he wanted, which was Marilee, and that he wasn't through trying. It sounded way too much as if he thought Grady would somehow find her and when he did … That thought sent a surge of bile down toward my stomach where it threatened to come right back up. Not now, I told it. I might be sick with fright, but there wasn't time to dwell on it. I rummaged in my pocket for my car keys, wondering if I needed someone to walk with me while I retrieved my car. I looked down the street, trying to gauge how near I could drive without being immobilized by emergency vehicles. Not very near. There was a tangled knot of them, making it impossible to see more than half a block. A figure appeared around the back of a fire truck, coming out of the gloom of the dim street lights into the glow of flashing emergency lights and the roar of noise still surrounding the ruined house. Another firefighter? Only this figure wasn't wearing a heavy coat and boots.

"Look." I grabbed Dan and pointed. "Look."

Everyone turned to stare, but no one said a word as the figure walked up to us.

"Holy shit," Leona said, "what happened here?"

Chapter Nineteen

It had taken awhile, but everyone had finally been rounded up and transported to my house, where they were sitting in my kitchen eating pot roast. Even Leona.

Everyone had gathered around her, alternating between exclamations of relief that she was alive and demands to know where she had been. She muttered something that sounded like "cigarettes" while she stared at what was left of the house. She didn't say anything more for a long time, ignoring the barrage of questions everyone threw at her, looking from the fire trucks to the paramedics, then back to the house.

Finally she looked at the crowd around her, not seeing the one person she was concerned for. "Did Marilee get out okay? And the baby, is he all right?"

"Yes," Anne said, "They're fine, thanks to Nathan. Only we didn't know where you were, and we were afraid ..."

Leona didn't seem to hear Anne. "What happened?"

Surprisingly, it was Susannah who answered. "They think it was arson."

"Arson." She shook her head as if in disbelief. "What'd he ...," her eyes shifted as she looked from Anne to the rest of us, "*whoever*, use to do that? It looks like ... something you see on TV."

"We don't know yet." Howard's face was grim. "But we're going to find out. Leona, we're glad you're safe. Anne, I have to go. Try and get home before morning."

That was all we got out of Leona. She listened while Anne explained the plan, watched silently while Nathan struggled to install the car seat base in my car, then claimed a seat on one side of it. Now she sat at my kitchen table, along with everyone else, eating pot roast while never taking her eyes off of the baby, who lay in his infant car seat close beside his mother's chair.

Marilee poked around on her plate, but very little got to her mouth. Leona, on the other hand, consumed everything put in front of her.

"This is great." She looked up and smiled. Unfortunately, her mouth was still full. "Only thing that would make it better would be a little something to wash it down."

Aunt Mary turned from the stove where she was still dishing up plates. "You have a full glass of water right there. But I can put the coffee on."

"Actually, I was thinking of something a little stronger." She looked around hopefully. "Something to help calm my nerves. It's been a pretty stressful day, you know."

"Then I'll make tea." Aunt Mary's tone left no doubt that was as strong as any beverage was going to be this night. "There's nothing like tea for stress. The English have known that for years."

If I hadn't been so distracted, I would have laughed. However, I was still trying to figure out who was going to end up in which bed, how I was going to come up with enough nightgowns and toothbrushes, and if my house was in imminent danger of being burnt down. I thought about the wine bottle, chilling nicely in the refrigerator. Leona had a point.

"My mom wants to know if you need any blankets or anything." Neil and Susannah walked in, cell phone still clutched in Neil's hand. "She thinks Susannah should come over to our house tonight. We have a guest room." He added this last bit of information somewhat hastily, probably because of the look on my face.

"Pat's got your wedding dress spread all over the bed in there, but she says she can fold it all up," Susannah added.

There was a lot of amusement in her tone. "She says, what else do you need?"

"Toothbrushes for openers. And diapers, but I don't suppose she has any lying around."

Neil laughed. "I don't think so, but we could run out and get some. Toothbrushes, too. Make a list."

"No." I was really tempted. I had no idea how long it had been since the baby had been changed, and I knew Marilee needed personal things as well. At least I could provide those. "I think we'd better wait and see what Anne and Nathan can dredge up. Besides, Dan made it clear he wanted us all to stay put until he sent someone over here."

"There's a squad car parked out front." That was the first I'd heard out of Gina in awhile. I hadn't noticed she'd left the table. I wondered if she had been looking out the living room window, watching for Grady's flamboyant truck. I'd been thinking about doing the same thing, but if Dan's squad car was out front, I could forget about Grady, at least for now. Besides, how could he possibly know …? That was easy. By now, the whole city council knew Dan had taken the girls to our house. So did half the fire department, the emergency services people, everyone either Anne or Nathan contacted for donations … He could find her, but you had to be half-witted to burn down the chief of police's house. Or break into it. Half-witted or desperate. Damn. I couldn't rule out either one. How had this happened? One minute I had nothing more pressing to worry about than a wedding that wasn't going the way I wanted and a few escrows that mostly were. Now I had a houseful of homeless people, one of whom was brand new, and whose mother was being pursued by his father, who thought nothing of torching a house to get to her. That thought made me break out in a cold sweat. The thought of a policeman outside my door was only slightly consoling.

"Has that policeman had dinner?" Aunt Mary was already reaching for a clean plate.

"I have no idea." There was a ghost of a smile on Gina's usually serious face. "Shall I go ask him?"

"Well, someone needs to find out. Neil, you go ask him. There's plenty here, and he can stand guard over us in the kitchen just as well as out on the street."

The sound of the front doorbell made me jump. My coffee mug jerked, and hot coffee sloshed over my hand. "Damn."

I started to push back my chair, but Aunt Mary was already handing me a napkin. "Are you all right?"

"Fine." I mopped up the mess, thinking I didn't need one more person in my already crowded kitchen, but that I'd have to answer. Maybe it was one of Dan's people coming to tell us that Grady had been caught and was on his way to jail.

It was a policeman, all right, but the only thing he brought was a healthy appetite.

"Hi, Ellen." Gary, the policeman, strutted into the kitchen with the confident air of an old friend. "Sure is nice of you to invite me to dinner. I haven't had more than a snack since lunch."

He wasn't alone. Neil followed him in, carrying a huge carton box. "Where can I put this?"

Anne was right behind him, lugging a box of her own. "This thing is heavy. Can I put it down here?" She gingerly set it down on the floor in front of the stove, abandoning it to bend over the car seat and coo at the baby.

"Well, look at you, all scrunched up. You're going to slide right out of there."

She started to pull one end of the blanket up, as if to better cover him, but Leona got there first. She almost pushed Anne aside in her rush to pick him up. "Here, I've got him."

Marilee looked stricken as she watched Leona pull the blanket up over the baby's feet, cradle him in her arms, and start walking him around the kitchen.

"Leona, "she began somewhat tentatively, "I don't

think—"

Leona ignored her. She started to bounce him up and down, making little crooning noises, a rapt expression on her face.

It happened so fast that it froze us all in our seats. That, and the fierce possessiveness with which she held him against her.

Nathan broke the spell.

"Hey, big guy." He walked over to Leona, slid one hand under the baby's head and took him out of her arms. "The last time I saw you, you were kind of smoky smelling." He leaned over the baby and sniffed. "You don't smell so great right now, either. I think you need your mom." He very tenderly placed the small bundle in Marilee's outstretched arms. She clutched him tightly to her, glaring at Leona.

Nathan smiled down at her, and his hand hovered for a moment, as if he were going to touch Marilee on the cheek. Instead, he let his finger run lightly down the cheek of the child.

Leona stood very still; her eyes blazed, boring holes in Nathan's back. Her gaze shifted to Marilee, anger and resentment ready to boil over. It was only when she dropped her eyes to the baby that her expression changed. The hunger in them was pitiful. And scary.

The baby started to squirm, his face reddened, and his mouth opened. His lungs were fully developed and he did his best to prove it.

"He's crying." Marilee looked terrified, but she still held him close to her. "What should I do?"

"Feed him." Aunt Mary and Anne spoke together. Aunt Mary was at the sink, scraping plates and loading the dishwasher; Anne rummaged through the boxes. "Look. Diapers. A little big, but still … and a little nightgown and a blanket. Thank God for people who donate."

"It's pink." Nathan picked up the nightgown and held it up. It was adorable. It also had pink rosebuds all over it.

"So's the blanket."

"It won't scar him for life." Anne pulled more stuff out of the box, held it up, examined it, and started putting it in piles. "I promise not to tell him, when he's fifteen, that we put him in a pink nightie the day he was born."

The cries coming from Marilee's arms were getting louder. She looked around wildly. Leona headed for her, but Aunt Mary got there first. "Let's get him changed and then you can feed him. It's too soon for your milk to be in, but he needs the colostrum. You are going to breast-feed, aren't you?"

Poor Marilee looked as though any references to breasts had, in her experience, nothing to do with feeding a baby. "I guess."

Anne paused in her unloading, and she and Aunt Mary exchanged glances. Aunt Mary shrugged; Anne sighed. A spot was cleared on the table, the baby laid out on it, and the necessary functions started. The baby screamed louder. Leona hovered over their shoulders, clucking at him, telling them the diaper was too tight, the nightgown too big, to take care with the cord, demanding that they let her do it.

"Marilee's going to take care of him." Anne sounded as if she was out of patience, and if Leona didn't back off, she'd give her the backside of her tongue.

Leona didn't seem to notice. Nathan took her by the arm and moved her so that Marilee could stand by the table.

"Are you sure his cord's all right? Does it look too red?"

"It looks fine. Here. Hold his legs up and put the diaper on like this. Good." Anne guided Marilee through her first lesson on diapering and helped her take off the hospital shirt and put on the new, pink nightgown. Leona never quit making comments or offering—demanding—to do it. You would have thought she was the doting grandmother. Or mother.

Nathan stood on the other end of the table, watching the whole procedure with a proud, nervous grin on his face.

"You're sure the cord's all right? Why does his—you know—bowel stuff, look so black? Is he supposed to be so—sort of folded up looking?"

I kept thinking the wrong people were agonizing over this child.

Aunt Mary settled Marilee in one of the kitchen chairs. Anne draped the pink blanket over her shoulder and the baby quit screaming. I could hear sucking noises. Success. Only, there were dark circles under Marilee's eyes and she kept yawning. Poor kid. Giving birth was supposed to be joyful. Painful, exhausting, but also joyful. All she'd had a chance to feel so far was pain and exhaustion. And fear.

The doorbell rang. Now what? I glanced at Susannah and Neil, but they were as mesmerized by the baby as everyone else. Why, I didn't know. All they could see was his feet. Gina glanced at me and started for the door. I waved her back and pushed open the swinging door into the dining room. The bell rang again. "I'm coming." Whoever was sitting on my doorbell was getting my best imitation of Aunt Mary displeased.

Rose stood there.

"Is Gina here?" Her face was pasty white, her breath labored. I looked around but didn't see a car.

"Yes," I said. "How did you get here?"

"I walked. Sal didn't want me to come. Is she all right?"

"She's fine. But you don't look as if you are. Come in." I took her by the hand and led her into the house. I really didn't want one more person in my kitchen—it was more than crowded—but I could hardly send her out into the night in the condition she was in. Besides, I was curious. I could understand being concerned, but this seemed like too much emotion. Everything about tonight seemed like too much emotion.

"No, I don't want to be a bother. I just wanted to know … I was so worried … that awful fire and no one could tell me."

159

She started to back away. I grabbed her before she took one too many steps backward and fell off the porch.

"What bother? We're all in the kitchen admiring the baby and all the stuff Anne and Nathan have collected. Gina will be delighted to see you." I pulled her into the living room without much resistance. Once in, she trotted past me through the dining room and pushed aside the swinging door that led into the kitchen. I followed, wondering whom she'd called and how she knew to come here. Small town grapevines can come in handy, but there was just too much information making the rounds tonight. I paused to glance out the living room window, reassuring myself that Gary, who had bolted the last of his food and fled when the baby started to cry, was once again sitting in his squad car keeping watch. I hoped he was. At least he was in the car. I followed Rose.

Anne knelt beside Marilee. The pink baby blanket was still draped over her from her shoulder into her lap. She had picked up one end and was staring at the baby underneath. The look of awe on her face made me smile for the first time in hours. She was finally getting some of the joy.

Rose sat at the kitchen table, which somehow had been cleared of dirty dinner dishes, talking earnestly to Gina. Aunt Mary and Leona were listening intently, Aunt Mary with an expression of extreme disapproval, Leona with avid curiosity. Susannah and Neil leaned, side by side, against the kitchen counter, Susannah with a damp dishtowel in her hands.

"So, I have the extra room." Rose leaned across the table, trying to get closer to Gina, to make her point. "That way you wouldn't wake anyone up. Five o'clock … not everyone wants to be up that early. And now that you are doing so much of the baking … anyway, I thought it would be a good idea."

Gina had both of Rose's hands in hers. "I can't believe you came all the way over here, just to see if I was safe. Why didn't you call?"

Rose's eyes shifted. "I thought … it isn't really that far … and I wanted to make sure …"

She wanted to make sure Sal didn't overhear her making the offer, I suddenly realized. Gina seemed to have the same suspicion. "Does Sal know you want me to stay with you?"

"Once Sal thinks about it, he'll be fine."

"Oh, Rose." Gina smiled at Rose and patted her hands but started to shake her head. "You are the sweetest thing in the world, but …"

"Where's your car, Rose?"

She looked up at me, as if she hadn't noticed I'd come into the room, but now that she had, she wasn't one bit pleased. Or maybe it was my question she didn't like. "I told you. I walked."

"Walked!" Aunt Mary sat up straight and glared at her. "You don't walk enough every day? It's a good two miles from your house to here. And how did you think you'd get Gina home with you? Both of you walking back? At this time of night?"

She had a point. The schoolhouse clock on my kitchen wall bonged out midnight.

"Well, decide something." Anne stood up heavily, holding her back. "Marilee is going to sleep sitting up. She's exhausted, and that's not good for her or the baby. And I'm not far behind her."

"It's decided." Aunt Mary's lips were set in a straight line. Yep. It was decided. "Gina is coming home with me. I'm quite used to getting up early, so that's not a problem." She looked at the piles of donated things. "Gina, see if you can find something to wear tonight in that pile and let's get going. We're all tired."

"We need to find something for Marilee to put on and get her into bed." Anne walked over to Marilee's chair and gently took her arm. "Come on, baby. We're going upstairs.

Where is she going to sleep?"

"In my room," Susannah said. "I'm going over to Neil's to spend the night. I'll go up and throw stuff in my backpack. She can come now; this won't take me long."

Marilee fought a yawn. She tried to get up out of the chair, still holding the baby. He must have fallen asleep, because she was holding the whole package gingerly, as if afraid that moving her arms too much would wake him up. Or break him.

"I'll take him." Leona, arms out, was in front of Marilee almost before I realized she was up from her chair.

"I've got him." Anne had the small bundle cradled in one arm and was helping Marilee to her feet with the other. "Leona, why don't you see if you can find a nightgown in the pile for her, and one for you, too. There are hairbrushes, toothbrushes, and toothpaste in that small box. There are some other things as well. Just bring up the whole box. Ellen, do you know where Leona is going to sleep?"

"The guest room, right next to Susannah's. She'll show you. There are fresh towels in the bathroom." I crossed my fingers and hoped I was right.

Nathan had taken Marilee over from Anne. He had her by the arm, half holding her up, and was headed out of the kitchen.

"You don't need to—" Anne said.

"Yes, I do." He let his arm slide around Marilee's waist. "Lean on me. That's right."

Anne watched for a second, sighed, and turned to Leona. "Let's go." She followed Nathan and Marilee through the swinging doors toward the living room and the stairs. Leona picked two nightgowns from the pile of clothes. Without looking at them she threw them over her shoulder and grabbed the box of other supplies. I doubted she cared one bit where she slept, or if she had a nightgown or anything else. She wanted her hands on that baby. I watched her push open the dining room door and hurry after Anne.

"That's settled, then." Aunt Mary walked over to the cupboard where I keep the plastic grocery sacks, took one out and shook it open. "Gina, put whatever you think you can use for tonight in here. Neil, you and Susannah drive Rose home. It's hardly out of your way at all. I'll take Gina."

She held up her hand as I started to object. "It's late. I'm not waiting for Dan to give me permission to do anything. Besides, Grady Wilcox doesn't care a fig about me or Gina."

There wasn't much I could say. It was late, and she was right. It was Marilee who Grady was after. "Call me when you get home."

She smiled at me and nodded.

Gina went around the back of Rose's chair and dropped her arms around Rose's shoulders in a gentle hug. "You're the sweetest, most thoughtful thing in the world." She planted a kiss on her hair. "I can't believe you walked all the way over here just to make sure I was safe. But I think this is best for right now." She let Rose go and frowned. "Sal won't give you a hard time when you get home, will he? Maybe you should stay at Mrs. McGill's also."

Aunt Mary looked as if she thought that was a good idea, but Rose shook her head vehemently. "No, he'll be asleep when I get home. If he woke up in the morning and found me gone ... I'll be fine. Mary, are you really sure you don't mind?"

She sounded almost relieved that Gina wasn't coming with her, almost as relieved as when she found out she hadn't been burned to a crisp. I wondered if she was thinking about Sal waking up to find Gina in the guest room. Might have gotten their morning off to a rocky start.

"Now, Mary ..." little worry furrows deepened in Rose's brow as she twisted around to look up at Gina, "you'll take good care of her, won't you?"

"I think I can promise you that." Aunt Mary smiled at Rose, but the look she gave Gina was speculative.

The kitchen door swung open, and Anne and Nathan

walked in. "The girls are settled. Marilee's already asleep, and, luckily, so is the baby. Leona says she can't go to sleep without a smoke first, but I assured her she'd sleep on the chaise outside if she lit up in this house." Anne's smile was tight.

Aunt Mary laughed out loud. "Couldn't have put it better myself. Gina, have you gotten what you need? Good. Let's go home. I'm beat."

Susannah, Neil, and Rose left out the back door, everyone else out the front. Aunt Mary waved to Gary before she got into her car. I waited until she drove off, then walked back into the living room and set the dead bolt on the front door. I'd leave the back door unlocked. Dan would be home sometime before dawn, and that's the door he would use. I stood in the middle of the room, thinking about that. I'd grown up in this house and couldn't remember my parents ever locking the back door. It hadn't even had a lock when I had moved back in. Dan was the one who thought we needed one. He called Mr. Leeds at the hardware store and the next day I had a dead bolt. Only, I never could remember to set it. Maybe, tonight, I would. Dan had a key. Did he have it on him? If not, he could wake me up. If I could sleep. I was exhausted, but not one bit sleepy. I walked back into the living room and looked out the window. The street was empty except for the black and white patrol car stationed in front of my house. No lights shown in any window in this respectable neighborhood, where all good citizens were in bed by ten o'clock and where crime was something that happened on TV. I'd bet there were half a dozen homes on this street with unlocked doors.

Headlights were shining. Someone had turned the corner and was slowly coming our way. Car? Truck? Grady Wilcox? I couldn't tell. I froze. What if he threw a firebomb at my house? He could open his window and lob it over here before Gary could open his car door. What should I do? Run upstairs and wake up the girls? The baby. Could we get the baby out? And Jake. My cat. Where was he? I hadn't seen him all evening. Under the bed upstairs? On top of the refrigerator? I stared out the window, watching the lights approach. I needed to move. But somehow I couldn't. Little beads of sweat pooled up around my hairline, and I could feel my heart beat faster, my breathing become shallow. If he threw something, I was right in the way. Move! The only thing that moved was my hand, reaching out to clutch the curtain. The lights slowed down. Move! I couldn't.

It was a Toyota Camry. Light blue. Not orange and not a truck. The Witherspoons from a couple of houses down had a Toyota Camry. The car slowed more. I could see the driver take a good look at the patrol car, then at my front window before gathering speed again. I watched it pull into the Witherspoon's driveway. I let the curtain drop and sighed. Just the neighbors coming home from the movies, or a friend's house, curious about a patrol car, sitting without lights in front of my house. My heart slowed to a more dignified pace and my breathing settled down. I'd been terrified for the second time in two days. Damn Grady Wilcox! I had never laid eyes on him, but the thought of him, what he might have done, what he still might do, reduced me to jelly. I could not let this happen. I would not let it happen. I would leave the back door unlocked, just as I always did, and march myself upstairs to bed and to sleep. I headed for the kitchen, meaning to turn out the light, but stopped. Dan would need it when he came in. He might also need the light in the living room. Should I turn on the staircase light? That might wake up one of the girls. I'd leave it off for now. And the stairs squeaked. Wasn't there a quilt in the hall closet? Yes. There it was. Maybe, because I didn't want to disturb anyone, I'd just lie here on the sofa where I could see out the window. That way, I'd be able to see Dan's headlights. Or anyone else's. Not that I was scared. It was just that … Jake sauntered into the room, purring. I picked him up, set him on the sofa and covered both of us with the quilt. Now I could relax and get some sleep. Only I didn't.

Chapter Twenty

"Not again." Dan rolled over and groaned. "I know newborns don't sleep through the night, but this is too much."

I had to agree with him, especially as I was the one getting up to help Marilee. He was the one going back to sleep.

"How many times does this make?" The question came out from under the covers a bit muffled.

"Before or after you got home?"

The answer was lost under the quilt.

I pushed my feet into slippers and managed to get my arms into the sleeves of my bathrobe. "Dan, since you're awake …"

"Who said I was awake?"

"You sound awake. And it's six thirty. Almost time to get up anyway. Dan, do you know where Grady is?"

"No."

"Do you know why he set the house on fire?"

"No."

"Do you know for sure it was him?"

"No."

I was getting exasperated. "You don't know much."

"I know I got home at two o'clock this morning, that every time I go to sleep that kid starts howling, and that I have a nine o'clock meeting with Dick Hadley. He's the fire chief."

"I know."

"Then you also know I'm going back to sleep for an hour. Maybe more if that kid shuts up. Good night, Ellie."

He turned over and buried his head under a pillow. The baby continued to scream. I sighed and headed for Susannah's —Marilee's—room.

The screaming stopped. I stood outside the door and listened to the quiet. I didn't know if he'd fallen back asleep or if Marilee had figured out that breast-feeding could be really easy. You didn't even have to get up. But since I was up and awake … Or was I?

I made it downstairs without tripping over Jake or anything else. The coffeepot was right where I'd left it. Somehow I managed to fill it with water and coffee with my eyes half closed. I was sitting at the table, wondering if caffeine would be enough to get me awake and moving again, when Leona walked in.

"I smelled coffee and thought I'd come down. Hope you don't mind."

My eyes snapped open at the sight of her. The nightgown she'd picked up last night was about three sizes too big. The light cotton hung in soft folds from the shoulders, the sleeves full and flowing. She had found a cord somewhere and had tied it around her waist, probably to keep the gown up off the floor. She looked like a medieval nun. Only, with Leona, I was fairly certain the resemblance was surface only.

"It should be finished in just a minute. Grab a mug off the hutch. Cream and sugar?"

"Yeah."

She headed for the hutch, lifted a mug off the shelf, took the lid off the sugar bowl, and peered inside. The cream pitcher sat empty and clean beside it. She ignored it. The refrigerator door opened. She straightened up and put the whole carton of milk on the kitchen table, the sugar beside it. The coffee gurgled to a stop.

"Where's your mug?"

"I haven't gotten it yet."

"You want I should—?"

"Thanks, yes." I don't know why I was surprised. Maybe because she hadn't made one move to help last night, because she seemed so ineffectual the only other time I'd seen her in a kitchen, the day I met her at the now defunct Grace House.

She took down another coffee mug, poured and pushed the full—very full—mug my way, and sat down opposite me, shoving away a pile of clothes. "Bunch of ol' junk." She liberally spooned sugar into her coffee.

"I hope you didn't lose anything you can't replace." I looked at the mug. How was I going to get that to my mouth without half of it ending up on the table? Or down my front?

"No. Didn't have much, anyway."

"But you had your purse with you? So, you have no clothes, but you still have some money, your checkbook, your driver's license?"

"Only money I had was what I made at the Yum Yum. I had that with me. I don't believe in leaving good money lying around."

Did she think someone at Grace House would steal it? "How about your other things? Your charge cards, checkbook, that kind of thing?"

She snorted. "Hell, nobody's goin' to give me a charge card. I've got a bank account but there's never nothing in it. As for a driver's license, well, I haven't had one of them for a while."

"So, the only thing you're really out is your clothes?" I wasn't sure how I felt about this. Could someone really have so little of their own in their life?

"I guess. No loss, though."

If the rest of Leona's clothes were like the ones she had on last night, she was right. "Then it's a good thing Anne and Nathan got all those people to donate. We're going to have to get this stuff off the table before breakfast anyway, so let's see if there's something here you can use. Gina and Marilee will have to have something also."

I pushed some of the clothes her way and started through a pile next to my coffee. The first thing I picked up was a T-shirt with a ripped neck and unidentifiable stains down the front. Why give something like this? It belonged in the trash or under my coffee mug. That's where it went, and I kept on looking.

"Here." I held up a pair of sweatpants with the tags still on. Size small. "These should fit you, and here's a sweatshirt." I held it up and, recalling the T-shirt, went over it critically. "It looks new. You'll need some underwear, but I don't think we're going to find any here."

"Never wear it." Leona took the clothes gingerly. "Guess these will be all right. For now. These should fit Marilee." She held up a pair of plaid flannel pants. They had a drawstring at the waist, and for a girl who had just given birth that seemed like a good idea. "She could use this as a top." The big shirt was—big, but it had buttons down the front.

"Did Marilee get her money out?" Leona threw out the words in an offhand manner, but I could feel her eyes on my face.

I was concentrating on the pile of clothes, dropping the impossibles on the floor, wondering how Aunt Mary could do this for all of the rummage sales she ran, so I almost missed her comment. "Money?" I dropped a size-forty skirt, decorated liberally with purple pansies, on the send to the rummage sale pile and looked up. "What money?"

"Marilee had some money saved. I don't know where she kept it. She sure wouldn't have been happy to lose it."

"How much money?"

Leona shrugged. "Enough to get her started somewhere else, least that's what she told me."

Money. Grady. Is that why he was looking so hard for Marilee? Had she taken—helped herself—to money before he kicked her out?

"Do they know who set the fire yet?" Leona watched

me out of the corner of her eye. Her hand on her coffee mug tightened. "Was it Grady Wilcox?"

"I don't know," I replied truthfully. "But I do know he was seen in the neighborhood about the same time."

"Idiot," Leona told her coffee cup softly.

"Do you know Grady?" I hadn't thought about that, I suppose because Leona was a whole generation older than Grady and Marilee.

"You could say so." She glanced up at me for a moment, then resumed staring at her light brown coffee. "We lived in the same trailer park. Until I got kicked out by the landlord. I wasn't late with my rent that often."

"So you knew Marilee also?"

This time Leona lifted her head and stared at me. "Yeah. Somethin' wrong with that?"

"Of course not," I said hastily. "It sounds as if you both ended up at Grace House at the same time."

"Humm."

I took another really good look at her. Bony arms, long sharp nose, thin lips tightly pursed together, dirty blond hair that hung limply down her back And she didn't wear underwear. Well, I guess it saved on the wash. Which we were going to have to do. Everyone who had been near that fire had smoke-saturated clothes.

But first, Leona needed to hit the shower. She was giving off a distinct smoky aroma, but hers was cigarette smoke. At least, I *thought* it was cigarette smoke.

"There's a shower in the little bath down here, right off the service porch." Thank goodness for Paul's Plumbing. The shower now worked.

She looked blank.

"Where the washer and dryer are." I pointed to the door, right beside the hutch.

She still looked blank.

"Everyone's going to be up soon. You can get yours in first."

"You telling me I need a shower? And there's one in that little bathroom by the washing machine?"

I nodded. "There are towels in the bathroom. And shampoo."

"Funny place for a bathroom."

"My father had it put in when my sister and I got to be teenagers. Said it was the only place he could go where no one banged on the door and shouted for him to get out. Anyway, it's all yours for the moment."

I didn't think she was going to move, but finally she got up, hitched her new clothes under one arm, and headed for the back porch and the little bathroom. She left her coffee mug on the table.

I picked my own mug up, wiped the bottom of it with the soiled T-shirt—which I dropped in the trash—put Leona's mug in the dishwasher, and leaned up against the sink, sipping. All the donated articles stared back at me, silently reminding me of the huge needs of Leona, Marilee, and Gina. How had they ended up at Grace House? Leona was easy. Chronically out of work, in and out of alcohol abuse programs, I wondered how many different jobs Grace House had tried to train her for. I had no doubt Ruthie, whose standards were high, wouldn't put up with her marginal performance for very long. What was it that Leona had said that first day? Something about her husband. He'd taken her kids and left. She had hinted that he'd been abusive. I wondered. There was a sullen air about her. Not open hostility, that would take too much effort, but more of a "I can't ever catch a break" attitude. Except when she was around the baby. She didn't want anyone to touch that baby, even his mother, and she didn't want him out of her sight. Well, most of the time. I hadn't seen her helping Marilee in the middle of the night. And she wasn't there when the fire started. What was so important that she left the house? It seemed strange. Although, if she really had needed cigarettes … I pushed myself off of the counter, walked over to the coffeemaker and refilled my mug. There was a convenience store about four blocks from Grace House. She could have walked there. If she had, her timing was sure good.

Water was running in the small bathroom. That was a good sign. I hoped. But it meant Leona would be back out soon, and Dan would be up as well. Pushing my coffee mug aside, I gathered up a bunch of clothes and carried them into the dining room. That table was a lot bigger and we didn't need it. At least, not for breakfast. Which I had better get started. Eggs? Or oatmeal?

Marilee was standing in the middle of the kitchen, holding the car seat by the handle, the baby asleep in it.

"Oh." She ducked her head, as if expecting a scolding. "I thought I'd come down. I smelled the coffee and ..."

I walked over to the hutch and took down a mug. A blue one with bright painted flowers. I filled it with coffee and handed it to her. "Cream and sugar are on the table. You might as well put him on that chair."

Marilee did as I instructed. She acted as if she'd had a lifetime of practice in being instructed. She sat down, put milk in her coffee, and started to sip.

"I wondered ... if the shower isn't in use ... do you think ... I don't want to leave him alone ... but ..."

"Dan will need to use the upstairs shower. Leona's in the downstairs. You can use it when she's finished. I don't think she'll be long. I'd be glad to watch the baby." Especially now that he was asleep. I didn't say that though. Instead I poured what was left of the coffee in the pot into my own mug and made a fresh one. We weren't going to get through this morning without lots of coffee. At least, I wasn't. I stared at the heavenly brown liquid as it began to fill the glass container and sighed. This was as good a time as any. The water had stopped running in the downstairs shower and I could hear the hair dryer I kept in there. The upstairs shower was going, so Dan would be down soon, and I had no idea when Aunt Mary, Anne, or Nathan would pop in. If I was going to ask Marilee any questions, as in—did you take your husband's money, do you still have it, and do you realize that you're putting us all in danger because he doesn't seem to care what he does to get it back?—I'd better do it now. However, I softened my approach a little.

"Marilee," I started as I pulled out a chair next to the baby. "I've been talking to Leona. I wondered—"

"I'm not going to get an apartment with her and that's that."

That took me by surprise. "Okay. I really wasn't going to suggest it, but I'm glad—"

It was as if she hadn't heard me. "I keep telling her I'm not going to, but she doesn't listen. If I did, I wouldn't have escaped from anything."

I wasn't sure how to respond, or even if I should. I wasn't even sure what she meant. Escaped from Grady? But he'd thrown her out. Hadn't he? And she hadn't escaped. Grady was doing everything he could to track her down. Escaped from her life before Grady? I wondered. There was a look on her face I'd never seen before. Her mouth had hardened, and she looked more like a woman and less like a terrified child than at any time since I'd met her. Her expression was—what? Determined. A sort of weak, scared determination, but still, it was there, and I was pretty sure it wasn't a new emotion. For the first time I wondered if Grady had thrown her out, as she said, or if Marilee had planned her escape.

She took her eyes off her baby and looked at me. "Leona's a loser like my mother."

I hadn't seen that one coming and it gave me a jolt. "How?"

She didn't even have to think about that one. "I love my mom, don't get me wrong, but my dad's told her she's a loser for so long, she's just given up. It doesn't make any difference what she does, it's wrong." Her eyes dropped back down to her baby and the lines around the corners of her mouth tightened. "It was the same with us kids. I'm not going to live like that anymore." She took a deep breath but didn't look up. "My mom's given up on life. So's my sister, and she's only fourteen."

She must have heard me catch my breath because she looked up at me. Her eyes held an expression much too hard for a girl of eighteen. "Leona's different. She's hit bottom so many times she's lost count. She keeps crawling back up, but it's usually on someone else's back, and this time it's not going to be on mine."

Pure, undiluted shock. That was what I felt. I'd assumed Marilee was a terrified kid caught in a life spiraling out of control. I was wrong. Oh, she was terrified all right, and she had every right to be. But she wasn't out of control. There was a core of steel somewhere in this kid and she was starting to let it show.

But she'd made some mistakes. Marrying Grady had been one of them, and I was very much afraid she was underestimating Leona. If she thought Leona was going to give up trying to get her hooks into that baby, she was making another one.

She stole another look at my face. "It's true. About my mom." Such a simple statement for such a terrible truth. "She's why I married Grady. I didn't want to be like her. I thought if I could get away ... My father was furious, but I'd turned eighteen, and he couldn't stop me. My mom tried to. Said I was going from the frying pan into the fire. She's always saying stuff like that. I didn't know what she meant. Things were great at first. Fun. Then I got pregnant."

The hair dryer had stopped. We didn't have much time. "Marilee, have you called your mother? Told her about the baby?"

"No." She reached over and stroked the downy hair on his head.

The sunlight came through the kitchen window and stroked it also. His hair was red. No. Golden. But it probably would be red. When he actually got hair. His skin had faded from the red of a newborn to a pale pink, more evidence he'd be a redhead. He had the same cameo-shaped face as his mother. I could picture him as a young boy, freckles, huge green eyes fringed with long lashes, enchanting grin, a Norman Rockwell kind of kid. Oh how I hoped he would have a Norman Rockwell kind of life! But no matter how determined Marilee was, I didn't think his chances were very good.

Marilee must have noticed the quiet in the bathroom, because she glanced quickly at the laundry room door. "My dad'd just tell me I made my bed, now lay in it. He won't let my mom do anything for me, either. Easier to just keep away. Besides, if she knew where I was, she'd tell my dad, and he'd probably tell Grady. I don't want to talk to Grady."

That was no surprise. Grady's pursuit of her had a frantic quality that wasn't very comforting. If he had set Grace House on fire, what was to stop him from doing it again? I wondered if I still had that fire extinguisher under the sink.

But Grady didn't know where she was, at least not now, and the most important thing was to keep it that way. For all our sakes. The second most important was to find out why he was chasing her so hard.

I opened my mouth to ask her about the money when Leona walked into the kitchen. The sweatpants and shirt she had chosen hung on her in much the same way the nightgown had, but her hair was clean, and she didn't smell of cigarettes.

She headed straight for the baby. "Oh, just look at the little bugger." Her hands were out as if she were going to pick him up.

"No." Marilee was half out of her chair. She grabbed hold of the baby seat.

"Don't wake him." I was right behind her. I grabbed Leona by the arm.

Leona looked as if we had slapped her. "I was just going to hold him. He wouldn't wake up."

"Oh, yes he would." Marilee's tired eyes were evidence that he'd woken up lots.

I positioned myself between Leona and the car seat, which Marilee was still holding, and tried to soften our kneejerk reaction with a smile. "Let Marilee get her shower first. And she'd better hurry; this kid seems to be on an "every hour I need to eat" schedule."

"You mean he cried last night?" Leona looked from one to the other of us. "I never heard him."

Marilee and I exchanged glances. I rolled my eyes. She sighed. "He cried. Can you watch him now, Mrs. McKenzie? I mean, Ellen?"

"Sure. He can sit right here and keep Dan company while he eats breakfast. You'll need some, too, and with luck, you can eat before he wakes up. Leona, is there a clean towel in there?" I got a blank look. "Never mind. Marilee, look in the little cupboard by the washing machine. I keep extras there. Do you have clean clothes?"

Marilee looked down at herself, at the T-shirt she'd elected to wear to bed, the one that barely covered her underpants. At least she wore some. "No."

"Here. We pulled these out a few minutes ago. They may not fit very well, but they'll cover you until we can figure something out."

I held out the pair of plaid knit pants and the oversized cotton shirt that buttoned down the front. She grabbed them and fled toward the laundry room door just as Dan walked into the kitchen.

He nodded to Leona on his way to the hutch for a coffee mug, picked up the cream pitcher, looked in, and looked at me. I nodded toward the table, where the sugar bowl and milk carton sat. Dan grinned slightly, filled his mug, ladled in a little sugar, and headed for the refrigerator. "There's no coffee stuff."

"I forgot to get it."

"There's no cream either."

"No. But the milk's not skim."

He looked at me, and for a moment I thought he was going to say something. I could feel myself stiffen. Brian would have blasted me. It wouldn't have made any difference if the Pope had been in the room. Dan sighed, picked up the milk carton, and looked at the label. He poured a little in his mug and headed back to the table, stopping en route to give me a quick kiss. "Get some today, okay?"

"Okay." I wanted to hug him. Hard.

"Hey, young man." Dan leaned over the sleeping baby as he took his first sip. "You had quite a night. Aren't you a little small to be able to make that much noise?" The baby slept on. Dan stood over him, studying him while he sipped his coffee. "He doesn't look very comfortable, all scrunched up like that."

I walked over and looked at him also. So did Leona. I could feel her need to pick him up

"He's used to being scrunched. He was only born yesterday."

"But that pad thing he's lying on looks lumpy. Can't you straighten it out?"

The phone rang. Probably Aunt Mary. "He's fine. And for heaven's sake, don't either of you touch him. You'll wake him up." I grabbed the phone on the fourth ring. It was my mother.

"Yours or mine?" Dan mouthed as I answered, "Uh-huh, probably, no, I don't think so, oh really?"

I pointed to my chest. He grinned at me and went back to sipping coffee. Leona watched him from over her coffee mug, her eyes shifting from him to me, then back to the still sleeping baby.

"Sure, Mom. That's great. Wonderful. Call you next week. Love you, too."

I must have looked a little stunned because Dan set his mug down on the table. "We need to talk?"

I nodded and headed for the dining room. He almost ran me over when I stopped. I walked back and grabbed the handle on the car seat.

"You don't have to do that." The look on Leona's face was surprise quickly replaced with fury.

"I promised Marilee I wouldn't let him out of my sight," I told her brightly and quickly followed Dan, who held the swinging door open for me. He didn't say anything until it had stopped swinging.

"Did you really promise that?"

"Not exactly."

"You really don't trust her, do you?"

"It's just that … well … no."

"What do you think she'll do? Grab the kid and run down the street?"

"Of course not. It's just that … It's not normal, the way she acts about the baby. It gives me the creeps."

I put the carrier on the table next to the piles of clothes. Dan stood in front of him, looking down, sipping his coffee, thinking about I didn't know what.

"Doesn't that kid have a name?"

"Not that I've heard," I said. "I'll ask Marilee later. Right now we have another problem." The door was completely closed, but I moved toward the living room anyway. "That was my mother."

"I gathered that."

"They're coming early."

"How early?"

I sighed. "Like around the fifteenth early. She wants to help."

"They want to come early." The look on Dan's face would have been funny if I'd been in a mood to be amused.

"She wanted to come even earlier. She thought she could help make the wedding dinner."

"You're kidding. Aren't you?"

This time I really did have to smile. Dan had eaten plenty of my mother's food and was well aware that we couldn't serve four hundred people nothing but fried chicken. And champagne, of course.

"I love your mother," he said hastily, "but ..."

"We both love my mother, but she can't cook. Especially for that many people."

"Do we have a caterer? How about that guy who wants to barbecue the tri-tip? I like tri-tip."

"It's New Year's Eve. It's probably going to be cold. If you want to wait until August ..."

The look he gave me said plainly what he thought of that idea.

"I have the number for another caterer. Someone Marilee knows. I'm calling him today."

"Marilee?"

"There's lots more to Marilee than I would have suspected."

"Good." Dan wasn't paying any attention to the subject of Marilee. He was thinking of my parents, and probably of his also. "Where are they going to stay?"

"Who?"

"Your parents."

"Good question. I'm sure they expect to stay here, but we're a little booked up."

"Yeah."

I watched his expression change. "Didn't you write an offer for Anne?"

I nodded. "A good one, too. Why?"

"How long before they can move in?"

"First I have to run the offer by the attorney; then I need to get it accepted. I have an appointment with him this morning. I'll leave as soon as I can get in the shower. But it could easily take ninety days to close it. There's financing and ... oh."

"What?"

"I just had an idea."

"I knew I could count on you." He grinned and reached out and hugged me. "Best little real estate agent in town, that's you. What are you going to do?"

"Rent it."

"What?" He stepped back and frowned at me. "How can you rent it?"

"It's called interim occupancy. The house is vacant, so we rent it during the interim while we wait for the escrow to close. It can get kind of complicated. I'll have to run it by Mr. Butler, but I think I can make it work. At least, I'll try. I wonder what I did with Anne's cell phone number."

"How fast can we get that baby out of here?"

"Listen, Mr. Chief of Police, taking them in was your idea. I'll do the best I can, but until I get further along … I don't know."

He looked at me with tired eyes. "Try to make it fast. If I'm going to do without sleep, I can think of better ways to stay awake than listening to a baby cry."

I laughed. "So can I. Believe me, I'll move heaven and earth to get them out of here."

A car pulled into the driveway and stopped. I stiffened and immediately turned toward the living room window. "Where's Gary?"

"I told him to go home when I got here last night. It's Mary."

"I knew that." But I hadn't. I had immediately thought of Grady. Coming after Marilee. Damn, if I were this jumpy, how did she feel?

The back screen door slammed. Voices echoed. Another car drove up and parked in front of the house. Nathan and Anne got out of that one.

Dan sighed. "I'll get the front door. You go organize the kitchen and then, Ellie, head for the shower. I don't care who you have to beat off. You need to get to that attorney. Let's find these people another place to stay."

I grabbed his arm before he could answer the bell. "There's one more thing."

The bell rang again. "I'll make this fast. Marilee had a lot of money when she came to Grace House."

Dan stopped abruptly and turned. "Are you sure?"

"That's what Leona said. I think she was counting on Marilee's money to get them set up in an apartment."

"Where'd—never mind. There's only one place she could have gotten it. How much money?"

"I don't know. Leona didn't know."

"Well. Isn't that interesting. Listen, meet me for lunch at the Yum Yum. We'll talk then. And you can tell me how your meeting went." I got a quick kiss, and he headed for the door. I picked up the car seat and returned to the kitchen.

Aunt Mary was in her element. Rummage sales are her charity of choice. She isn't choosey about the church they raise money for, or the cause. To her, they serve dual purposes. Money gets raised for causes that need it, and articles of clothing and household goods that are still perfectly good don't end up on the trash heap before their time. Proof of her belief in the value of recycling goods through rummage sales is her own wardrobe. Most, if not all, of what she wears comes from them. The effect is often somewhat bizarre, but it doesn't seem to bother her. So she isn't patient with others who are a little more particular. Or perhaps a little less brave.

I walked into the kitchen to find her holding up a dark brown shapeless dress liberally sprinkled with red and yellow flowers. It was truly hideous. She was eyeing Marilee speculatively. "This will fit, and it will look lovely on you."

"It's too big." Marilee could scarcely restrain her horror.

"Not much. And look. Buttons down the front."

I thought Marilee was going to cry.

"I don't think so." Poor kid. Someone had to come to

her rescue. "She looks cute and comfortable in what she has on. Find her another big shirt like that one and more soft pants. Where's Gina?"

"At the bakery. She insisted. It had to do with yeast." She pulled a pair of soft looking navy pants out of the pile. "How about these? Oh. Maybe not." Her hand went through a huge hole in the knee. "Well, we'll find something. Put all the stuff you girls can't use aside. I'll take it home later for the St. Stephen's sale next month."

The front door slammed. I started for the living room, only to meet Nathan and Anne, followed by Dan. He grinned at me and disappeared into the kitchen. We all followed him.

"Got to leave." He refilled his mug then turned to address the crowd. "Listen up, everyone. Marilee is to stay in the house. She is not to be alone. Anne, how about Leona?"

"Ruthie says she doesn't need her today."

Anne looked a little disgruntled at this. Leona didn't. She brightened right up. The house would be empty. No one around to stop her taking that baby away from Marilee whenever she wanted. She stared at him as he started to squirm in his mother's arms. I could almost feel her need to reach out and take him. I could see Marilee shrink back a little and tighten her hold on her son.

Evidently Anne had seen it also. "I'd feel a lot better if we had someone to stay with both of you. I'm sure Grady wouldn't dare break in here, even if he knew where you were, but still ..."

"I'll stay." There was Nathan, standing beside Marilee, looking down at her, gently touching the baby's head. The smile he gave her was tender, the finger he used to stroke the baby's head gentle. "I'm doing paperwork today and can do it here just as well as at the office."

Marilee looked confused. She probably wasn't used to men who were tender. She might be used to men grinning at her like sick puppies, though.

Leona scowled.

Anne glanced at me, rolled her eyes, and sighed. "Good idea, Nathan. I'll feel a lot better knowing they won't be alone."

I sighed also and headed for the stairs and the shower. Aunt Mary called after me. "Gina and I will be here for dinner. I'll bring meatballs."

Dinner. I sighed again, longer and harder, and kept on going up the stairs.

Chapter Twenty-One

Sam Butler's office was on the second floor of one of the oldest buildings in town, the only one that had three floors. The top floor used to be the Odd Fellows Lodge. Dances were held here when women wore dresses with pinched waists and trailing skirts, and when the dresses sported fringe and knees were rouged as well as cheeks. During the Second World War it was the local service men's canteen. The town girls handed out Cokes and cigarettes and danced to big band music. The town matrons rolled bandages and watched. During the afternoon, people lined up to give blood. It had been empty for years, a piece of our history quietly disappearing, until a group of local businessmen bought it. The transformation was not quite complete, except in Mr. Butler's office. There, it was magnificent.

In Mr. Butler's office, the original oak crown moldings, the door casings, and the high baseboards that sat on the well-worn oak floors were all in perfect condition. The heat and air-conditioning ducts were placed discretely so as not to detract from the elderly elegance of the room. His desk was a huge relic of a bygone era, but it gleamed with polish. So did he. In this small town not many men wore suits. Wool slacks, khaki pants, sweaters over plaid shirts—if you wanted to get spiffed up—jeans, if not. T-shirts and L.L. Bean jackets were the uniform of choice. Mr. Butler wore a gray suit with a subtle darker stripe through it, a stiff white shirt, and a red figured tie that I thought I'd seen in the Metropolitan Museum of Art catalog. He had a full head of very white hair, flinty blue eyes, and a stern look about his mouth. His nose was long and thin, his face was, of course, clean-shaven, and there wasn't a trace of humor anywhere. This was not going to go well.

He gestured toward a green leather chair that sat in front of his desk. Straight-backed with no arms, it was obviously not meant for either comfort or prolonged occupancy.

"Coffee?" The offer was made somewhat absently, out of polite habit. I had the feeling he would have been surprised if I had accepted.

"Thank you, no."

He nodded and flipped open a file. "I've gone over this offer. You think this is a good price?"

I had brought the comparables that I had shown Anne and Aunt Mary the day before. Silently, I handed them to him. Silently, he accepted them.

Finally he leaned back in his chair and, with two fingers, rubbed the bridge of his nose.

"Are these all of the inspections that are required?"

"All that are required for single family occupancy. There will be things required by the city before they will issue a conditional use permit."

"Such as?"

"We'll need one bathroom that is handicapped approved, windows that meet fire escape requirements, doorknobs fixed so toddlers can't open them, things like that. I've put them in as contingencies and asked the seller to pay for them. It's all there on page five."

He almost smiled. He'd read page five carefully and probably knew every ordinance the city had ever dreamed up by heart. He wanted to know if I did also. "You've put together a good, solid offer. I don't think we're going to have to change much of this at all."

I could feel a glow of pleasure creep over me. Several veteran agents had warned me about attorneys, about the problems some of them created. Of course, there were those who had saved the deal by knowing just what to do and doing it in a timely manner, but the others—the ones who were either determined to drag out their billable hours or to make sure everyone knew how vital they were to the transaction—seemed to be in the majority. At least they dominated the stories I'd heard. So I'd been prepared for multiple small changes, a nitpicking of minute points. I hadn't been prepared for praise.

"I see you have left out the financing and title information." He nodded as if this were a wise thing. I wasn't about to tell him it was simple ignorance.

"Grace House is a charitable tax-free entity. I'll supply escrow all of the information they need, if we get that far. As for the financing …" He smiled, but it was a rueful smile, no mirth in any part of it. "It turns out that will be easy. We'll be able to pay cash."

That I was not expecting. "Cash?"

He nodded. "Surprised?"

"Well, yes. Nothing Anne or my Aunt Mary said led me to believe … I was expecting financing to be a problem."

"Your aunt Mary?" One eyebrow rose slightly. "Are you Mrs. McGill's niece?"

It was my turn to nod.

"Wonderful woman, Mrs. McGill. Very efficient."

I tried hard not to laugh. "Yes, isn't she."

He looked at me a minute over the tent he'd made of his fingers. "There's a good reason they didn't tell you. They don't know yet."

I must have looked confused, because his smile got just a tad wider. "Doctor Sadler left all of his estate to Grace House. There's more than enough money to buy this new house, and when the insurance claim for the fire is settled, there should be enough to fund some extras. That daycare center Anne keeps going on about, for instance."

I sat very still. Rigid. I felt like crowing with joy for Anne, for all the women who needed Grace House so badly, but there was a sadness that it came from such a tragedy. Poor old Doctor Sadler.

"How long …" I didn't want to seem like a mercenary real estate agent only trying to quickly close a deal, but I needed to know what to tell the seller. I had an even larger obligation to the buyers. It was called fiduciary relationship. There was another real estate term that applied. Time is of the essence. Besides, I had a houseful of Grace House inhabitants that needed to go someplace else.

"Hmm, could take up to six months to settle his estate. Depends on court calendars, that kind of thing. And we don't know how fast the insurance claim will be settled."

I blanched. I had a horrible vision of Leona trailing around my kitchen the day after the wedding, eating leftover wedding cake and commenting on how someone should take down the Christmas decorations. She'd also be trying to take the baby out of Marilee's arms, him screaming, Marilee protesting, me having a nervous breakdown. "I thought we could … maybe … offer to do an interim occupancy?"

He said nothing for a moment, just stared at me. I felt like I had in school, when I'd made a really dumb error and Mrs. Compton, my sixth grade teacher, had handed me back my paper and stared at me in disgust.

Finally, he gave that small smile again. "Interim occupancy. You think you can get him to agree to that?"

"I don't know. I can try."

"Well, I'll tell you what. I think I can offer a way to help convince him. Tell him we'll close in ninety days, even if the estate isn't settled, so we'll only have to rent back for whatever period you can arrange. You should be able to get them in within a couple of weeks, if the seller is agreeable."

"How can we do that?" I couldn't believe him. He was an attorney! Where were we going to get the money, and exactly who was going to guarantee it would be there?

"Don't look so horrified. Only I'm glad you are. Shows you're thinking. I have some friends. If necessary, we'll do a short term loan to Grace House. We will, of course, put it all in writing. Go see what you can do, and I'll write up the occupancy agreement and the funding guarantee." He finally gave me a genuine smile. "You actually seem pretty intelligent. I think we can get this one done."

I didn't know whether to feel complimented or to throw something at him for that rather condescending statement, but, given the circumstances, decided on neither. I stood up, rather dazed, and said, pointing at the offer still lying on his desk, "Can you sign that for me?"

"I can, but I won't. Not yet. But I'll have my secretary draw up an intent to purchase, outlining all the terms you've put in your offer, and the things you and I have just discussed. I'll make sure he understands that the funds will be there if all of the other contingencies are met. See if we have an agreement in principle, and then we'll draw up a contract. She'll fax it to you."

He handed me back my contract and comparables, checked to make sure he had copies in his file, and closed it. Our meeting was over.

I thanked him, at least I think I did, and turned to pick up my purse and briefcase from the floor beside my chair.

"Oh, Ellen, by the way—may I call you Ellen? —I'll tell you one other thing."

I turned to face the desk again, my mind more on how I was going to present my offer than what he was going to say.

"I've been Owen and Francis Sadler's attorney for years." The gravity, the grimness, of his tone caught my attention. "Grace House was everything to Francis. It was her wish that everything they had be left to keep it going." He paused and once more rubbed the bridge of his nose. "Owen wasn't so enamored. He felt that Anne was too soft. Wasn't guiding some of the girls … women … with a firm hand."

I found myself starting to protest. His hand went up. I stopped.

"Owen had some rather definite opinions. Anyway, he had decided to change their will ... *his* will. Grace House was going to be left only a token. I advised him against it, but he was adamant."

I stood, unable to move, all kinds of things going through my mind. "Had he ...?"

"Signed it? No. Our appointment was tomorrow."

I could feel my stomach turn over. Emotions were bombarding me on all sides. Relief that Grace House had been saved, horror over the way that it had been saved. Could this be the motive for the terrible way that Dr Sadler had died?

"Anne. Have you told her this? She will be so ..."

"Why, Anne knew. Owen told her what he intended to do. That's why I was so surprised when she started to look for a larger house. She didn't mention it?"

Chapter Twenty-Two

I stared at the phone I had just hung up, feeling both euphoric and depressed. I reached for my coffee mug and took a healthy swallow, wondering how it was possible to simultaneously feel such extremes. Yuck. This tasted worse than the stuff Gary had given me in the cemetery. I pushed it aside and thought about the morning.

The phone call had been good news. Our offer had been accepted. Not only accepted, but the owner was thrilled the house was going to be used for such a good cause and was more than willing to exchange a rent back period for a longer escrow. He was even willing to make the necessary changes to obtain the conditional use permit. Within reason, of course. A dollar limit was mentioned that sounded reasonable, even generous. It seemed he'd had a niece … Everywhere I turned, someone had somebody they knew, loved, had heard of, who could have used a place like Grace House. The bad news was that Anne and crew couldn't take occupancy until we got the changes made. That meant city inspections, bids from contractors, home inspections, termite inspections, and probably others I couldn't think of right now. The owner thought it could all be done in about two weeks. I thought we'd be lucky to get them in by Christmas.

Anne thought that was just fine. It gave her time to get her paperwork together and the house ready. Would the owner let her paint? I'd ask. It gave Aunt Mary time to get her donations collected. She was already on the phone, arranging for living room furniture, beds, towels, pots and pans, everything she could squeeze out of people. Could she use my garage to store things? I gulped. My garage was already overflowing, and now we had Dan's stuff to deal with, but I said I'd try to make room. And it gave me the necessary time to get all the inspections done. I had the termite report already. The listing agent was an old hand at this. She not only knew what to do, but she did it. However, we still needed a home inspection, which was my responsibility to arrange. I also had to arrange for the city inspector and confirm everything that they were going to require, and there was a whole folder of other disclosures I needed to go over with Mr. Butler before I sat down with Anne and Aunt Mary to explain it all to them.

Anne. Sweet-faced, kind Anne, dedicated to Grace House and the women who stayed there. Anne, who wouldn't hurt a fly. Or would she? She knew Doctor Sadler was going to change his will. Could she have …? Not possible. But I couldn't dismiss the notion. She'd almost lost it all; no new Grace House and maybe not enough money to keep the old one going. Doctor Sadler, on whom she had relied to keep his promise to his dead wife, had been about to snatch all that away, and she knew it. Anne knew it.

I refused to even consider that thought, but it kept nagging at the back of my brain, giving me a gigantic headache. I pulled my desk drawer open and rummaged through it for the Advil I knew was hiding in there. I washed two of them down with what remained of the cold coffee, shuddered, and opened the escrow support people file on my computer. I scrolled down, looking for the number of my favorite home inspector. She was always booked weeks in advance, but I hoped for a cancellation. Maxi would know every requirement the city would throw at us.

I had a vision of my folks arriving, expecting to stay in the house they'd owned for so many years, now occupied by their daughter and granddaughter, helping to set up the tree, wrapping presents, Dad and Dan drinking eggnog while Mother and Aunt Mary stuffed the turkey … No. Aunt Mary and my mother in the same kitchen would never work. And it really wouldn't work if Leona, Marilee, and the baby were still there. I could picture my father knocking on the downstairs bathroom door, newspaper in hand, demanding to know how much longer, while Leona … I shook out another Advil and swallowed it dry while I picked up the phone and dialed.

Maxie was booked solid, but when I got through telling Sallie Jo, her partner, what I needed done and why, I got squeezed in. It seemed she had a sister …

"Congratulations." Tim McGibben, office manager and chief cheerleader of our ten-person real estate office, stood in front of my desk, beaming at me. "I hear you got a deal put together on the Gray place. Who bought it?"

News sure traveled fast in small towns. "Grace House."

"Really?" He looked surprised. "How'd you land them as a client? Oh. Right. Mary McGill is your aunt. How long is the escrow?"

I outlined the offer for him and told him about the interim occupancy. He frowned. "Those things can backfire on you. Be careful."

"Sam Butler is the attorney for Grace House. He's helping me."

"Well, in that case." He nodded. "Sam's a good man. He won't let you make any mistakes. But if you need help, let me know." Having given my ego that little boost, he left.

I looked at my watch. Ten minutes after twelve. Time to meet Dan for lunch. I had been going to make a list of all the things I needed to talk to him about but hadn't had time. I still didn't. Oh well. Anything I missed at lunch I'd ask over dinner. No, I wouldn't. Dinner was going to be a mob scene. After we went to bed? If I could keep him awake long enough. Damn. Life was just getting too complicated. I grabbed my purse, pushed the "do not disturb" button on my phone, and left.

Chapter Twenty-Three

"I ordered for you. Well, Ruthie decided." Dan sat in our favorite booth, the one in the back, away from the kitchen and the glass case with all the Yum Yum fruit pies and coffee cakes in it. There was a cup of coffee in front of him, suspiciously light in color. I glanced at the metal cream pitcher. Drops of cream dripped from the spout. I turned my attention to the specials handwritten on the chalkboard clearly visible from where we sat. Chicken fried steak and mashed potatoes was one, the other was Mandarin chicken salad. Guess who was getting what.

"Your arteries are clogging." I pointed to his coffee cup.

"Good afternoon to you, too." Dan laughed at me.

"I'm serious. You're eating way too much fat stuff. I'm going to feed you oatmeal every morning for the rest of the year."

"Thank goodness there's not much left of the year."

"Dan, this isn't funny. Now that I've found you again, I have no intention of losing you to something as stupid as clogged up plumbing. You have to be more careful."

He looked a little startled then smiled at me. "I can't tell you how much I like the sentiment in that statement, even if I don't agree with the content."

"Now listen …" I parked my purse on the bench beside me and leaned over the table to make my point.

"I am." The smile was gone. "Did you get the house?"

It was my turn to smile. "Yup. It's a done deal." I held up my hand to stop his next question. "And I arranged the rent back as well."

This grin went from cheek to cheek. "I always knew

193

you were fantastic, and you just proved it one more time. When do they move out?"

"Two weeks, if we're lucky. Maybe more."

The smile faded. "Two weeks? They'll be moving out just as your folks arrive."

"I know, but it was the best I could do. I need to get them a conditional use permit even for the rent back and that means some alterations before the city will approve it. The owner wants to do the termite repairs at the same time. But, Maxi is going out tomorrow to do the inspection."

"Maxi Freedman?"

"Yep. She's good."

"And her uncle is the head building inspector for the city."

I gaped at him. "I didn't know that."

"Now you do." He grinned. "So at least we know the inspector will show up when he's called."

"Which is a good thing. Now all we have to worry about is getting a contractor who'll take on a job at this time of year, whether the weather will stay dry—because they are going to have to take out some doors and replace some of the old windows—tenting the house—it's full of termites—getting the offer signed, and opening an escrow."

"You have to do all that?"

"Plus some other things. But Aunt Mary is doing the other stuff."

"Such as …?"

They need furniture. You know, beds, dishes, a table, that kind of thing. She's on the phone right now, squeezing donations out of everyone she can think of. She wants to use our garage to store the stuff she collects."

"Good luck getting anything else in there. So, we have the baby for two more weeks?"

"As well as his mother. And don't forget Leona."

"It would be hard to forget Leona."

Ruthie, part-owner of the Yum Yum and one of Dan's

biggest fans, arrived with our food. "Hot tea. Too cold for iced." She set the mug down and slid a plate of salad in front of me. Dan got a platter overflowing with meat and potatoes, swimming in cream gravy, a few nicely steamed carrots that I knew he wouldn't eat, and a basket of biscuits—hot, high, and smelling wonderful. Those would be gone before we left. I might even have one. Just to help Dan's arteries, of course. A dish of small butter patties appeared, and a larger dish of the Yum Yum's special apple butter. I was definitely having a biscuit. Ruthie stood back, hands on her hips, to survey the table. She must have been satisfied, because she smiled.

"You got that problem with the flowers solved, Ellen?"

Small towns are good for many things. Privacy is not one of them. "I have a call in to the florist. Should hear today."

She nodded. "It'll work out. Saint Stevens is a beautiful church. Even red ones will look just great."

I wondered how many other people in town knew about my flower dilemma. Probably the whole town. They most likely were making book at the barbershop on whether I'd get white or red poinsettias for the altar.

"We can all hardly wait. This is going to be the best wedding we've had in years." She paused, and her eyes twinkled. Actually twinkled. I thought only Tinker Bell could do that. "You know, some of the folks around here, especially the older ones, were real disappointed when you two went off and married other people. They've been waiting for this for a long time. Some, around forty years." She chuckled, checked Dan's cup, found it full, eyed my mug—it also was still full—and trotted off to oversee other customers.

"Forty years?" Dan raised an eyebrow at me over his forkful of potato.

"I guess they had us down the aisle when we were still in diapers."

"Speak for yourself. I was way beyond that when you

were born."

Dan is only two years older than I, so I doubted his statement, but that wasn't what was on my mind.

It wasn't on his either. "Tell me more about Marilee's money."

"I don't know anymore. I started to ask her this morning, but everybody converged on the kitchen before I got a chance. Do you think that's why Grady is stalking her?"

His fork, fully loaded, returned to his plate. "If there really is any money, it sure would explain why he's so determined to find her. We've been watching him for some time." He paused, as if wondering how to word the next sentence. Or wondering how much to tell me. "The little creep's been acting as some kind of middle man for a Mexican group who are making meth around here. We think they ship most of it down to the LA area, but some has been showing up on the local market. Thanks, in part, to Grady Wilcox. Seems he speaks a little Spanish, and lots of these guys don't speak much English. If Grady forgot to fork over their share of the sales he made—well, it might not be good for his health. Or his immediate future. Could account for his anxiety." The fork went up again and was returned to the plate empty.

My fork stayed on my plate. This was a twist that had never occurred to me. "And you think Marilee's money might be ... oh dear God in heaven. No wonder he's frantic."

His fork, reloaded, had once more made its destination, and there was a pause before he answered. "Ellen, listen." He leaned forward, ignoring his still half-filled plate. All traces of humor were gone, replaced with an intensity I rarely saw in him. "I need to know how much money she has and if she took it from Grady. And, if she did, what, if anything, she knows about where he got it. Anything she can tell us about who he's been working for." He paused again and leaned back, pushing his plate aside. He reached across the table and took my hand. "I don't like asking you to do this, but I need help."

"You what?" I was stunned. This was police stuff. I'd been on the fringes of Dan's murder cases before and my help had not been received kindly. But this time ... I wasn't quite sure how to react.

"All I want you to do is talk to Marilee, so don't start thinking about playing detective. There's a better than even chance she won't know much, Grady not being the kind of guy to confide in the little misses. But I'd be surprised if she doesn't have some idea of what he's been up to and just a name—one name, a description of one of these guys, even a meeting place—could help."

I thought about this while I picked at my salad. "If Grady goes to jail, she's free of him, at least for a while. She can get a divorce and go on with her life somewhere else. I think she's pretty determined to do that."

"Then talk to her. Let's see if she's willing to part with whatever information she has."

"You're asking her to give me information that could get her husband arrested."

"Yes." He didn't have to sound so unhappy about it.

"Why me?"

"Because she's scared to death of me. She cringes when I walk by. I think she's scared of all men."

"She's not afraid of Nathan."

"No." Dan stopped for a minute and thought about that. "She certainly isn't afraid of him. However, I can't ask Nathan to do this. I need you to talk to her; she seems to like you, and I think she'll open up to you. She can't have much loyalty to Grady. See if she'd be willing to help us."

I put my fork down and pushed away my half-full plate. "If Grady got that money from selling meth, it's not legal. Is it?"

"No."

"So, the government could claim it?"

"Yes."

"So do you really think she'd tell me if she had it?"

I didn't like this much. It didn't look as if Dan did either. However, sometimes …

"Think of it this way. If Marilee helps us, I'll have more to charge Grady with when we find him, and the faster we find him the less likely he is to do damage—to her and to us."

"You sound pretty certain Grady threw that firebomb."

I've known Dan Dunham since I was born. When we were kids, I could read his moods and tell what he was thinking. Most of the time. I still can. Most of the time. When his eyebrows come together, he's not pleased. When he pulls in his upper lip and sort of sucks on the edge of his mustache, he's trying to decide something. He did the mustache thing.

"We're almost positive it was him."

I thought about the way Grace House had looked smoldering in the moonlight. I thought about how close Marilee, Nathan, Gina, and the baby had come to being incinerated. Not only was bombing the house cruel and dangerous, it was stupid. Driving Marilee out so he could get the money made no sense at all, but I couldn't think what other motive he could have. I'd heard that prolonged drug use made your brains scrambled eggs. That your circuits got warped or something. So did your judgment. If that was Grady's problem he was doubly dangerous and there was every reason to think he'd try again. A ripple of fear ran through me. The next time it might be our house that went up in flames. "Okay. What do you want me to ask her?"

"If she got her money from Grady, and if she knows where, and how, he got it. I especially want to know if he owes part of it to someone, and who that someone is. And if she has any idea of who might have told him where she was."

"You don't want me to ask if she still has the money?"

"What for? She's going to say it got burned up along with everything else."

I smiled just a little. "Yes. That's probably just what she'll say. If, of course, she says anything."

"And if that's what she says, she may be telling the truth. As a matter of fact, I don't see how she could have gotten it out. From what Nathan said, he barely got *them* out. But Grady's not likely to believe that and I'd love to get him off the street before he finds out where she's at. And I'd really love to bust up that meth lab."

Somehow the meth lab and the people who ran it didn't scare me nearly as much as the thought of Grady throwing a gasoline filled pop bottle through my front window. And, since half the town must know by now that we were sheltering the fire victims, it seemed all too possible that Grady might pay us an unwanted visit.

I looked at my salad and my stomach rebelled. Dan had eaten only half of his huge lunch as well. Grady Wilcox was turning out to be better than the South Beach Diet any day.

"Let's get out of here," I said. "I'll think of some excuse and go by the house and talk to Marilee."

Dan nodded, let go of my hand, and pushed back his chair. He reached for his wallet but I stopped him.

"Wait. There's something else, something I wanted to ask you."

He waited, half out of his chair, a wary look on his face. "What?"

"If one parent signs adoption papers, is that legally binding on the other parent?"

"What are you talking about?"

"Grady Wilcox signed away his rights to this baby. He put him up for adoption. Does that mean they can take him away from Marilee?"

"Grady did *what*? Does Marilee know?"

"Everyone at Grace House knew. Gina knew; she told me. Evidently Doctor Sadler got Grady to sign everything and then was going to use that to pressure Marilee into doing the same thing."

Dan sat back down. Hard. "That old ... so and so. What a rotten thing to do. But it sounds like him. He always knew best and he didn't much care what anyone else wanted or thought. I remember one time when I was a kid ... never mind. To answer your question, no. Marilee couldn't be made to give up her baby on Grady's signature alone. He gave up his rights, not hers. She'd have to be proven unfit by the courts." Instead of pushing back his chair again, he picked up his almost empty coffee cup. "Where are you going with this?"

"What makes you think I'm going anywhere?"

He gave me the look.

"Okay, okay. Leona. I've been thinking about Leona. She wants that baby."

He started to say something but I put up my hand to stop him. "You think I'm making too much of her, but I'm not. She's obsessed with him. If the baby was adopted, Leona would be just as grief stricken as Marilee."

"So," Dan said slowly, never taking his eyes off me, "you think Leona—what?"

"I don't know, but it's one more reason for her to hate Doctor Sadler."

Dan stared at me for a moment, took another sip of his coffee, made a face and put it down. He looked around, caught Ruthie's eye, and motioned for the check. "Motives for killing the good doctor don't seem to be in short supply, but evidence is."

He pulled his wallet out, thumbed through the bills then stopped. "Are you going back to our house right now?"

I glanced at my watch. "Yes. I have to be back at the office later, so now would be a good time. And Leona isn't there."

"How do you know that?"

"Because I just saw her cleaning off that table right

behind you. Ruthie must have called her in after all."

Dan dropped some money on the table before he turned to me. He wasn't smiling. "Be sure you tell Nathan not to leave her alone. We haven't found Grady and until we do … I wish I could tell you that there was no way he'd find her, and even if he did, there was no way he'd try to get at her while she's with us. But I can't." He slid his arm around me and pulled me close to him. "But I can tell you we're looking for him. Hard. And we'll find him. We have enough evidence to arrest him for arson and I'm going to try to get attempted murder thrown in. Hang in there with me. I'm not going to let anything happen to you or Susannah."

He dropped a kiss on the side of my ear and let me go. I made myself smile up at him.

"I know that," I said. "I'm not really scared. Just a little nervous."

What a lie. We both knew I was scared to death. The only reason I didn't insist that Susannah come home was because I thought she was safer at Neil's house. Well, at least she wouldn't end up a piece of burnt toast. But I didn't want Dan worried about me. He had quite enough to keep him occupied.

"I'll tell him."

Dan looked around impatiently. "Where's Ruthie? I've got to get back." He looked down at the money, did some mental arithmetic, and added another dollar. "This should cover it. If I'm wrong, she knows where to find me." His attention came back to me. "See if you can find out if she has any ideas about where Mr. Wilcox may have gone to earth. That truck of his is hard to miss, but so far, we're missing it."

"I'll try."

"And call me right after you get back to the office. Promise."

I smiled. "I promise." I started to give him a peck on the cheek when there was a crash. The metallic sound of a metal tray connecting with the floor was immediately followed by the unmistakable noise of crockery breaking. It was finished off with a loud "shit." Both Dan and I whirled around to look toward the kitchen. A very greasy looking Leona was standing in the doorway, staring down at a mass of broken dirty dishes. An angry Ruthie was rapidly advancing toward the blocked kitchen door and the seemingly immobile Leona. Dan and I exchanged looks and headed, rapidly, for the front door.

As I drove toward home, I realized I hadn't mentioned Anne Kennedy. I'd told him about the will, that there would be enough money to pay cash for the new house, all the good stuff. I'd even told him Doctor Sadler was going to change his will. But I hadn't told him Anne knew about it. I couldn't. Eventually I would have to. Wouldn't I? Damn. I would go home and see if I could get Marilee alone and carefully, gently, get a few answers. Then, before I called Dan, I'd stop by Aunt Mary's and see what she thought.

Chapter Twenty-Four

Nathan sat at the dining room table, surrounded by piles of clothes and stacks of files, working on his laptop. There wasn't a sign of anyone else.

"What are you doing home?" He blurted this out, stopped, and reddened. "I didn't mean … you startled me."

I smiled, hopefully not too brightly. "I came to pick up all of the discards for Aunt Mary's rummage sale. Do you know where the big box is?" The living room was empty, and so was the street in front of my house. The swinging door that led to the kitchen was propped open. The kitchen, too, was empty. I listened. No crying baby, no soft voice trying to comfort it, no harsh voice telling Marilee what to do. I'd tried all the way home to come up with a good excuse for popping in, when I'd told them all I wouldn't be there until after four. I didn't want it to appear to be checking up on them, and I didn't want Marilee to think I had made a special trip to interrogate her. The clothes seemed like a reasonable excuse, and it would get them off my dining room table. Now all I had to do was find Marilee and get her alone so we could talk. "Where are the girls?"

"Marilee's asleep upstairs. The baby fussed most of the morning, and she's worn out. Leona was on the phone for an hour or more, then said she had to go to work. She left about ten. I haven't seen her since."

He probably would soon. I doubted if Ruthie was in the mood for third or fourth chances. Leona was a grade F employee, and she didn't give the impression she was trying to move up the alphabet.

"Are you going to stay until the others get home?"

"Isn't that what Chief Dunham wants me to do?" There was a determined set to Nathan's jaw and I didn't think it was entirely because Dan had assigned him the job of protector of mother and baby. Nathan had already assumed that role. "I've got my cell phone and plenty of stuff to do. Might just as well do it here." He stopped and looked up at me, anxiety written on his face. "If you don't mind, of course."

No, I didn't mind. Except it was going to be hard to get to Marilee with him constantly standing guard, and with Leona, who would undoubtedly be here when I returned, looming over the baby, ready to snatch him up at the first opportunity. "Well." I let my car keys dangle a moment, thinking. "I guess I'd better get back to the office. Have you had lunch?"

"Marilee fixed us something before she went upstairs." The anxious look intensified. "I hope you don't mind. She's a great little cook, and she cleaned everything up."

Nathan was going to have to get over this anxious stuff. It didn't go with his role as protector. Besides, it made me irritable. "No, Nathan. I'm glad she did."

I turned to go, but he stopped me. "The clothes."

"What?" I turned back, not realizing at first what he was talking about.

"Aren't you going to take the clothes?"

Of course. That's what I'd come for, wasn't it. "Ah, yes. Do you know where the box is?"

"I put it on the back porch. I'll go get it."

He clicked save before he pushed back his chair and headed for the porch. I watched while he wrestled the box back into the dining room. We stuffed it with all the things neither my guests nor almost anybody else I could imagine would ever use again.

"Where's your car? I'll carry it out for you."

I let him.

"I'll be back in a couple of hours." I took off for the

two-block drive to Aunt Mary's. I hadn't planned on actually going there, but I wasn't driving around with all that junk in my car either. Besides, maybe I could spot Leona. She'd have to be walking. Maybe I'd give her a ride. On the other hand, if Ruthie had fired her—and I'd be pretty darned surprised if she hadn't—maybe I wouldn't. She could walk off some of the bad temper I was sure was boiling over about now. Losing another job wouldn't help her campaign to get Marilee to share an apartment with her. Besides, Marilee's money may have gone up in smoke. And if it hadn't … I wasn't sure which was worse.

I slowed down as I turned into Aunt Mary's quiet tree-lined street. Her white cottage sat halfway down the block, her cracked concrete driveway empty. Damn. I really wanted to get rid of these old clothes. And I would. Her front bedroom was always filled with rummage sale stuff, and her back door was never locked. I'd just lug the box into the bedroom and stash it with all the rest of the stuff.

The box was awkward but not really heavy. I got the screen door open and was in the kitchen, on my way to the hall, when I heard voices. One voice. And it wasn't Aunt Mary's.

Chapter Twenty-Five

"Yes, I found them."

The coldness in Gina's voice stopped me in my tracks. That was Gina, wasn't it? I listened, almost involuntarily, wanting to be sure. Gina's voice was always soft, serious, but never biting, cold or sarcastic. This voice …

"She's not a bit the way you described her. She's a sweetheart. He's … a sick old man."

It was Gina. There was a pause while she listened. Should I announce myself? I didn't want to eavesdrop. But I was curious. Who was she talking to, and who was she talking about?

"I'm not coming back. I told you that."

Not going back where?

The box shifted, and I pushed it into the wall to keep it from falling. It made a scraping noise. Damn.

"Someone's here." The tone of Gina's voice changed. It got softer and caution crept in. She didn't want to be overheard. Why?

"I'll call you back in a few days. No. I won't give you my phone number." The phone was hung up, and Gina was moving my way.

"Ellen, I didn't hear you come in."

I knew my face was red. I hoped she didn't think it was embarrassment because I was eavesdropping, which it was, but because I was wrestling with the awkward box. I started to come up with an excuse but—just for a second, with the light behind her—she reminded me of something. Or someone. Then she moved, and the moment was gone.

"I'm looking for my aunt. These are the leftover

donations none of you could use. I thought I'd put them with her rummage sale stuff."

"Oh." She looked at me, then at the box, which I still had jammed into the wall. "We moved all that into the garage. There's a table in there. Here, let me help you." She took one end and started to back up into the kitchen.

"I can get it," I said. "If you'll just open the door … "

She was right. The table in the garage was piled high, and there were boxes pushed under it, stacked around it. There was enough good junk here to stock several sales, and enough unusable rubbish to fill several trashcans. I shoved my box in a corner, straightened up, and smiled at Gina. "Do you know where my aunt Mary is? I wanted to talk to her. About dinner tonight." I added that last bit hastily. Gina had been watching me appraisingly, as if she wondered how much of her conversation I'd heard. It made me uneasy.

"No. She wasn't here when I came back for lunch." She paused for a moment, smiled a sad little half smile, and went on. "I needed a break from Sal."

"Oh. But isn't this late for you? I mean, I'd think you'd need a break long before this. It's after one o'clock."

"I'm supposed to quit at around two, but it depends … Rose seems tired, so I'll work later today. Sometimes, well, I just have to get away for a few minutes."

"Sal can be a bit much," I agreed. "Are you going back? I could give you a ride."

"A bit much," she repeated. There seemed to be genuine amusement in her smile, probably for the first time since I'd met her. "I think I'd have described him … another way. Thanks for the offer, but I think I'll walk. Shall I lock up?"

Lock up? If she did, Aunt Mary would never get in again. I wasn't at all sure she owned a house key. "No, don't bother. I think I'll wash my hands before I leave. That box is pretty dusty."

I had no idea if Gina believed that one or not, but she

nodded, turned, and started down the street. I closed the garage door and walked back to the house.

There was a familiar smell in Aunt Mary's kitchen, a warm cake smell I hadn't noticed until now. Aunt Mary surely hadn't baked for dinner tonight. Had she? I looked around. On the counter three layers of what looked like sponge cake rested on racks, which sat on cookie sheets. I walked closer. The cake layers had been drenched in some kind of syrup, something with—they smelled like espresso. What on earth was Aunt Mary up to? She was a great cook, everyone knew that, but she didn't usually ... Gina? No. It couldn't be.

Puzzled, I continued on into the dining room. The phone was on the old built-in sideboard, right where Gina had left it. I stared at it. It was a new cordless one with all the latest features. It had a screen that lit up and showed you the number you were calling. Or the one calling you. Or the last number you dialed. I'd given that phone to Aunt Mary for her birthday, only last month. She'd claimed to love it, but I knew she had no intention of using all those wonderful features. She knew who she was calling and who was calling her, and she didn't need a screen to tell her.

However, *I* did like those features. I had no idea who Gina had been calling, but the phone could tell me. Should I? Of course not. That would be a terrible invasion of privacy. Wouldn't it? But we were in the middle of a murder investigation. Well, Dan was. I wasn't. But if I could help in some way ... and I wanted this murder solved before the wedding. Even more, I wanted Grady Wilcox caught and put behind bars. Sturdy ones. It seemed very possible he was the murderer, but even if he wasn't, he'd probably burned down one house trying to get to his wife. I'd feel better knowing he was locked up. If he wasn't the murderer ... Of course, there was no reason to think Gina ... but from what I had overheard, accidentally, of course, it sounded as if she were talking about Rose and Sal Ianelli, that she'd come to

Santa Louisa to find them. Why? I thought of her standing in the light for that brief moment. The picture Rose had shown me of the first Gina superimposed itself on that image. No. It wasn't possible. How could that be? Talk about far-fetched. I picked up the phone and hit redial.

The number appeared on the screen. I hurriedly wrote it down.

"Baker's Bakery and Deli. May I help you?" The woman's voice sounded out loud and clear.

A bakery? I had no idea what I'd expected, but not that. Now what? "Ah, I'm looking for—"

"Yes?"

"Gina Baker?"

I could almost feel the stillness coming from the other end of the line. "Who is this?" The voice was still loud, but now it was hostile.

"I'm an old friend of hers, from high school, haven't seen her since I left town, and thought I'd look her up."

"Yeah? Well, that was a long time ago. She got herself married."

"Oh." She wasn't married now. But if I were a friend from long ago, I could continue to play dumb. "How wonderful. Can you tell me where to get in touch with her?"

"No. I don't know where she is. She took off after her husband died. Left me here to run this bakery all by myself. She knew I couldn't do it all alone anymore. Haven't been able to for years. But does she care? Oh, no. Not her. Some daughter she turned out to be."

"Her husband died?" I'd thought about divorce, but it had never occurred to me that she could be a widow.

"Got himself killed in one of those pileups in the fog on Highway Five. I told her to come back and live with me. But would she listen? Not her. She just took off on some fool errand of her own, and now she says she's not coming back. If you see her, tell her she's an ungrateful bitch." The phone went dead.

Well! Wasn't that interesting. It was crystal clear why she didn't want to live with her mother. It explained a few other things as well. Poor Gina. Widowed. I'd always pictured widows as old ladies who lost their husbands after years and years of marriage and had children and grandchildren to lean on. Didn't sound as if Gina had anyone. I thought about her, outlined in the dining room doorway, sunlight behind her. And I thought about the photograph Rose had shown me. There was one logical answer as to why Gina had come to Santa Louisa. Only, it wasn't logical at all. It was impossible. Wasn't it? I put the phone back on the sideboard but stashed the slip of paper I'd written the number on in my purse. Invasion of privacy was no longer an issue. An answer to my very big question was.

Chapter Twenty-Six

I found Aunt Mary. She had, of course, been collecting for Grace House and her back- seat was loaded down with boxes. I helped her unload, put the coffee on, and made her sit down while I brought her up to date on what I knew and what I suspected.

"First, you can forget about Anne Kennedy as a suspect. She's the most grounded person I know."

"But she knew Doctor Sadler was going to change his will."

"So did the attorney."

"He didn't have a motive. Why would he kill Doctor Sadler?"

"No reason at all. But Anne didn't have one either. Doctor Sadler wasn't the only person who gave money to Grace House. We'd have managed."

I didn't say anything. She might be right. But I doubted we'd be making an offer on the blue house on Elm Street if Doctor Sadler were still alive.

"You need to talk to Hermione Turner."

"Who?"

"Hermione Turner. Don't laugh. Her mother was addicted to English novels. Hermione was Owen Sadler's nurse for years. She ran his office, knew all of his patients, and kept him from driving too many of them away with his bossiness. He really was a good doctor, and everybody knew it. He just couldn't keep from wanting to run everybody's personal life as well as their medical one. Hermione had a way of soothing the feathers Owen ruffled. If what you suspect is true—and the more I think about it, the more I think you may be right—she'd know."

So, instead of going back to my office, I headed out to Shady Acres.

Retirement for Hermione didn't mean a sweet little thatched-roofed cottage on a quiet village lane. It meant a single room and wheelchair, into which she barely fit. Hermione was not a small woman. There was more than enough room on her lap for the blue point Siamese that stared at me with unblinking blue eyes. Her brown eyes were just as piercing.

"Why do you want to know?"

There were a number of ways I could have answered that question, some true, some not so true. I looked around the small room. It was lined with overflowing bookcases. The single bed had a depression in the middle—a testimony to Hermione's excessive weight—but the bed was neatly made. There were pictures on the antique dresser. Children? Grandchildren? I didn't know, but there were a lot of them. A laptop computer sat on a roll-around table by her wheelchair, a printer close by. The small TV was on mute, but it was turned to the local PBS station. The CDs displayed on the nightstand were an eclectic collection of classics and jazz. This woman's legs might not work well anymore, but her brain was clicking along just fine. Truth was called for.

"I think Gina came here looking for Sal and Rose Iannelli. I believe she thinks they are her grandparents. My aunt, Mary McGill, said you would know if that were possible."

She laughed. A huge, rolling belly laugh. The cat looked at her with deep reproach and left. He looked at my lap, rejected the possibility, and jumped up on the bed, where he proceeded to clean himself.

"So Mary thought I'd know. Well, she's right." The laughter left and she got very quiet. Finally she sighed and nodded. "Guess it won't hurt to talk about it now. She's been dead … what? Close to thirty years? And now the doctor's gone, too." She peered at me closely. "Do you think this might have anything to do with who killed him? Is that why you want to know?"

That caught me completely by surprise. I hadn't planned on talking about my vague suspicions, because that's all they were—half-formed, shadowy things. I couldn't imagine how, or why, Gina could be connected to Doctor Sadler's death. Still … "I don't know."

She kept looking at me, studying me. She sighed again. "Ginseng," she said, not looking at the cat, "come here."

The cat looked up, then very slowly—making sure we both knew that moving was his idea, not hers—he stretched, gracefully left the bed, landed on the floor, and sprung into her lap. She didn't speak again until he had kneaded her dress a little, turned around twice, and settled himself.

"She just might be their grandchild. Gina, Sal and Rose's daughter, had a baby." Again she fell silent.

I wasn't sure she was going to say anything more. She sat very still, absently stroking the cat, evidently reliving something that had happened a long time ago. Should I speak? Get up? Leave? She had told me what I had come to find out. Sort of. But before I could move, she refocused on me.

"Sal was furious when he found out. I don't know how long Rose had known, but they didn't tell Sal until she was so close to the end it couldn't be hidden any longer." She shook her head. "I can still hear the yelling. Him yelling at Rose, saying it was all her fault for not keeping a closer eye on Gina, Rose crying, Gina screaming back at her father, saying none of it was her mother's fault and to leave her alone. The older girl—I can't remember her name—tried to run interference, but it was no use. They were all in our office. Not to make sure Gina had prenatal care, but because Sal wanted Owen to abort her." She shook her head in disbelief. "Can you imagine? She was about eight months gone."

She stopped again. The cat pushed his head into her

hand and turned up his purring a notch. His demand for attention seemed to soothe her because she smiled, resumed stroking him and went on with her story.

"Owen said she had to deliver it but didn't need to keep it. He knew someone who was looking for a baby to adopt. Actually, Sal knew them too. They had a bakery in Salinas."

A bakery? In Salinas? I thought about Gina's phone call. Oh, my.

Hermione's mouth gave a twitch of disapproval as she went on. "Owen—Doctor Sadler—always knew someone who wanted to adopt, and God knows, there was always some poor girl who needed to give up a baby. Anyway, Sal couldn't wait to get onboard with that idea, especially since he knew them and thought they were good people. Actually, I don't think he cared much. I think he mentioned their "goodness" to make Gina and Rose feel better. It didn't work. Gina had a fit. Said she was going to keep it. Rose, poor Rose, wrung her hands and cried; the other daughter just kept hold of Gina's hand and looked frightened. Owen wanted to make arrangements to check her into the hospital when the time came, but Sal was having no part of it. She was to deliver right there, in our office, where no one would ever know she'd had a baby. Until then, she'd hide out in her bedroom. We were told to say she had mononucleosis. That's good and contagious so she couldn't have visitors." She stopped again, and this time I'd swear there was a tear in her eye. She reached up and wiped it away before she went on. "Before long, Gina went into labor. They kept her at home until her pains were coming every couple of minutes. By the time she got here she was bleeding. Placenta Previa. We got the baby out but couldn't stop her from hemorrhaging. Rose kept pleading for them to take her to the hospital, but Sal just kept saying for Owen to fix her. He couldn't." She paused again, took a deep breath, and finished. "The baby was a girl. They gave her to the adoptive mother before she was all the way cleaned up."

I handed her the box of tissues that sat on the dresser. "What happened then?"

She blew her nose, causing the cat to dig his claws into her legs. "Ouch. Ginseng, you rotten spoiled thing." The cat ignored her and resettled himself. She scratched his ears, wiped her nose again, and finally looked up at me. "Nothing happened. The adoptive parents had already signed all the papers. She, the mother, had come equipped—diapers, blanket, bottle." Hermione paused again. She wasn't looking at me, but at the memory of that awful night. "She was a sour-looking woman. The man, he looked nice. He held the baby and kept cooing at her. He looked so happy. The woman barely glanced at her. Took her as soon as I'd clamped the cord. Said they had a doctor at home. She and her husband left. I didn't have much time to think about it. Gina was bleeding pretty bad, we couldn't get it stopped, and then she died."

There was another long pause. She absently stroked the cat, blinking back tears. I wondered if her tears were as hot with rage as the burning lump in my throat I was trying to swallow. How could he! How could they! To give away a child with no more thought than giving away a puppy in front of a grocery store, and then to just let the girl die because Sal didn't want the neighbors to know she'd disgraced him. I'd read about things like this, but in another world, another century. That it could happen here, in this town, in this century, seemed impossible. But it had.

Hermione took in a deep, shuddery breath and went on. "After Owen pronounced Gina dead, Sal just stood there, stony faced. Finally, he asked Owen to make all the arrangements and write "heart failure" on the death certificate. I think Rose was in shock. She kept staring at Gina, shaking her head and moaning. No, no, she kept saying. Then the sister had hysterics. She started screaming at her father, not very nice words either."

"What did Sal do?" I hesitated before I asked that

question. Hermione was obviously having a hard time reliving that terrible night. I wasn't sure I could go through much more of this, either, but somehow I had to know.

"He hit her. Told her to be quiet, and when she wouldn't, or couldn't, he smacked her right across the face. I've never seen anyone do that before or since."

I hadn't either. "Oh, how awful. What did the girl do? What did Rose do?"

"Nothing. Absolutely nothing. I'm not sure Rose even knew it happened. Like I said, she was in shock, just not functioning. I wanted to do something, give her something, but Sal pushed them both out the door. Rose was sort of frozen. The girl was sobbing, but not so loud anymore, and she was holding her face. She kept trying to look back at her sister, but Sal just shoved them both out the door, again ordering Owen to take care of it."

"And did he?"

"No." The tears disappeared. Hard lines formed around her eyes and mouth. "I did."

I didn't think I could ask any more questions. The whole thing was making me a little sick, and even if I could think of any, I didn't want to know any more. Besides, I didn't think Hermione could stand to answer.

"I'm sorry," I said.

"Yes. We all are."

"I didn't mean to …"

She sighed. "I know you didn't. It's just that … well … it was a terrible night. One I'll never forget." She stroked the cat. He purred and kneaded her lap some more. She seemed to gain comfort from that, because the next comment came out a little stronger. "So, what are you going to do now?"

"I don't know." I was still shaken by her tragic tale. I wondered how much of it, if any, our Gina knew. There didn't seem to be any doubt that Rose and Sal were her grandparents and that she'd come here looking for them. Of course, an overheard phone call wasn't proof, but still. Why else was she here after all these years? Curiosity? Baker's Bakery. A name you couldn't forget. "Do you remember the name of the couple who took her?"

"I never knew it. Adoptions were the only files I didn't do." She leaned back in her chair and closed her eyes. They opened with a snap. "Do you think this young Gina murdered Doctor Sadler?"

It was exactly what I was wondering but didn't want to say out loud. "I honestly don't know. Why would she? It doesn't make any sense."

"Revenge. For her mother's death."

That seemed more than a little dramatic. But it had crossed my mind as well. "How would she even know how her mother died?" I deliberately let doubt show in my voice. "And, if that could possibly be true, why wouldn't she go after Sal? No, I don't think Gina killed anybody."

Hermione's brown eyes peered at me intently. The cat sat up and his blue eyes peered at me as well. "But it would be interesting to know who her adoptive parents were, and if they really did own a bakery, wouldn't it?"

I nodded, but slowly. I already knew they owned a bakery.

"Those files are all in the back room of his office. I'll bet I can find out who those people are. If I can find out their name, can you ask around and see if this Gina is the one they adopted?"

I wasn't prepared for that. I hadn't thought past knowing if the first Gina had had a child. She had. Was this Gina that child? It seemed more than likely. So, the next question had to be, did she know how her mother died? That her grandfather had let her bleed to death rather than allow people to know she was giving birth to an out-of-wedlock child? She'd come to Santa Louisa looking for them. She'd said as much to the woman on the phone. But had she come seeking revenge? Somehow, I couldn't make that fit with the serious but kind woman I knew. I thought of her tenderness with Rose, her empathy for Marilee, her genuine concern and help getting Janice to a safe house ... No. Gina couldn't be a murderer. But one thing was certain. Gina was at Ianelli's to learn something, and it wasn't how to make bread. And she hated Sal.

"Get me their name."

Hermione nodded. "I'll call you."

I nodded also, reached out to pet the cat, thought better of it, and left. There was a whole, difficult evening before me, and I had several more things to do before I tackled it.

Chapter Twenty-Seven

Something was going on in my front yard. The car ahead of me slowed to a crawl, almost stopping before it drove on. There was another car across the street, engine idling. I could see the driver staring in my front yard. What on earth was going on? I sped up. My front yard was full of people, all staring at my roof. It was a little early for Santa. What were they looking at? A fire? Oh, no. Grady had found Marilee. Fear gripped me with an iron hand. But there was no fire. No Santa either. Just Nathan balancing himself on a gable while Neil stood at the top of a very high ladder, handing him something. Christmas lights. They were putting up my Christmas lights. Only, they weren't my lights.

Marilee, Leona, Gina, and Aunt Mary were clustered on the lawn, making hand gestures and evidently shouting instructions. Susannah was with them, also shouting, but not pointing. Instead, she held the baby. She shifted him, much too confidently, to her other arm so she could wave at me as I pulled into the driveway. The strains of "It's Beginning to Look a Lot Like Christmas" wafted through the car as I opened my door. Maybe it was. But it wasn't the kind of Christmas I'd had in mind. I had envisioned a small tree decorated in white lights and a string of icicle lights hanging from the rafters. Simple, subdued. What I had were strands of multi-colored lights strung to outline every upstairs window as well as the roofline. They were also in place around the downstairs windows. And where did all of those electric candles in little brass holders come from? They were in every downstairs window, surrounded by fake holly. I'd never seen them before. I looked at Aunt Mary, who was beaming.

"Michael's or a rummage sale donation?"

"Rummage sale. I got enough for my house and yours."

I looked at them again. They were kind of pretty. Vintage looking. Like my house. But what was happening on the roof was not.

"Pull that wire tighter." Neil did something with wire and a large wrench and Rudolph rose to perch on my rooftop. A huge plastic Rudolph with the brightest nose I'd ever seen. Two other reindeer appeared behind him. Donner and Blitzen, I presumed, unless it was Comet and Cupid. I watched in dumb horror while Nathan and Neil fastened them down.

"Where did they come from?"

Aunt Mary had the grace to look uncomfortable. "Actually, Nathan bought them. From the Methodist Christmas sale. They had a lot of ... uh ... decorative things. He thought the baby would like them. After all, it's his first Christmas." She grinned. "I think he's going to donate them to Grace House for next year."

But this year they were at my house, on my roof, along with enough colored lights to make Times Square green with envy. At least it was only reindeer. No sleigh. Yes. A sleigh. It came up next, right behind Cupid. Or Blitzen. I held my breath, waiting for the inevitable. I didn't have long to wait.

"Is it secure?"

"No. Let me tighten this one more ... that got it. Now. We're ready for the big guy. Susannah, hold the baby higher so he can see."

The baby was two days old. Did those two really think he cared? But Susannah obligingly held the baby up a little higher. She looked way too natural holding him. And I didn't like the smile she and Neil exchanged one bit. I was going to be a bride, for God's sake. I wasn't ready to be the mother of the bride and certainly not a grandmother.

"Are you all ready? Here he is."

The sight of Nathan plopping Santa into the sleigh erased all thoughts of Susannah and Neil. This Santa sat at a jaunty angle, one arm flung over the side of the sleigh. His cheeks were indeed as red as cherries. So was his nose. His grin was a little blurry, as if his cocoa had been liberally laced with something a bit stronger than whipped cream.

"Okay." Neil peered over the top of the roof and waved at Gina, who waved back with what looked like a remote in her hand. "We're ready. Can the baby see?"

No, the baby couldn't. He couldn't see anything yet, didn't know who Santa Claus was, and cared about nothing but his next meal. That didn't stop his two "uncles." They couldn't have been prouder of their work if they'd been about to open on Broadway.

"Hit the lights, Gina."

My house blazed. Red, yellow, green, blue, every window, the front door, the roofline, came alive with lights. So did lighted collars on the reindeer and the runners on Santa's sleigh. How had they done it? Why had they done it?

"We outlined the front window, Mom." Susannah was standing next to me. She handed me the baby. "So the Christmas tree will stand out. That was Neil's idea. Don't you just love it?"

That wasn't quite the way I'd have put it, but I nodded in agreement anyway. I wondered what Dan would think. He had expressed approval of the white lights—the understated look I'd described. This was not understated.

Neither was the roar of the engine that drowned out Elvis, who was bemoaning the fact that his Christmas was turning out blue. It effectively froze all of us in place.

"Get Marilee inside."

Nathan almost fell off the roof as he slid down the gable toward the ladder. Neil jumped to the ground, barely making it out of his way. Gina grabbed Marilee by the arm and propelled her toward the front door.

"Bring the baby," she yelled. I wasn't sure if that was for

me, or for just anyone. However, Susannah grabbed him out of my arms and followed, Leona on her heels.

"I had him," she yelled after Susannah, who paid no attention. "God damn it." She caught the front door just as it started to slam in her face.

Nathan took the steps in one jump, grabbed the door, pushed Leona inside and disappeared after her.

The engine noise got louder. Aunt Mary and I turned to stare at the corner, bracing ourselves for a gaudy truck and Grady.

A car full of teenagers took the corner on two wheels, the driver revving the engine as it settled back down on all four. We could hear the squeals of laughter over the blare of the music that had nothing to do with Christmas as they shot by. One of them pointed up at my roof and waved.

"Can you overdose on adrenaline?" Aunt Mary finally said. Her voice sounded weak and a little shaky. Exactly the way I felt.

"I don't think so." My voice came out not much stronger. Adrenaline evidently subsides as quickly as it rises, and I was feeling a bit shaky in the legs. "Dan's got to find that damn kid. None of us can take much more of this." I put my arm around Aunt Mary and gave her a squeeze. She looked up at me and smiled, or tried to, and patted my hand.

Neil came around the corner of the house. "It wasn't Grady?"

"No." I took Aunt Mary by the arm and headed for the house. "But it might have been."

"It's kind of hard to believe he'd … you know … do something."

"Believe it," I told him. But I knew what he meant. Horror, violence, fear, they weren't a part of our lives and we had a hard time grasping that they were real. Only, this past week, the murder of Doctor Sadler, the escape of Janice, the destruction of Grace House, had gone a long way toward convincing me.

"Yeah." Neil nodded soberly. "Go ahead on in. I've got to finish tightening up the sled." He looked at the house and smiled. "Looks pretty good, don't you think?"

I looked up at it also. It was ablaze with lights around every window, lights draped over every bush. There were candles welcoming weary travelers, and Santa on the roof. I started to laugh.

"What's the matter? Don't you like it?" Neil looked anxiously at the glowing house. "We could take some of it off."

"Actually, it looks pretty good. Festive. And, God knows, we could use some 'festive' about now. Leave it." I took another look, then turned toward Aunt Mary. "Except for the slightly tipsy Santa. The Methodists should be ashamed of themselves."

"Why do you think they had it in their sale?" she said with a wry little smile that showed me she was back to normal. "Come on. Let's go see about feeding all those people."

Gina and Susannah were setting the table in the dining room. Nathan was holding the baby. Leona, looking sulky, leaned up against the counter and stared at him, while Marilee peeled potatoes. The oven was on, and something smelled wonderful.

"Old fashioned meatballs. I told you I'd bring some."

I nodded. Aunt Mary had, but I'd forgotten. The day had been a little full, and somehow dinner for this mob had worked its way to the bottom of my list of "things to do."

"I thought we'd do garlic-mashed potatoes. They'll be great with the meatballs." Marilee finished the last potato and set it in a large pot she'd filled with cold water. She wiped her hands on the dishtowel draped over her shoulder and turned toward me. "You do have garlic … Oh."

My surprise must have shown on my face. I shouldn't have been surprised. Everyone kept saying Marilee knew her way around a kitchen, both catering and the home variety, but evidently I hadn't been listening. She was taking charge of dinner with the same confident attitude Aunt Mary always had displayed.

"I'm sorry, Ellen. I didn't mean …"

"In the hydrator, in that little plastic carton." I smiled to let her know I was fine with both the potatoes and the use of my first name.

I watched her bring out the carton, open it and examine the contents. She frowned, but set it down on the counter. "I guess they'll be all right. Do we have anything for salad?"

I should have gone to the grocery store. "There're carrots. We can cook those."

"I brought French bread. It's a day old, but if we butter it and wrap it in foil, it should be fine. I also brought a cake." Gina stood in front of my silverware drawer, counting out forks. Her smile was grim but satisfied. "For some reason, Sal didn't mind a bit when I took them."

Aunt Mary looked at her sharply but said nothing.

"I don't think we're going to starve." Susannah came into the kitchen with a handful of leftover napkins. She placed them in the drawer and picked up the French bread. "Do I slice this stuff all the way through or leave a little crust on the bottom?"

"Either way," Gina said.

Susannah was having a great time playing house. Or was it something else? The way she wielded the bread knife was awkward yet enthusiastic, and I recalled her pride in her pot roast only a couple of days ago. I watched her face when Neil came in the back door, the smile she gave him—warm, confident, welcoming—and something inside me lurched. I turned to look at Nathan, who was still holding the baby, and watched Marilee give him the same kind of smile.

"Makes you feel old when this happens, doesn't it?" I hadn't seen Aunt Mary, or maybe I was so absorbed in my realization that Susannah had grown up I hadn't noticed her.

"When what happens?"

She smiled at me and patted me on the arm. "Should we wait dinner for Dan?"

Anne appeared at the back door carrying two sacks of groceries. "Help! These things are heavy."

Someone had remembered the grocery store. I held the door. She set her sacks on the kitchen table and smiled broadly at all of us. "It smells wonderful in here. I brought some eggs, milk, that kind of thing. Ellen, I got your message. I can hardly believe it."

"Did you bring butter?" Marilee was already emptying the bags. "Coffee. Good."

"Butter? I think so." Anne dismissed groceries with the wave of a hand. She was only interested in the new Grace House. "I've got so many ideas, so many things I want to do. Paint first, then we have to get rid of those dreadful rugs, and that wallpaper! " She laughed. "Then we'll work on getting the daycare up and running. We've needed it for so long, and now ... finally!"

"Daycare?" Leona's eyes widened. It was the first word she'd spoken in a long time. She pushed herself away from the counter, where she had been leaning staring at Nathan and the baby, and turned her attention to Anne. Her interest sent a shiver up my spine.

Marilee took the baby from Nathan and sat on one of the kitchen chairs, preparing to nurse him. She threw the small blanket over her shoulder and fumbled with the buttons on her shirt. The baby disappeared under the blanket. Marilee shifted him on her lap a little before she looked at me anxiously. "How long before we can move in?"

I hesitated. At least two weeks, and I doubted if we could get everything done by then. "Before Christmas." I crossed my fingers and held them behind my back.

"Before ... Oh." Gina looked from Anne to Marilee to me. "I thought we were going to rent it until the escrow closed."

"We are," Anne said. She looked around the room, trying to include them all. "I know how hard this is on all of you, but we have to get some things done, inspections and things, and also permits from the city."

"It's a lot harder on Ellen and Chief Dunham than it is on us." Gina frowned as she looked around. "They've got company coming for Christmas, a wedding a few days after that, and we've thrown Susannah out of her room. That's all right for a couple of days, but I don't think …"

"That's okay. Gina can keep staying with Mrs. McGill and me, and Marilee will get an apartment. We're going to anyway." Leona, who had said nothing since the subject of daycare had been dropped, spoke almost defiantly. The room became very still. Gina stopped scrubbing carrots. Susannah, who was on her way to the dining room, hands full of water glasses, stopped and looked at me. Her expression clearly said, "Here we go." Nathan started to speak, but a small wave from Anne stopped him. I transferred my gaze to Marilee, who looked amazingly serene. She shifted the blanket and moved the baby to her other breast. "No. We're not getting an apartment. I'm going to finish my GED, go to the community college, and I'm going to take that job with Central Coast Catering. Anne says we can stay at Grace House for a while, and that's where I'm going as soon as we can move in." She looked up, directly at Leona. "I told you that. Yesterday."

"Yeah. But I didn't think you meant it."

"I did."

Marilee's hand quivered a little as she held the baby, and her eyes were lowered, but there was a set to her jaw line, a tightening around her mouth. Marilee wasn't going to let her child grow up the way she had.

I glanced at Leona. We were all looking at Leona, holding our breaths, waiting for her to explode. She didn't. She stood in the middle of the kitchen, her hands clenching and unclenching, her mouth pinched. Her eyes locked onto the baby, watching as Marilee adjusted him, wrapped the blanket a little tighter, held him closer. Then she exhaled, her hands relaxed down by her side, and her shoulders dropped. "Sure. Whatever you think's best."

That wasn't what I'd been expecting. Evidently it wasn't what Aunt Mary expected either, because she looked at me and raised an eyebrow. I shrugged slightly, puzzled but relieved. None of us needed another of Leona's tirades.

"So what are you going to do, Leona?" Gina's voice was soft, thoughtful, as if she really wanted to know. But Leona didn't take it that way.

"Whaddya mean?" Her fists started to clench again.

"Are you going to stay at Grace House, try to get your own place, or what?"

The belligerence on Leona's face faded to confusion. Her eyes wandered around the room, coming to rest on the baby. "I don't know. I guess I'll have to think about it."

Silence greeted that statement.

"We'd all better think about it." Gina turned back to the sink, but the carrots were scrubbed. She stared at them for a moment then walked over to where Marilee still sat, the baby now over her shoulder, sound asleep. "Especially Marilee." She laid her hand lightly on the baby's cheek then squeezed Marilee's shoulder. "She's had a rough few weeks. She needs a little stability."

"I'm not too sure Chief Dunham will let her go anywhere until they find Grady."

Nathan had his hand on Marilee's other shoulder. She looked up at him, then around the kitchen at the rest of us.

"Then they better find him fast before he does something else."

"You think he will?" Marilee had just confirmed my worst fear.

"Count on it."

I already was, and I didn't like it one bit. But where were they all going to go? Especially Marilee and the baby. I couldn't think of any place safer than right here. Unless, of course, we could furnish one of Dan's cells with a nice bed and some towels … probably not.

"You think he'd come here?" Leona didn't look scared, just interested.

"If he found out I was here, and he thought he could get away with it." Marilee looked scared.

Susannah also looked scared. She put the lid back on the pot, where the potatoes were beginning to give off a lovely garlic smell. "Why is Grady so determined to get to you? What would he do if he found you?"

Marilee didn't answer right away. She held the baby a little closer and let her hand run down his cheek, stroke his fuzzy head. "I don't know."

I didn't buy that one for a minute. Neither did Anne or Aunt Mary. And they didn't know about the money. I was sure that what Grady wanted was his money back, and probably for a very good reason. If his hide was on the line, that made him all the more dangerous. Somehow I was going to have that talk with Marilee. But not right this minute.

Marilee tucked the baby firmly in the crook of her arm, pushed herself out of the chair, and headed for the stairs. Leona stepped in front of her, arms out.

"He need changing? I'll do it for you. Just sit there and rest."

Marilee clutched the baby closer, if that were possible. "Thanks, but I'll do it."

She pushed past Leona and walked out of the room. A red flush crept up Leona's neck and onto her cheeks but immediately faded, leaving her face white and pinched. She didn't look at any of us. Instead, she pushed through the swinging door that led into the dining room. I was afraid she was going after Marilee. Evidently Nathan did, too, because he took a couple of steps toward the door, but the clinking of silverware stopped him.

"We need more knives." Leona appeared back in the kitchen, her face rigidly under control.

"How many?" Susannah opened the silverware drawer and handed a bunch to Leona. Aunt Mary jumped right in. "Gina, are those carrots ready to go on? Susannah, want to try your hand with potato mashing again? I guess we'd better not wait for Dan."

The mood in the kitchen settled down into a more or less normal hum, but an undercurrent of unease remained. Leona seemed sullen and unresponsive, but that was not abnormal. Gina seemed as if she were a million miles away. Silent all through dinner, she hardly noticed when Anne left. Everyone was silent. Aunt Mary kept trying to get a conversation going, describing the wonders of the new home and suggesting dragging out more of my Christmas decorations. Nothing worked.

Susannah and Neil left as soon as the last plate was placed in the dishwasher. Susannah pleaded the need to study for an upcoming test and Neil made vague comments about a term paper on the mammary glands of dairy cows that was due immediately.

"Coward." I gave her a peck on the cheek.

She grinned. "Better you than me. You think it will really be two weeks?"

"At least."

"Guess I'd better pack more clothes tomorrow."

Nathan was the next to leave, but not before he'd followed Marilee up the stairs, holding the baby in the carrier. She had eaten almost nothing, and her face looked drawn and pale. His expression was grim when he came back down. "She should still be in the hospital. Resting. Enjoying that child. Not hiding out from that son of a … sorry." He muttered thank you for the dinner, and he, too, was gone.

Dan walked in the front door as Nathan walked out.

"Any news?" Nathan asked.

Dan shook his head. Nathan hesitated, looked toward the staircase, sighed, and closed the door behind him.

That left Aunt Mary, Gina, Leona, Dan, and me.

Aunt Mary sat Dan down at the table and set the plate of food in front of him that we had been keeping warm.

"These potatoes are wonderful."

"Forget the potatoes. Have you found Grady? Do you know any more?"

Fork halfway to his mouth, he looked at each of us in turn. "We're working on it," he said, his face expressionless. I knew that look. I gathered up the rest of the silverware and headed for the kitchen but was stopped by Leona.

"You mind if I watch TV?" She edged her way closer to the living room, ignoring the rumpled napkins and soiled tablecloth still to be removed from the dining room table. Gina and Susannah had already picked up all the plates and loaded the dishwasher. Aunt Mary and I had put away the few leftovers and wiped down the counters.

"No." I gathered up the napkins and headed for the back porch and the washing machine. I'd get the tablecloth when Dan was finished.

"What do you want to watch?" I asked.

"There's a rerun of *Bay Watch* on."

It was also time for *Mystery* on PBS. It was the first episode of a dramatization of an Elizabeth George novel that I had been waiting to see. My resolve to get them the permits they needed and moved into the new house in no more than two weeks went up one more notch.

"Gina and I are going." Aunt Mary's voice right behind me made me jump.

I quit stuffing in napkins and turned around. "You don't want to watch *Bay Watch*?"

"No." She grinned. "A few too many shapely thighs for me. It makes me lonely for the body I never had." The smile faded. "Are you going to be okay? This is not easy. A wedding to plan, Christmas, people coming from all over …

That alone is enough to give anyone a nervous breakdown … but add a houseful of refugees and a nut like Grady Wilcox running around throwing firebombs and … It's too much."

"I love the way you put that. Makes me sound like Super Girl or some kind of martyr."

You're neither," she replied a bit tartly. "But that doesn't make it any easier."

I had to laugh, which felt nice. "You're right. It's not easy, but it isn't for them either. Besides, you have one of the refugees. How are you and Gina getting along?"

She looked thoughtful. "Beautifully. She's polite, considerate, and she's teaching me how to make sourdough bread."

"I have a few things to tell you about Gina."

"You found Hermione?"

"I did."

Aunt Mary looked toward the kitchen. It was empty but she dropped her voice anyway. "And …?"

"Sal and Rose's daughter, the first Gina, had a baby. A girl. She died in childbirth and the baby was adopted."

"In childbirth. So that's how she died. I never quite believed that mononucleosis, damaged heart story. Poor thing. And that means this Gina really could be …"

"I think she is. I think she came here looking for them. Why, I don't know." I paused. Just thinking about what I was going to tell her made me a little sick. It would be even harder for her. "Hermione says Gina's mother bled to death right after the birth. She was at Doctor Sadler's office. Sal wouldn't let them get her to the hospital where she just might have been saved."

"He what? Oh, no. You must be mistaken." I watched the color drain out of her face. "Sal loved his girls. He would never …" Tears welled up in her eyes. I'd never seen Aunt Mary cry. I didn't this time, either. She swiped them away angrily. "Dear God in heaven. He really did that?"

I nodded. "That's what Hermione said, and she had no reason to lie."

"And you think Gina found out and came back to … You don't really think …" Aunt Mary was having trouble processing all this. I didn't blame her. So was I. But she had one thing clear. "And Rose has lived with that all these years."

"Yes."

Aunt Mary shuddered and took in a deep mouthful of air. "And the baby?"

"Adopted. Doctor Sadler arranged the whole thing before she ever gave birth. Gina wanted to keep it, but Sal wouldn't hear of it. He didn't want anyone to know his daughter had disgraced him."

She didn't say anything for a moment. She didn't have to. Sal and Rose were her friends, had been for years. The thought that Sal could stand by and let his daughter die rather than have the neighbors know … That was something you read about in Victorian novels, not something your neighbor, your friend, would do. I could see her struggling with it. I wanted to say something, do something to make it easier, but there was nothing. If only I hadn't told her. But I'd had to. Gina was staying with her, Gina was staying in this town, and I was sure the reason she had come was rooted in that long ago tragedy. And now, one of the people involved in that tragedy was dead.

Gina's voice brought her back to life. "Mary, are you ready? Oh … I didn't mean … are you all right? "

"Fine." Aunt Mary didn't look fine, and the look she gave Gina was a mixture of all kinds of emotions.

"We were just talking about Marilee." I quickly dumped soap in the washing machine and closed the lid. Where that lie had come from so easily I didn't know, but I was grateful. "We're both a little shook up by this whole thing. It's all so awful. That poor girl."

I twirled the knob and started the machine. On which

cycle I had no idea and I didn't care. My lie seemed to be working. Gina was nodding.

"Do you really think Grady threw that firebomb hoping to get her when she ran out?"

Gina's face went blank for a moment, and she just stared at me. Whatever she'd thought I was going to say, it wasn't that. "I really don't know. It's hard to believe anyone could be that dumb. What if she hadn't gotten out or ..."

Or what if she hadn't gotten the money out? Gina didn't have to finish that sentence. I could see it on her face. She knew about the money and she was sure he had set Grace House on fire.

"Mary, are you ready? I still need to put that cake together tonight." She handed me the tablecloth and turned to go.

"What cake?" Why was she making ... the layers on Aunt Mary's counter. "Did you make those layers I saw today? They smelled wonderful. What are they and what did you pour over them?"

Gina smiled. "Espresso. Real Italian espresso. They're sponge cake and I'm making Tiramisu. A very special one for one of our ... Sal and Rose's old customers."

Gina turned to go and Aunt Mary started to follow her. "I'll talk to you tomorrow," she said. "I'll call you."

I reached out and grabbed her arm. "Wait. Gina's making it? Not Sal?"

She looked at me a little pityingly. "Gina's made all of the special things that have appeared in that bakery lately. I thought you'd figured that out by now." She turned on her heel and hurried through the kitchen.

I stared after her, still holding the tablecloth. Of course. Why hadn't I seen it? Sal was short of breath just walking from the kitchen to the front of the store. Baba au Rhum, Lemon Semolina Cake, flaky, buttery pie crust ... Sal couldn't make any of those. But Gina ... what was she after? If all she'd wanted was to find her family, to see where she came from, she'd done that. She hadn't, to my knowledge, announced to Sal or Rose that she was their granddaughter. So what did she want? Whatever it was, it wasn't baking instruction.

I stuffed the tablecloth in the washing machine and headed back to the living room and *Bay Watch*.

Aunt Mary had better count on that phone call tomorrow. We had a lot to talk about.

Chapter Twenty-Eight

"Why didn't we bring over my little TV?"

Dan sat on the edge of the bed, looking at a corner of the chest of drawers, three drawers of which now contained his clothes, the top of which didn't hold a TV.

"We'll get it tomorrow."

"Right. But what are we going to do tonight? It's too early to go to bed. To sleep."

The last part was said with a leer, which I ignored. "It's ten o'clock. If you're not sleepy, you could read a book."

Dan looked around the room. "You only have those sappy mysteries you read. Don't you have a Tom Clancy or something?"

"You're in a good mood." I walked over to the bookshelf and picked out a Dick Francis. "Read this. You'll love it."

He opened it, read the inside cover blurb, and shut it. I couldn't believe it. How could anyone not read Dick Francis once they'd opened the book?

"I'll start it later."

He got up, went to the window, stared out, dropped the curtain back down, crossed the room to stare at the phone, then crossed back over to the bed, sat, and immediately got back up.

"What's the matter with you? Ever since you've come home you've been—is it the Christmas lights? I didn't know they were going to do that and I certainly didn't know about that awful Santa Clause and the reindeer. We can … "

"Christmas lights? No. Of course not." He started to grin. "You should see the look on your face. You look just like Mary when she's not happy with someone. I sort of like the Santa. Of course, if he were driving that sleigh on the street, I'd have to pull him over for a sobriety test. It's not that."

"Then what is it? You're strung so tight I could twang you."

Dan didn't say anything for a minute. "We've had some lab results on what started the fire."

"Oh." I took a deep breath. "And?"

"It was pretty much what we thought. A glass bottle filled with gasoline. He stuffed a rag in it, then lit the rag and threw the bottle over the fence. He doesn't have much of an arm. It hit the side of the garage instead of the window, which was probably the target. If it had gotten inside, the fire would have spread a lot more quickly."

"Meaning they might not have gotten out in time?"

"Meaning that's a possibility."

I felt a sinking feeling in my stomach and sat down on the edge of the bed. "Also meaning you're convinced it was Grady. So, if you already know that, why are you so jumpy? Just go pick him up."

From the look on Dan's face, I was afraid it wasn't quite that easy. I was right.

"If we could find him, we would." There was bitterness in Dan's tone that I hadn't heard before. Bitterness and frustration. "How a little punk like that—somebody's helping him. Someone's given him a hole to hide in, from us and from his 'buddies.' But he can't stay there forever. And when he crawls out … I hope we get to him first."

I wasn't so sure I did. If Dan got him, he'd only go to jail. If his "buddies" found him, well, if what I'd heard was true, Grady Wilcox might not bother anyone anymore.

"Why do you keep looking out the window? Do you think he might …?"

Dan let the curtain drop back over the window and came back over to sit beside me on the bed. "No." He paused, glanced over at me, took my hand and stroked it lightly. "I don't know." His thumb kept tracing patterns on the back of my hand. He meant it to be comforting, I knew, but instead it was distracting. "There were a lot of people there, around that fire, who knew we took Marilee to our house. Someone told Grady she was at Grace House, and that someone could very well know she's here as well." He paused, both stroking and talking. I was pretty sure he wanted to go on with the stroking, and that he didn't want to say what he was about to say.

"Grady is a punk, in every sense of the word. He's also not very bright; most of them aren't. In addition to selling, he's using. And he's managed to run up a very big bill. The money Marilee took was to pay that bill."

I could feel myself go cold. I really knew all this, or certainly suspected it, but to hear Dan lay it out so clearly …

"How do you know all this?"

"The idiot went to The Watering Hole after the fire. After a few beers, he started complaining how his great plan didn't work out and how he was going to have to think of something else." Dan looked at my hand. "Or did you mean the part about the money?"

I gulped a little. "That part. How do you know that?"

He touched the index finger of my left hand and smiled. "A wedding ring is going to look nice on your hand." He stretched out his own hand. "Won't look too bad on this one either." He sat quietly for a minute. "Are you sure you don't want an engagement ring?"

"Yes. No. Yes, I'm sure. Just a plain band, one that matches yours. Dan. How do you know, for sure, that these drug people are after Grady?"

"Moles."

"What?"

He smiled. "Not the kind that wreck the lawn." His smile disappeared. "Our county, and all the police departments in it, try to work together to … get rid of these people. One way is to plant someone inside, someone who feeds us information. We've known about Grady for a while, but he's pretty small. We were hoping to prune this particular tree a little higher." He dropped my hand, got up, and walked over to the window. "Looks like we're going to get our rain after all."

I wiggled off the bed to stand beside him, staring out the window. The clouds were lower, dark, partly obscuring the street light down the block. I watched as the first small drops fell, barely dampening the sidewalk. The wind had kicked up, blowing the few remaining leaves around in circles, bending the bare branches of the elm tree in my front yard in a bizarre dance. It was the kind of scene you see in movies right before something horrible happens.

Finally Dan spoke. "Have you had a chance to talk to Marilee? I thought you were going to call me." He didn't sound mad, but not exactly happy either.

"Oh. No. I keep trying, but I can't seem to get her alone, then I went to see Winifred and everything else happened and … Oh, Dan. I'm so sorry. I forgot." I felt terrible, as if I'd let him down. And I had. He'd asked me to do something and I hadn't. Things happened, and I forgot. If I'd forgotten to do something for Brian, he would have thrown it up to me for months. Years. Dan brought it up because he was concerned, for me, for Marilee, for all of us. It made me feel worse.

He put his arm around me and gently squeezed. I slipped mine around his waist and leaned into him. "It's all right. But next time, keep in touch, all right? I worry about you." He pulled me close and placed a feather-soft kiss on my check. "She probably couldn't help us much anyway, but I'd like to know if she got that money out or if it burned up."

"Would it make a difference?"

"If we could somehow get the word to Grady that the money was gone, he might be less interested in chasing her."

Maybe. If he believed it was really gone. I couldn't stop

the shiver that ran through my body. Grady Wilcox was taking up far too much of my time and energy. And although I'd never laid eyes on the man, I already despised him.

Dan and I stood close together, watching the rain make puddles on the front walk that glowed red, green, blue, like little pools of luminous paint.

"I should go down and turn off the Christmas lights." Dan said.

"What do you suppose happens to Santa when he gets wet?"

Dan laughed. "Not much. If you're hoping that tipsy grin will wash off, I think you're out of luck." He started to turn but I tightened my hand on his arm. He stopped and I took a deep breath.

"Dan, after lunch today I went to visit Doctor Sadler's old nurse. It's one of the reasons I forgot to call you. She's at Shady Acres, confined to a wheelchair, but there's nothing wrong with her brain. She told me some things you ought to know."

His arm tightened around me about halfway through my story. He held me so close against him I could barely breathe. After I'd finished, he didn't speak immediately, just watched the rain. Finally he took a deep breath and let it out slowly. "The things we do to each other."

I let my head rest on his shoulder for a moment. "Do you think Gina could have killed Doctor Sadler? I know it doesn't seem possible, but then, why would she come here if not for revenge of some sort?"

"Gina doesn't seem the revenge type, but if I've learned anything in all these years of police work, it's that people surprise you. All the time. However, if that's why she's here, why not Sal? He was the one who let her mother die."

"I don't know. But someone killed him, and unless it was someone who just happened to find an angel arm and thought it would be fun to bash in an old man's head, the people at Grace House seem to have a corner on motives."

"Grady because he wanted to find Marilee, Gina for revenge—I still can't believe Sal—and who else? Marilee was in no condition to wander around cemeteries lying in wait for old men. Besides, all she had to do was not sign the release papers."

The rain was coming down harder, throwing itself against the window, leaving streaks on the glass. I could see Dan's reflection in the glow of the Christmas lights. He seemed to be waiting, for what? Another name? Leona came to mind, but he had already refused to believe her need for that baby was anything more than a normal woman's wanting to help. Leona wasn't normal. But it was another name I was thinking of. Anne Kennedy. Only I couldn't make myself really believe that either. And I couldn't say it.

"I'm going to use the bathroom before Leona comes up." I stretched and turned away from the window.

"Good idea. I'll run down and turn off the lights."

Dan started down the stairs and I gathered up my nightgown and slippers and headed down the hall the other way. I stopped at Marilee's door and listened. All was quiet. I hoped it stayed that way. The television was still blaring away downstairs so I figured I had plenty of time. A shower? No. In the morning.

I exited the bathroom just in time. Leona was coming up the stairs, a rebellious look on her face, followed closely by Dan.

"Would you like to use the bathroom first?" His tone was oh, so polite, but his patience was wearing thin. I'd known him a long time. I could tell. Leona couldn't.

"Letterman wasn't over."

Was she addressing me?

Evidently she was, because she waited for a response. When she didn't get one, she glared at both of us, pushed open the guest room door, and let it shut behind her. Loudly.

"Guess it's my turn." Dan stared at the closed door for a minute then went into the bathroom. I could hear the lock click. Afraid Leona would walk in on him? I sighed and returned to our room.

I was propped up in bed with Jake on my knees when Dan returned. He wore green and black plaid pajama bottoms and a white T-shirt. The same thing thousands of men wore to bed every night, but I was willing to bet not one of them looked as good as he did.

"Ready?"

I nodded. He moved Jake over, climbed in on his side and turned off his bedside light. I snuggled down and turned off mine. I loved this time, warm and safe in bed with him. Usually the evening didn't end for a while, but tonight … somehow tonight all I wanted was to be held. I was emotionally and physically exhausted. I wasn't sure how to tell Dan how I felt and I could feel myself tense up. I'd felt like this often with Brian, but for very different reasons. Never with Dan, and I wasn't sure how to make him understand.

"Come here."

I did, bracing myself to say something. What, I didn't know. Only, I didn't have to.

Dan put his arm around me and held me close. He reached up and gently pushed the hair back off of my cheek and gave it a light kiss. "This seems to be the night for tragic tales."

"What are you talking about? We don't need any more tragedy."

I pushed myself up to lean on one elbow but Dan pulled me back down and cradled me against his shoulder.

"I talked to Anne today. She's pretty close-mouthed about her people, and she should be. But I got to thinking about Leona's jacket and decided to ask a few other questions while I was at it."

I had to laugh. "You mean she didn't hand over their

files?"

"She politely told me I'd have to get a court order for that."

"What did she say about Leona's missing jacket?"

"That we don't know if it was missing and since everything got burned up in the fire, there's no way to find out."

Damn. "She could have hidden it somewhere else."

"She could have. And there may not be a bloody jacket."

"She had motive, means, and opportunity. Aren't those the three things you look for?"

"Proof helps. She did tell me one thing about Leona, though. Something I hadn't realized."

Dan's voice changed. I couldn't read his expression. "What?"

"Leona's last name."

"It's Wilson, isn't it? So what?"

"It's Wilson now. It used to be Carter."

"I don't understand. Why do you care what her name was?"

There was a long pause while Dan stared at the rain streaked window. Jake got up and draped himself over my legs again. I didn't move. I just waited for whatever was coming next.

"I had a friend in high school named Kevin Carter. Hadn't seen him in years. One day, while I was working homicide in San Francisco, I got a call. Seemed Kevin had joined the Santa Louisa police department. Only he wanted to change locations, and he wanted to do it right away. He asked if I could help. I made a couple of phone calls. He got a good job with the police department in Redding. Six hours drive north of here."

A chill ran up my arms. This was leading someplace I was pretty sure I didn't want to go. "And what does Leona have to do with Kevin?"

"She's his ex-wife. The mother of his kids. She was arrested for child neglect. Evidently she was falling down drunk on a pretty consistent basis. Kids were two and three, something like that. Kevin was the arresting officer." He stopped, glanced at me out of the corners of his eyes before he went on. "I found all this out later. After Kevin got full custody of the kids, Leona got six months in the county jail. When she got out, Kevin was gone."

"Has she seen the kids since?"

"Not that I know about."

I thought about the first day I'd met Leona. She'd said something about her cop husband. I got the impression that day that he'd abused her also. That she was a victim. Well, maybe she was, but not the way I'd thought. Leona was weak, more than weak. Unstable was the kindest way to put it. I thought about her losing her kids, what that might have done to her. "Adam."

"Who?" Dan said.

"That's what Marilee decided to call the baby. Do you think Leona could have told Grady where Marilee was?"

"I don't know. She knows him. She and Grady lived in the same trailer park."

"But, why? She wants … wanted … to get a place with Marilee and the baby. Telling Grady where he could find Marilee wouldn't get that accomplished."

"True."

"Someone told him."

"Also true."

I felt hot suddenly, in need of air. Leona, Marilee, Grady, it was too much. I climbed out of bed and headed for the window. The street was empty. No Grady, no old truck, no firebombs, no police car was disturbing the peace of this sedate neighborhood. A neighborhood where everybody carved pumpkins for Halloween and left their porch lights on, where everybody put up Christmas lights the day after Thanksgiving and had a block party every Fourth of July with a potluck dinner and boxed fireworks for the kids. "Where's Gary?"

"I sent him home."

I let the curtain drop and turned back to look at him so fast I almost tripped. "You what?"

"Don't worry. I've taken precautions."

What did that mean? I thought about it for a moment and decided I didn't want to know. Instead I walked over to the bed and looked down at him. "Now do you see what I mean about her? She's … off."

"I have to admit, Leona has some problems. And, Ellie, you can come back to bed."

I climbed back in. My feet were cold and I put them on Dan's legs.

"Thanks," he said but gathered me close. "All right, tell me about her."

I told him about Marilee's last confrontation with Doctor Sadler and about her calling the bakery, crying.

"Leona saw Grady's truck heading toward the cemetery and made a big point of telling Gina. I guess she left soon after that. She was supposed to go back to Grace House, but she could have made a detour."

"She was on foot?"

"Yes. She could have gone looking for Doctor Sadler. She had time. I got to Grace House around two o'clock, and she was just eating lunch. That leaves almost an hour for her to make a ten minute walk."

"It does seem as if we have to take another look at Leona. Why was she at the bakery? I thought she was working for Ruthie."

"Ruthie gave her the afternoon off."

Dan laughed. "I wonder why." The laugh faded. "And Gina was there by herself?"

"I think so. Rose was away getting Sal's lunch or something. I don't know where Sal was."

"And Leona knew Grady had signed the adoption

papers and that Owen Sadler was badgering Marilee to sign as well?"

"Yes. Everyone at Grace House knew. Doctor Sadler told Leona she was a fool if she thought she could set up housekeeping with Marilee."

Dan didn't say any more. Neither did I. We lay in the dark, close together, listening to the rain on the window and to our thoughts. Pretty soon I heard light snores and I rolled out from under Dan's arm. Sleep seemed like a good idea, only it refused to come. I kept thinking about motives, how they were like roads on a complicated map. If you could just follow them, you could reach your destination. Or solve the crime. All the roads on this map led back to Grace House.

The rain stopped around one o'clock.

Chapter Twenty-Nine

Weak sunshine shone through the window. I opened one eye. It looked as if the sun didn't want to get up any more than I did. I opened the other eye and waited until I was able to make out the time. Seven o'clock. Too early to get up but too late to go back to sleep. A shower and some coffee. Maybe that would do it.

I had to go into the office but wasn't awake enough to choose what I would wear. Clean underwear and knit pants and a sweatshirt would do for now. I gathered it all up and headed downstairs to start the coffee. I'd leave the upstairs bathroom open for Dan. Or whoever got to it first.

I was sitting at the kitchen table, coffee mug cradled in both hands, when Dan arrived. He still looked half asleep when he came down the stairs.

"You're a fine woman, Ellie, my love."

The coffee was primarily responsible for that statement. I'd remembered the creamer, and he poured a generous amount into his mug.

"What were you doing on the phone at two thirty this morning? Something to do with Grady?" I had just fallen into a deep sleep when the phone rang, but instead of waiting to find out the reason for the call, I turned over and put the pillow over my head. Grady Wilcox had robbed me of enough sleep. He wasn't getting what was left of that night.

"No. Something to do with a bunch of kids who got high and thought it would be fun to smash a bunch of car windshields." He paused to take another sip. "Ah. Wonderful. I don't think they're having so much fun now."

Another sip. "Neither are their folks."

"Serves them right."

"The kids or their folks?"

"All of them. What about Grady?"

"No sign of him."

"So now what?" I was also cranky. I needed more coffee and another four hours of sleep. I was only going to get the coffee.

"We keep looking. In the meantime, someone has to stay here with Marilee and the baby. Adam? Is that his name? I don't want them out of this house."

Just the thing to get my day off to a good start. I thought of my Christmas gift list, which was getting longer, not shorter. I'd left messages for the florist, who hadn't called me back, and for the caterer, who also hadn't called. I was scheduled for a final walkthrough on one of my escrows. I also needed to find out if we had loan approval on another. And then there was Minnie, my little very senior citizen, and her family, whose condo had termites and had to tented and vacated for at least three days. They were not going to be thrilled. Maybe they could get her into Shady Acres early.

I sighed deeply and took another large swallow of coffee.

"You all right?" Dan looked at me anxiously.

Somehow that made me feel better. "I'm fine. Just a little overwhelmed, I guess. I don't want to face all the stuff waiting for me at the office, I don't want to badger the florist, and I don't want to call that damn caterer one more time. I don't want to think of Christmas shopping and especially of wrapping gifts. And I really don't want to think of my house burning down. I hate Grady Wilcox. None of this would be happening if it wasn't for him."

"You're going to blame him for the florist not calling you back and your escrow problems?"

"I would if I could think of a way."

Dan looked for a moment as if he was going to laugh.

He didn't, probably because of the look on my face. "We'll find him. You'll feel a lot better when he's in jail."

"What if you don't?"

"Someone's going to find him, and it better be us. If his buddies get to him first, we'll probably find him floating off the end of the Pismo Beach pier."

"If that's the case, be sure to get the names of the guys that throw him in. I'd like to send them a thank you note."

This time Dan did laugh. He put his mug down on the table, pulled out a chair, and took my hand. "We could elope."

"Don't tempt me. Besides, that wouldn't solve who killed Doctor Sadler."

"No. It wouldn't. But ..." He put my hand down, patted it, and picked up his coffee. "How about, you give me the caterer's number and I'll call him. He'll call back the chief of police."

"Would you?" I couldn't believe it. Brian would never have even thought of such a thing. "You'd actually do that?"

"Sure." He smiled at me over his mug. "It's my wedding too." He took a sip and gave me a very serious look. "But you'll have to be okay with whatever he and I decide."

"As long as its not creamed chicken on toast."

"Not a possibility. Now, let's figure out who's going to stay with Marilee this morning."

"I can't."

"Do you have an appointment?"

"No. Well, sort of. I have three escrows I have to close before next week. I want to get all this settled before Christmas so I can get married."

"Is the new Grace House one of the escrows?"

"No. But finalizing this interim occupancy, getting the permits from the city, scheduling the inspections that I'm responsible for ... all that is."

"I like your priorities. So, who can we get to stay here?"

"I don't know. Nathan said he could come right after

lunch, but he has obligations until then."

"Gina?"

"No. Gina can't leave the bakery."

Dan quit sipping coffee to look at me. "You know, Ellie, I really don't think I can take her to the station. There's got to be somebody."

"I'll stay with her."

I hadn't heard Leona come in, but there she was, trailing around in that medieval looking nightgown, heading for the hutch and the coffee mugs. You would have thought she'd done this every morning for the last year.

"No." Dan and I spoke in unison.

"Why not?" Leona took her full mug, pulled out a chair, and sat down. "Is this cream?"

She picked up the pitcher, poured a generous amount into her mug, stirred, and with the same spoon helped herself to sugar. I could see brown drops on top of the sugar bowl and around the rim. I watched with what I hoped was an impassive face. Dan watched also, then looked at me with a grin he didn't even try to hide.

"I just love incentives, don't you?"

I thought about throwing the sugar bowl at him.

Leona blew into her coffee mug.

"Grady might know where Marilee is." Dan erased the smile and turned a serious face to Leona. "If he came calling, you'd be no match for him."

"Neither would Gina. But I could get to a phone, which is about all anyone could do."

Dan and I looked at each other. I made a face at him that I hoped said, "Do something," but before he could, Marilee appeared carrying Adam in one arm, the empty baby carrier swinging from the other. Amazing what a couple of days can do. She held him crooked into her arm as if she'd been carrying babies for years. Setting the carrier down close to the last remaining chair, she walked over to the hutch. She didn't even hand Adam off to me while she poured herself a cup of coffee.

"What about Grady?" She set the mug on the table, pulled out the chair and carefully sat down, looking at each of us in turn, eyes wide with anxiety. "What's he up to now?" She looked down at the sleeping baby and cuddled him a little closer.

"We think Grady set the fire." Dan's voice was even, matter of fact, as if he didn't want to upset her. He didn't.

"Of course he did." The fact had been accepted from the beginning. It was what he might do next that filled those green eyes with fear. "He'd do anything to get at me." She set her cup down and stared at Dan. "Does he know where I am?"

"We don't think so, but we don't know."

Dan looked over at me. His raised eyebrow and slight head jerks made it clear that he wanted me to do something, but what? He looked at Marilee, stared at her actually, then looked back at me. I got it. I was to ask her about the money.

"Now?" I mouthed it, jerking my own head at Leona, raising my own eyebrow.

He nodded. Okay. If that was what he wanted. I turned to Marilee, reached out and patted the baby gently, smiled brightly, and took a deep breath.

"Marilee, you know that Dan is trying to keep you safe." I thought I'd start out gently, with a positive statement. And that was as positive as it got for the moment.

"Get Grady and put him in jail. That ought to do it."

I tried again. "They're looking. Marilee, just why do you think Grady wants to find you so badly?"

"Don't know." She looked down at Adam and bent over a little to adjust his blanket. Avoiding me?

"Could it be because of the money?"

Her head jerked up. She looked at me, then her gaze shifted to Dan. "I don't know what you're talking about."

"Yes, I think you do." I tried to sound gentle but at the same time firm. It had never worked with Susannah; I wasn't at all sure it would work with Marilee, but it was worth a try.

It didn't. She shook her head, still looking only at the baby. "I don't have any money."

"But you did."

"What if I did?"

Firm was getting easier. Gentle was getting harder. "If you did, and that's why Grady is trying to find you, then we need to know. Before he burns down another house, like maybe this one."

Tears dripped down on the baby. "I needed that money. Grady wasn't going to do anything for the baby, and I had to have something so I could get away."

"How much was it?"

Marilee wiped a tear out of her eye but ignored the question. Gentle was wearing very thin.

"Do you still have it?"

"No." She looked up at me, all innocence. I'd seen the same look on Susannah's face when she was trying to make me believe a particularly big whopper, and it made me wonder if I'd just heard another one.

"What happened to it?" Dan had finally decided to jump in.

"It got burned up." He also got the innocent look, only this time it was tinged with anger. "Grady decided to do something stupid—not a first for him—and it cost us both."

"Do you know where Grady got the money?"

Marilee's eyes shifted to Leona with a glare that would have soured milk. Leona was going to be blamed for telling us about the money. It wasn't going to advance her chances of teaming up with Marilee. From the flush that crept up Leona's face, she got the message. Marilee transferred her attention back to the baby, and her face softened. She adjusted the blanket again around the sleeping child, pulling it tighter around his little face. "Probably selling meth. That's what he usually did." She got up and grabbed the handle of the baby carrier. "I've got to go change him. Why don't you ask Grady where he got it?"

"That would work," Dan agreed, "but unfortunately we don't know where he is. And it sounds as if he owes that money to someone. Someone who isn't very patient. Someone who's making Grady nervous. Until we find him, we'll have to go with Plan B."

Marilee stopped. She paused for a moment before turning to look suspiciously at Dan. "What's Plan B?"

"Keeping you and the baby safe until we find him."

"Get Nathan. He won't let anything happen to me." She looked down at the baby. "Us."

"Nathan can't get here until about noon."

Marilee looked at me as if I had deliberately planned it that way. "Why?"

"He has other clients scheduled." Dan spoke calmly, logically, bringing her attention back to him. He was favored with a look that was even more suspicious.

"So Adam and I'll just sit here and wait for Grady to show up."

Dan sighed. I must remember to tell him how well he kept his temper. It was a challenge.

"I'll send Gary or someone over right after I get to the office."

"In the meantime, I'll be here," said Leona, satisfaction in her voice.

The look Marilee gave Leona was wonderful to see. Amazement to amusement to disbelief. "How are you going to protect us if Grady decides to break in?"

"We got a phone here, don't we?"

"Right. A phone." Marilee looked from Dan to me, as if she thought this was some kind of big joke. "How about Anne? Where is she?"

"What's the matter? You don't think I can handle that punk, Grady?"

Marilee sat back down as if her legs would no longer hold her. She seemed to sink before our eyes. "You couldn't handle Billy Ray, and all he did was get drunk. Grady's high on something most of the time. No way could you stop him." This wasn't bad temper. Marilee was scared to death.

"Look, I have a lot to do, but most of its phone calls. Why don't I go to the office, get my files, and come back? Grady won't dare try anything if we're both here."

I could have kicked myself the minute the words were out. I needed to concentrate, and it was going to be a whole lot harder here, with a crying baby and a whining Leona, than at my office. Besides, I wasn't one bit sure my presence would intimidate Grady. The look on Marilee's face kept me from taking back my way too generous offer.

"Oh, would you?"

"Sure." I gulped but went on as brightly as I could. "I'll be gone about an hour; Nathan will show up right after lunch, and I'll go back to the office then."

"She can't do anything I can't do," Leona said, her anger barely under control. Why, I wondered. Hurt pride? Or had I spoiled her chance to wrestle the baby out of Marilee's arms.

"Marilee, are you all right with this? It'll only be for about an hour." It wasn't all right with me, but I couldn't see what else to do. I had to get my files, all of which were neatly stacked on top of my desk. "We can lock all the doors."

"It'll be fine." There was resignation in Marilee's eyes, but they glared when she looked at Leona. "It's early. Grady won't even be out of bed yet." She hugged the baby a little closer. "Just get back as soon as you can, okay?"

Dan didn't look happy about the situation either, but it didn't look as if we had much choice. "I'll get someone to do a couple of drive-bys. Call me when you get back here," he said to me. "Who knows? Maybe, by that time, we'll get lucky and have Grady nicely tucked away in a jail cell." He patted Marilee awkwardly on the shoulder, looked pointedly at Leona, then walked onto the back porch, shut the outside door, and clicked the dead bolt. "We'll go out the front.

Leona, lock the door after us. Ellie, got your key? Good."

I followed him out, wondering how I had gotten myself into any of this. Elopement sounded better all the time. Tonight maybe. We'd come back when Grady was arrested. Grace House would be ready to move into. Maybe we'd even wait until Adam was ready for kindergarten. Aunt Mary could feed the cat.

Dan climbed into his car and fastened his seat belt. I leaned in and he gave me a chaste kiss on the cheek. I felt like June Cleaver. Only I don't think she had ever been this scared.

"I love you, Ellen Page McKenzie soon to be Dunham. Be careful. And call me as soon as you get back to the house."

He rolled up his window and started down the drive. I watched him go, stunned. Dunham. My name would be Dunham. Of course it would. Wouldn't it? Why hadn't it occurred to me before? Did I want to be a Dunham? I didn't want to be a McKenzie. That kept me too close to Brian and a life I was only too happy to leave behind. And I didn't want to be a Page. Well, I didn't want to be a Page the same way I used to be. I was a woman, not a girl. True, I still lived in the same house I lived in when I was a Page, but that didn't mean … this was going to take some getting used to. Checking account would have to be changed, social security, and real estate cards. Damn. I started back toward the house, bathrobe clutched tightly around me, wondering how to get directions to the closest nunnery.

Chapter Thirty

It was closer to an hour and a half before I got back. The house was still standing, no strange cars were out in front, no smoke curled out from under the back door, and no howls of rage or pain emanated from the kitchen or any other room. The only sound was the shower running upstairs.

I walked slowly through the downstairs, looking for someone. Anyone. The baby carrier was gone, so was the diaper bag. Upstairs? Must be. I climbed the stairs, wondering why the house felt so empty.

"Leona?" I called out when I got to the top of the stairs. "Marilee?"

"In the bathroom."

Okay. I knew where Marilee was. Where were Leona and the baby? Unease was giving way to alarm. I threw open Susannah's door, heedless of anyone's privacy needs, but it didn't matter. It was empty. No bag with bottles that had come from the hospital, no little donated nightgowns of any color, no diapers or lotion on top of Susannah's white wicker chest. No baby on her blue and white checked bedspread. No baby anywhere.

Leona was sleeping in the guest room. My stomach clenched before I opened the door. Empty. Really empty. No clothes on the unmade bed. The closet door was open. Nothing inside. The top of the chest of drawers was bare. I ran back to Marilee's room. Gone. Dear God in Heaven. Gone. I sank down on the end of the bed while the enormity of all this tried to sink into my brain, but it didn't have time. Marilee walked in, wrapped in a towel, looking damp and lovely.

"Hi, Ellen. You got back earlier than I thought. Where's Leona?"

That was the question of the moment. "I don't know."

I watched her face change. The smile faded, replaced slowly by panic as the awful reality sank in. She clutched her towel tightly as she looked wildly around the room. "Where is Adam?"

"I don't know that either. What happened here? When did you get into the shower?"

"Ten, maybe fifteen minutes ago. The baby was asleep downstairs; Leona was up here. I think she was on the phone. There's one in this room."

"Then what happened?"

"She came down and said why didn't I go up and take a shower while he was asleep. She'd stay right by him. At first I didn't want to, but I really needed … I made her promise not to pick him up. Where is he?"

Marilee's voice was getting shrill and she had started to move around the room. "Are you sure he's not downstairs?"

"I'm sure. Marilee, get dressed. I'm calling Dan."

"Everything's gone. She took him."

She stood in the middle of the room, quite still, clutching the towel around her. I thought, incongruously, how glad I was I bought oversized towels and reached for the phone. It rang before I could pick it up.

"Ellen, this is Gina. Do you know where Dan is? Something's happened, and I need to talk to him."

"Something's happened here, too. Gina, I have to go. I'll tell Dan you need him."

I started to hang up but what she said stopped me. "Ellen, tell him Grady was here. He threatened Sal, said Rose knew where Marilee was and Sal did too, and they'd better tell him. Only about then, his cell phone rang. He actually answered it. Rose says he grunted a few times, then he said something like, "No kidding. I'm on my way," smacked Sal across the face—why, I don't know—and ran out. So be careful. He's getting frantic."

"Dear God in Heaven. I think I know who made that call. Adam's missing, and so is Leona."

I heard a gasp. "Oh, my God. She wouldn't ... Yes, she would. I'll be right there."

"No, don't. Stay—"

There was no point in saying more. The line was dead. I glanced at Marilee, who was still standing frozen in place in the middle of the floor. She looked as white as the towel she still clutched. I hoped she'd keep breathing and not pass out on the rug. My last first aid class had been in Girl Scouts, and I'd failed mouth to mouth. Or did you wave smelling salts around? I dialed 911. Fastest way I could think of to get Dan.

Chapter Thirty-One

My house was again crowded with people. I'd managed to get Marilee into pants and a sweatshirt before everyone descended. Aunt Mary arrived first. How she knew trouble had been brewing, I had no idea. I was just glad to see her. Gina burst in next, looking as pale as Marilee. She immediately put her arms around her and sat with her on the living room sofa. Dan arrived right after.

"We've got people out looking for them everywhere." He was squatting down beside the sofa, talking to Marilee in the gentlest of tones. She didn't look soothed. She looked almost comatose, her face white, her eyes staring at nothing. Only her hands, which were tearing little pieces of fringe off the sofa pillow she held tightly in her lap, indicated she heard him.

"Train station, bus station, she can't have gone far, and she's pretty conspicuous carrying a baby. We'll get her."

"It was Grady she was talking to." Marilee wasn't talking to us, at least not exactly. It was more as if she were confirming something to herself.

"Do you know that or are you surmising?" Dan made the question matter of fact. No demand, no threat, he was like a man trying to coax a frightened dog out from under a bush. Not a bad analogy, I thought, as I watched Marilee gradually focus on him.

"I heard her say, 'I'll be ready,' as I was coming up the stairs, but I didn't know who she was talking to. Then."

"Is that when she offered to sit with the baby?"

"Yeah. I was going to go back down and get him, put him in the bathroom with me, but she said go ahead, she'd be downstairs anyway, she'd watch him. Take my time, wash my hair. It'd make me feel better. So I did." Tears finally started to drip. No screams, no hysterics, just tears that made furrows down the side of her face to splash, unnoticed, onto her sweatshirt.

A uniformed officer entered the room and gestured to Dan. We all looked at him, expecting him to say something, do something. I know I held my breath. His face remained impassive. Dan got up and walked over to him. They talked for a minute. He turned and left. Dan returned to our little group huddled around my sofa.

"Does Grady have a cell phone?" he asked Marilee.

She nodded. "It's one of those where you have to prepay. Half the time there's no minutes left on it."

Dan nodded. "Why would Grady hit Sal? Threaten him?"

"Ask Sal." Marilee looked mulish. "Why are we talking about cell phones and Sal? Why don't you find my baby?"

"We're trying, and we did ask Sal. He wasn't talking. Why?"

"Because he's a stubborn old man." Gina put Marilee's hand back in her lap and looked up at Dan. "Marilee used to work at the bakery."

Marilee gave a sort of laugh. "I lasted a week. Longer than a lot of girls."

"Rose told me about it," Gina went on. "Sal couldn't stand Grady coming around, accused him of stealing cookies."

"Cookies." Marilee said. "Day old cookies. Who cared? Sal was a pain in the ass. I quit before he fired me. Only thing I felt bad about was Rose. She's a saint."

"Is that why Grady went to the bakery?" Dan asked Gina. "Because he thought Rose might know where she was?"

"Maybe. I don't really know. I do know Rose hid in the back room while he was there. After he was gone, she came out. Put ice on Sal's face. Grady had slapped him pretty good. About then is when I got there. Sal wouldn't let me call you, just said we're all going to work, just like every day. He also said I was fired. Again."

"Yeah." Dan stood up. I heard his knees creak. "Sounds like Sal. So, what did you do?"

"Called here. I thought I'd better warn Marilee and Ellen that Grady was over the edge. If he'd slap an old man like Sal, God alone knows what he'd do to Marilee if he found her."

"Are you going back to the bakery?" I couldn't help thinking about Rose, how distraught she'd be. She had come to rely on Gina these last few weeks, not only to do most of the baking but also to act as a buffer against Sal. And, although he wouldn't admit it, Sal needed her also. He could bluster all he wanted, but he could no longer keep up with the work.

"Of course." Gina gave a tight little smile that had nothing to do with humor. "I have bread rising right now. Someone has to take care of it. Someone has to take care of Rose, too. I came over because I was worried about Marilee but also to give Sal a cooling off period. The old ..."

Gary walked into the room. All heads swiveled to stare at him. He paused, looked at us anxiously, and shook his head. "Nothing." He looked at Marilee, and his lips tightened. "But we're looking. That ol' Leona, she hasn't been gone that long. We've got the highway closed, someone's checking the bus station, and I've called the airport. We'll get your baby back."

Marilee's fingers clutched the pillow so tightly they turned white. The fringe on it was almost gone. It lay scattered over the sofa, some piled on the carpet. I never cared much for that pillow anyway.

Dan watched the massacre of the pillow. He looked up at me. I shrugged; he nodded and went into his police chief mode. "Under the circumstances, I think we need a Plan C.

It seems pretty obvious Grady now knows exactly where Marilee is, and he's going to try for her as soon as he thinks he can. Without getting caught."

"Why didn't he come over before? Leona must have been the one who called him, but she left with the baby. Marilee was here alone. That would have been an ideal time."

"Good point, Ellie. And I don't know the answer, but I'd bet it was something Leona told him. We'll find that out when we find her. In the meantime, Marilee is going someplace else."

"She can come to my house." Aunt Mary was already planning—a meal, bedroom linen, commandeering a baby crib from a friend for when Adam was returned, who knew what else. But there was no doubt she was ready to spring into action.

"No. She's coming to the police station. Maybe not the most comfortable place, but the safest. Gary is going to stay here. We need to get all these cars away from the house, make it look as if no one is here except Marilee. I don't know why he didn't try to get to her before, but I don't believe for a minute he's not going to try again. Only, Gary will be waiting."

I watched Gary blanch. Traffic stops, picking up juveniles for petty pilfering, stopping domestic fights, dealing with DUIs, all these kinds of things he was used to. He had even gotten used to the occasional homicide. But lying in wait for a frantic young man to break into a house where he would be waiting, all alone, seemed to be new. And not welcome. He gulped a couple of times and started to say something to Dan.

"Something the matter, Gary?"

"No." Gary gulped a couple more times. "Not a thing. Good idea you had. Sure. I'll be here, waiting."

A small smile had formed under Dan's mustache. I doubted Gary saw it. "If you see him, or see his truck ... It's orange, isn't it?" He looked at Marilee, who nodded. "Call it in. You'll have backup right away. I just don't want anything to keep him from trying to break in."

Gary looked marginally reassured. Marginally.

I wasn't. I looked around and wondered what would happen if Grady did break in. I wondered if I should put my favorite blue and white lamp up on the bookcase, move my grandmother's milk glass vase. I sighed. Quietly, I hoped. Maybe not.

"Gary came with me, so there won't be any cars out front. Ellen, you take Marilee in your car. Mary, how did you get here?"

"I walked, of course." Of course she had.

Dan's smile broadened, but he wiped it away instantly. "Gina? Did you drive?"

"No. I walked also. I needed to let off a little steam."

"Well, you're not walking back. Ride with Ellie. She'll drop you off."

"Now?"

Dan nodded.

"Let's go," I said.

Aunt Mary was instantly on her feet, pocketbook in hand. Gina started to get up but sank back down. Marilee hadn't moved. She just kept staring straight ahead, plucking at the pillow.

"Come on, sweetie. You need to be someplace safe when that baby is returned to you." Gina took Marilee's hand and tugged. Marilee didn't budge. She slipped her arm under Marilee's elbow and pulled her to her feet. It didn't look as if Marilee could remember how to walk. "We've got to get out of here so they can catch that bastard you're married to. And when they catch him, they'll get Leona and your baby also. Let's go."

A few of her words got through to Marilee. "You're sure?"

"Positive." Gina gave her a gentle tug and she started

forward.

"I'll see you all out to the car." Dan already had the front door open. He took Marilee's other arm, guided her down the front walk, and made sure she was in the backseat. He reached over and fastened her seat belt, then helped Aunt Mary get in beside her. Gina occupied the passenger seat as I slid behind the wheel.

"Go straight to the police station. I'll be there just as soon as I finish here."

I assumed he meant he needed to have a heart to heart with Gary without an audience. "Are you all right?" He leaned through my window and spoke quietly into my ear. His hand rested on mine, and the squeeze he gave it was barely perceptible.

"Fine," I assured him. "Just fine. But for God's sake, find that baby."

There was no smile now, only a hard glint in his eyes that didn't speak well for either Leona or Grady. "We'll find them both. And soon. Now, get going."

I did.

Chapter Thirty-Two

I headed for the bakery first. It would have made sense to drop off Aunt Mary at her house, but since she had no intention of leaving Marilee alone with only me to take care of her, and since Gina backed her up completely, we drove right past her house.

I pulled up in front of the bakery, surprised that I'd found a parking spot so easily.

"It looks pretty quiet in there," Aunt Mary commented.

"It does." Gina stood on the curb for a moment, staring at the huge plate glass window filled with birthday cakes, cakes for christenings, and, of course, wedding cakes. I doubted that she saw them. I did. But worry about wedding cakes belonged to some other life, one that didn't contain missing babies, demented kidnappers, and violent idiots bent on destruction to get what they wanted.

"Here's where I get yelled at." I could see her take a deep breath and slowly let it out. "But better me than Rose."

Aunt Mary climbed out of the back and trotted around to the passenger side. She climbed in and fastened her seat belt. That she was going to dictate our route I had no doubt. "We'll call you just as soon as we find Leona."

"Good." Gina turned back toward the car. She reached across the seat and gave Marilee a hug. "She can't have gone far. You'll find them." She gave her hand another pat and closed the door.

She was still watching us as we drove away, her words ringing in our ears. I hoped she was right, but the feeling of dread that had been building since I'd walked through my front door to find Leona and the baby gone kept right on building.

"Go down Pine Street."

It's easier to give directions from the front.

"Why?"

"Because."

"Because we go by the Greyhound Bus station?"

"Oh, do we?"

As if she didn't know. "Dan's people are checking all the stations."

"It's not out of our way."

"No. It's not. And you never know, but don't hold your breath that we'll see them."

"Go slow."

I slowed to a crawl. The houses on Pine are old and small, a neighborhood where single-family homes are mixed with duplexes, interspersed with small home-style business. All of them back up to alleys. If I was Leona, I thought, and wanted to catch a bus without anyone seeing me, I'd go down those alleys.

"Check the alleys," Aunt Mary said.

"That's what I'm doing."

"Why are we going up this alley?" Marilee said. It was the first glimmer I had that she was aware of anything but her own paralyzing fear.

"Because if Leona has a grain of sense, she'll stay off the streets."

I could feel Marilee lean forward, could almost feel her start to hope again. "You think so? Go down that one."

I turned down the alley that dead-ended into Apple Street. It contained nothing but several empty trash bins and an old sofa. No Leona and nowhere for her to hide. I paused when I got to the corner, looking both ways, wondering where to go next. I had to turn one way or the other because the bus station parking lot was straight ahead.

There she was, standing in line, waiting to climb onto

the Greyhound bus that was slowly loading. The baby carrier was at her feet, the L.L.Bean tote bag I'd bought Aunt Mary for Christmas slung over her shoulder.

"Look," I said, pointing toward the bus. I put the car in gear and headed across the street, trying to resist the almost overwhelming temptation to gun the engine and go roaring into the parking lot.

"Hurry," commanded Aunt Mary.

"I am. But I can't run down the passengers. Here. Get out. I'll pull into that parking spot."

I slowed down and came to a halt on the street side of the bus. I didn't think Leona had spotted us yet. And Marilee hadn't spotted Leona.

"What are we doing?" She leaned forward over my shoulder, straining against her seat belt. "Why aren't we checking more alleys?"

"Get out." I practically shoved Aunt Mary out the door. "Go grab her. I'll be right behind you."

She was out the door and around the bus with really amazing swiftness for a woman her age and size. And she'd grabbed Leona. I could tell because the yelling had started. High pitched yelling that belonged to Leona, but other voices were joining into the din.

"Leona's trying to get on that bus," I told Marilee. "Go help Aunt Mary stop her while I call nine-one-one."

I don't think it registered at first, but when it did, Marilee was out the door and running, screaming "Adam" at the top of her lungs. There was more noise at that bus station than there was at a Friday night high school football game when our team had made the winning touchdown. There was even more noise as my message got relayed to police headquarters. The police station was only a couple of blocks from the bus station, so almost instantly sirens started to howl. Men were running toward the station on foot, a black and white careened into the parking lot, and Leona didn't get on the bus.

I managed to park the car—even with the back door open—and paused only long enough to slam it shut before I ran for the bus. Leona stood off to one side, screaming, crying, and handcuffed. Marilee had Adam in her arms, crooning to him, clutching him, and crying.

"That's my baby!" Leona was sobbing. She struggled to get her arms back in front of her and aimed a kick at the policewoman holding her. "He's mine. He gave him to me."

The bus passengers were standing around, mouths gaping, not knowing what to make of this. I could hear the murmurs, "Who's the real mother? Can't be that red-haired girl. She's too young. Must be. The other one's nuts."

They had that last part right. The bus driver was out of the bus, looking at his watch, and loudly bemoaning his schedule while trying, vainly, to get his bus loaded. Finally he managed to attract the attention of one of the policemen milling around. "I've got to get out of here. Can I go now?"

Dan walked around the side of the bus, headed our way, but stopped when he heard the bus driver.

"Get moving." He waved him on. "We won't need you."

The passengers slowly loaded, everybody jostling to get a window seat just in case more drama erupted. The doors shut with a final whoosh and the bus pulled out, leaving us on the platform. Leona was still screaming, insisting the baby was hers. They gradually degraded into heartrending sobs as she stared at Marilee and Adam.

I don't think Marilee heard her. She held Adam close, touching his cheek, kissing his hair, almost smothering him in her need to feel him next to her.

I don't think Aunt Mary heard Leona either. She kept patting Marilee on the arm, standing on tiptoe to peek at the baby, telling her that she knew all along that she'd get him back. She looked as if she might start crying as well. But her tears wouldn't have the anguish behind them that Leona's had.

"Don't you dare cry," I told her.

She beamed at me. "I have no intention of doing anything of the kind." But her eyes were moist.

Dan came up behind me. "Good job. We'd checked this station only a few minutes ago, but evidently not the women's bathroom."

"Dan." I reached out for him, not realizing how unsteady I felt until I had him to hold onto. "Dan, Leona …"

"It's okay. We've got her and Marilee has the baby. We're going to take her …"

"Dan, no. I know that. It's what she … she was screaming …"

"She certainly was."

"No. Listen. Grady gave her the baby. She didn't just take him. Grady …" I couldn't go on. He'd traded his own child, his son, for information on where to find his child's mother. I'd been shaken when I heard about Sal, but this … "He gave her that baby and she told him …"

Dan gathered me to him and I went willingly. The need to be held was almost overpowering. "I know, Ellie. I was pretty sure that was how it went down. Now …"

His cell rang. He looked at the screen and flipped it open.

Two black and whites and a fire truck, sirens screaming, went by, followed closely by an ambulance. I stared at them, waiting for them to turn into the bus station, but they kept going. One of the detective's cars left the bus station, siren going full blast, right behind them. Dan snapped his cell phone shut and pulled away from me.

"Seems we have another little problem." His face was white under his tan and he looked a little sick.

"You've found Grady?" But that wouldn't be a problem. Unless … my house!

"No. Not Grady." He paused, looked at me, then reached out and took hold of Aunt Mary and held her tightly. "It's Sal. He's at the bakery. Someone's beaten him to death with a rolling pin."

Chapter Thirty-Three

At first, Dan wasn't going to let us go with him to the bakery. His resolve didn't last long. Aunt Mary had no intention of leaving Rose to the tender mercies of the police, and I had every intention of finding out exactly what had happened. My first thought was Gina. That she was guilty I had no doubt. Hermione had been right all along. Gina had come here seeking revenge for her mother and now that revenge was complete. First Doctor Sadler, now Sal. But why now? Something horrible must have happened. Sal must have done something that made Gina lose control, something to do with Rose? All I could think was … how tragic. That lovely woman, so talented, so kind, and now her life lay in ruins. For some reason, I didn't think about Sal's life. And, I realized, that was the supreme tragedy.

Nathan had shown up at the bus station. How he knew I hadn't time to ask. He announced that Anne was also on her way and that he was taking Marilee and Adam back to my house. No, Dan said. We still didn't know where Grady was, and the safest place for both of them, at least for now, was the police station. We'd meet them there as soon as we could. Nathan was not pleased, but he bundled them into his car, and when we last saw him, he was following the police car that contained a still sobbing Leona. She was destined for a holding cell, Marilee for Dan's office. Neither would be very comfortable.

The scene inside the bakery was beyond horrible. Sal lay on the floor behind the counter. He looked, if possible, even worse than Doctor Sadler had. Blood was everywhere. So was the crime team. Some of them were Dan's people, but some had on county sheriff's jackets. The home team was only going to get part of the action on this one. Gina and Rose were huddled in a corner toward the front of the bakery, as far away from the body as possible. Rose sat in one of the bentwood chairs pulled up to the old oak table, her back to the crime scene, looking oddly demure in her high-necked gingham dress. It made her look a little dowdy and more than a little old. Someone had put a cup of coffee in front of her, but it didn't look as if she'd touched it. Gina stood behind her, wrapped in her baker's apron, her arms around Rose, holding her, patting her like one would a distraught child.

"Go over there," Dan said. "I don't want any of you to contaminate my crime scene." That was one command I was happy to obey. One glance at what was left of Sal was enough. Besides, I wanted to talk to Gina. Only, I wasn't sure how to start, or what to say. I started with the obvious.

"What happened?"

Gina looked at me and sighed. Rose didn't appear to notice that I had said anything or that I was there. She didn't even seem to notice that Aunt Mary had pulled up the other chair and had taken her free hand.

"Grady. Rose said it was Grady Wilcox. He came in here threatening Sal, demanding to know where Marilee was, and when Sal wouldn't tell him, he picked up the rolling pin and hit him with it. Several times. Then he left."

The rolling pin. Yes. It was there on the floor. Someone was taking pictures of it. I took a couple of steps toward it but was stopped by a sheriff's deputy. It didn't matter. It was the large one I'd seen when I'd been in the kitchen with Gina. The one with the piece out of the handle, showing the metal bar that ran through it. A shudder ran through me. Partly horror, but largely relief. Grady was guilty. Gina hadn't done it. Only, something about this wasn't right. Why would Grady come back? He knew where Marilee was. Leona had told him. He'd given her the baby so she would tell him.

I took a closer look at Gina. Her face was pasty white, and her hands clutched the back of Rose's chair, the knuckles bloodless. Her eyes were firmly fixed on the top of Rose's head and her answers had come from lips so stiff they looked frozen.

"Did he come through the kitchen?" I asked her.

"What?"

"Grady. Did he come in the front door or did he come through the kitchen?"

"I don't know." For the first time she looked directly at me, then around the room. I could see her gaze rest on the rolling pin. "He came through the kitchen."

"Are you sure?"

"Yes." Her "yes" had the ring of truth, but her eyes didn't meet mine.

Someone else was coming through the kitchen. There were two raised voices, one of which was shouting very explicit four-letter words. A pot banged. I thought it was a pot. Something metallic. There was another hollow thud. More voices, and a man, a boy really, was propelled through the door. A boy with dirty blond hair, red-rimmed blue eyes, and a long face. There was an open sore on the side of his nose. There were others on his arms, left bare under the black T-shirt he wore. On the front was a white and red fire breathing dragon with initials that didn't form any word I'd ever heard of. He was followed, more like pushed, by Gary.

"Hey, Chief. Will you look who came calling? Thought he'd let himself in by the back door." He grinned at me and gave Grady, for this could be no one else but Grady, another push. "I'm afraid your screen is torn. He sorta wanted to leave as soon as he saw me. I'll come over tomorrow and fix it."

"My, my." Dan walked across the room to stand in front of them. "Grady Wilcox. You know, we've been looking for you." He examined Grady closely before turning

271

to Gary. "Why did you bring him here? Why not take him directly to the station?"

"I was going to but I heard over the car radio about Sal. Thought you might want to have a talk with this ... him."

Dan nodded. "Good job, Gary."

"Yeah? How come?" Grady shook himself loose from his captor and stood, legs apart, hands cuffed behind his back, staring at Dan with what I supposed he thought was an innocent look. It made him look slightly feebleminded.

"Why, we thought we'd arrest you."

"Why? I didn't do nothin'. What are you arrestin' me for?" He kept jerking his hands as if he could make the cuffs separate. All he was going to get for his efforts was sore wrists.

Dan watched all this calmly. "Oh," he used that voice that sounded so mild and yet was so deadly, "how about arson? And selling drugs? And murder?"

"Murder?" Grady sounded genuinely astounded. "I never murdered no one. Who got murdered anyway?"

"Him." Dan pointed to where Sal lay. Someone had drawn a chalk outline around the body. A flash went off. More photographs.

Grady took a couple of steps closer and blanched. "Oh shit. I didn't do that. I never ... why would I do that? Oh shit. I'm going to be sick."

"Not a good idea." Dan's face was as closed down as I'd ever seen it, eyes hard, mouth tight. If Grady got sick, he might have reason to get even sicker. "Thomas, help Gary get this little piece of ... him out of here. Take him to the station and book him. Start with arson and go from there but get him in a cell. And don't forget to read him his rights. I'll be back there before too long."

Rose had watched all this with no evidence of interest. She sat on her chair, staring ahead, as if no one else was in the room. Every few minutes she'd turn in her chair and look at Sal's body, almost as if she was checking to make sure he was still there, showing no sign of hysteria, grief, or anything but numb acceptance. I watched her, wondering, looking at her hands, how still they lay on the table, how quiet her breathing was under the high-buttoned front of her dress. Her dress. Her collar. There was a damp spot on her collar. How had that happened? I looked back up at Gina. Her fingers tightened on her grandmother's shoulders. I closed my eyes and wished I was any place else in the world but where I was, but wishing wouldn't make this go away.

"Wait," I said. "Wait a minute. Are you going to book him for murder?"

"It seems like a good idea. Why?" Dan looked at me suspiciously.

"Give me a minute."

"What are you going to do?"

I pulled Rose's chair out from the table a little in spite of Gina's weak "no" and knelt down in front of her, trying to get her attention. Finally she looked at me.

"Why, Ellen. When did you come? How nice." She started to smile but it faded only half formed. "We've had a little accident. Sal fell down."

That wasn't at all what I had expected. An accident? Did she really think … but I had to go on.

"Rose, see that man over there?"

"Which one, dear."

"The one in the black T-shirt."

"With that awful dragon on it?"

"Yes." I had to suppress a smile at that one. "Do you know him?"

"Why, yes. He's Grady something or other. He's married to that sweet Marilee."

"Was Grady here earlier today?"

"Yes. He came here and yelled at Sal. Said terrible things and hit him in the face. He wanted to know where Marilee was. Sal didn't know. I did, but I hid. In the back room."

I could feel Dan right behind me. His hand was on my shoulder. "Ellen, you can't … "

"Wait." I let his hand stay there but got in one more question.

"Did Grady come back? A little while ago? Did he hit Sal with that rolling pin?"

"Oh no, dear. I did that."

Dan's hand tightened on my shoulder. I heard Aunt Mary gasp, and Gina gave a sob. Quiet gradually spread across the room as everyone realized what Rose had said.

Gina clutched Rose more tightly. "No, she didn't. I did. He was on her, wouldn't let up, and I hit him. With the rolling pin."

Everyone's eyes were now on Gina. Everyone's but mine. "Rose, where is your apron?"

"My apron?"

She looked down at herself as if she hadn't realized she no longer wore it. I looked at Gina. So did Dan. So did everyone else in the room. She stood behind Rose, in her immaculate white apron, a picture of despair.

"Go on," I heard Dan say softly. So I did.

"Why did you hit him, Rose?"

She looked up at me with much the same expression she had the day she showed me the picture. Unrelenting sorrow. "He was going to make Gina go away." Tears appeared. Just a couple. She lifted a hand to brush them off. Her hand had dirt on the fingernails. Or maybe that dark stain was something else. "I couldn't allow that again. I'd lost her for so long; I wasn't going to lose her again. He just wouldn't listen. So I hit him." She paused, staring at the body. "He's been lying down a long time. He's going to be really mad at me when he gets up, but I couldn't help it." She looked up at me, then turned to Aunt Mary, whose eyes were brimming. "You and Ellen have to help make him see reason. You will, won't you? Anne Kennedy did last time, but she's not here. Is she?"

My eyes were also brimming and blinking didn't help. "No, Rose. Not yet. And we'll help you in any way we can." Gina stood behind her grandmother, rigid. She glared at me, willing me to stop, but I had one more question to ask. "Is that why you hit Doctor Sadler, Rose? Because he wanted Gina to go?"

"Yes, of course. He was going to make her go away. He said Sal was right, she was trouble. I tried to tell him, but Owen never did listen. Just like Sal. He made me so mad." She sighed. "He took Gina's baby. My granddaughter. Did you know that? Just gave her away. I told him not to. I told Sal also. No one listened." She paused, as if mulling all this over. "I was going to lose her again. Gina." She frowned. "Did you know there were two … no. That can't be right" She paused again, than shook her head slightly, as if to clear it. "I told Owen … Did you know he died? I went to his funeral."

I couldn't tell if she knew she'd killed him or not. She didn't seem to realize that Sal was dead, either. I could feel tears running down my face. They were running down Aunt Mary's also, but she never let go of Rose's hand.

"Gina." Dan didn't raise his voice, and he looked a little sick, but his tone left no room for anything but hard truth. "Where's Rose's apron?"

Gina bent down and rested her cheek on Rose's hair, then raised her head and looked helplessly at Dan.

"Gina."

"I rolled it up and put it in the freezer," she whispered

I didn't want to say anything more. Words had become physically painful, hot pieces of metal scalding my mouth, but I had no choice. "There are two aprons in that freezer, aren't there, Gina. And there are latex gloves in the pocket of one of them."

I've never seen such pain on anyone's face. The look Gina gave me held no recrimination, no hate, no blame, just pain mixed with despair. She nodded.

I've never seen Dan's face like that, either. Rage, sorrow, frustration, all mixed together. I knew he loved his job, but I was certain that right then he'd gladly trade it to the garbage man. He turned around and faced the room. "You, get Grady out of here. Get him booked. Arson. One of you check that freezer."

I went on. It was as if I couldn't stop. Everything had come together, a truth I didn't want to deal with, and, somehow, if I said all of it, told everything I knew or suspected, I could get rid of it. "And today. You washed her hands and tried to get the blood off her collar. It's still wet."

Dan stared at me, gently turned Rose toward him and looked at her collar before he turned to Gina. "Did you really think you could get away with that?"

"I didn't know what else to do." Gina looked back at Dan, despair heavy in her voice. Her arms tightened around her grandmother.

Dan shook his head. There was anger, and anguish, in his voice. "The rest of you, finish up. You guys," he gestured at the photographer and the man with the chalk, "are you done? Then get the … Sal, out of here." He turned back to Rose, but a whiney voice interrupted.

"I've got a right to a lawyer. I get a phone call and an attorney. You can't frame me, and you got no proof that …" Grady's voice faded away under the force of Dan's stare. It would have withered wood.

"As God is my witness, if I wasn't a professional, I'd ..." He addressed every one in the room. "You all saw this. I never laid a hand on the little … Get him out of here."

The whines turned to soft mutters as he was led away. Dan turned back to Rose, who looked up at him with a small smile.

"Dan, how nice. Did you come to talk about the wedding cake? Sal will be so sorry he missed you. I'll tell him when he gets up. Oh." She looked at where the body had lain, then around the shop, mystified, lost.

I didn't think he was going to keep it together. I didn't think I was. We both swallowed, hard. Dan looked at me. I reached around and grabbed his hand and squeezed it. He squeezed back, slowly withdrew it, squatted down in front of Rose's chair and took both of her hands in his.

"Rose, listen to me. That's right." He stopped and took a deep breath. "You have the right to remain silent …"

Chapter Thirty-Four

The church was beautiful. This New Year's Eve night was crystal clear, stars hanging low in an inky sky, making the jewel tones in the stained glass windows glow. Inside, the church was alight with candles. Large candelabras flanked the altar, smaller ones sat on it, and there were actually lit candles in glass hurricane lamps that hung on every other pew. The ones in between were decorated with white satin bows into which were tucked sprigs of fir. I worried, briefly, if with all those candles the fire department would shut us down. Only, the fire chief and most of the fire department were here, so probably not.

Tubs of fir trees surrounded the altar, trimmed with tiny white lights. Tubs of white poinsettias, whose throats and outer leaves were brushed with pink, sat everywhere. A white runner covered the central aisle. Where it had come from, I had no idea. I hadn't ordered it. Or had I?

I stood in the vestibule beside my father. Pat and Susannah, looking elegant in their dark green gowns, kept milling around, greeting last minute guests, pushing open the entry doors to the church, coming back to tell me that neither Dan, his brother Don, Neil, nor Reverend Miller were out yet, but that Dan's mother had taken her place.

Dan's mother was the picture of calm. She had appeared at the church with Dan's father, dressed beautifully in a deep rose-colored dress, and given me a hug. "You look so beautiful, Ellen. I've wanted you for a daughter-in-law for a long time."

"Oh," was all I could say. I started to get teary, but she pulled out a tissue, blotted my eyes, and instructed me not to dare cry. My makeup would run. I laughed, and my makeup was saved.

My mother wasn't quite so calm. She'd been dithering for days, worrying about everything. She'd asked me at least ten times if I liked my dress and by the way where was it. I didn't lie. I told her my friend Pat had it and was making some alterations. I just didn't tell her how many.

Tonight she kept looking at me, a bit teary eyed, as I stood beside my father. "You look just beautiful. I knew that dress was you the minute I saw it." A slight frown wrinkled her face. "But I thought the skirt was, you know, fuller. The sleeves seem different, too. And wasn't there a veil?"

I smiled. "I love it. It's beautiful."

My father looked down at me and winked. "I saw the dress before your mother sent it to you. Your friend did a great job with her ... alterations."

My father is a very patient and perceptive man.

Neil appeared and offered mother his arm. "I think it's time for you to go up now. Besides, I've got to get back and prop up Dan."

I made a face at him, and he grinned. Mother took his arm and they entered the church. It wouldn't be long now.

Susannah came up to us. "Did you see Gina and Marilee?"

I nodded.

"Nathan's sitting right beside Marilee holding the baby. Do you think that will work out?"

"I don't know," I said. "Anne seems to have her doubts, but Nathan's a good man. And a persistent one. Only, Marilee's got ideas of her own. If they work out the way she and Gina have it planned, well, who knows."

Gina was going to remain in Santa Louisa. She was taking over the bakery. Her aunt Gabrielle, her mother's only sister, had flown in as soon as she had heard what happened. She had made all of the funeral arrangements for her father, but without any evidence of extreme grief. That she'd saved for her mother. However, Rose was residing at Shady Acres in their Alzheimer section and seemed, on the whole, content. It was a lockdown facility, and the judge was more than willing to commit her. Dan had said she'd never stand trial. She kept asking, not without trepidation, when Sal was coming back, and seemed to slip easily between present and past. I wasn't sure Alzheimer's was her problem, but at least she was comfortable, well taken care of, and seemingly content. More than she would have gotten at the county jail, which was where Leona and Grady still languished. I felt terribly sorry for Leona, in spite of what she had done. What a waste of a life. Grady was busy wasting his as well, but somehow I had less sympathy for him.

"What is Marilee going to do at the bakery?" Susannah turned her grandfather around and straightened his tie. "There." She stood back and examined him. "My, you do look handsome." She gave him a quick peck on the cheek, and he beamed at her.

I beamed at both of them. "The girls have gone into a partnership. They are talking about a coffeehouse kind of thing. Breakfast, lunch, and later, when Marilee has enough experience, maybe some catering. Could work."

"A partnership? How could Marilee do that?"

How indeed. I thought about lumpy baby car seats and almost grinned. "They must have worked something out."

"Well, if Gina is running it, it'll work out fine."

Pat, who had been keeping watch, started to wave to us. "We're starting. Oh, there's your aunt Mary sitting right beside your mother." She grinned at me. "And there isn't one single poinsettia on her dress. Susannah, get up here. We're about to go."

I could hear the organ. Susannah and Pat took their places at the door and, as it opened, started their slow glide up the aisle. My father and I took our places, ready for my grand entrance. I couldn't see Dan. But he must be there, waiting for me. A pause, then the music changed. Here comes the bride. That was me. The congregation stood. It was time.

I slipped my arm through my father's, and we moved to the open door. He looked down at me and whispered in my ear, "You ready?"

Again, I looked down the aisle. There he was, waiting, watching for me. He caught sight of me and smiled. I smiled back.

"I'm ready."

"Be happy, baby."

"Thanks, Dad. I already am."

Kathleen Delaney, a retired real estate broker, has authored three other Ellen McKenzie mystery novels, using her real estate experience to guide Ellen. The scenes in the bakery kitchen required extra research. (Bakery people are not only generous with their knowledge, but also with their Cherry Danish.) Besides her novels, Kathleen has contributed to several anthologies, won a national award for short fiction, and published several articles. She lives in a century-old house in South Carolina, enjoying her two dogs, and eight grandchildren.

You can find Kathleen online at
www.KathleenDelaney.net
www.KathleenDelaney.camelpress.com.

CPSIA information can be obtained at www.ICGtesting.com
Printed in the USA
LVOW071446271011

252382LV00001B/10/P